Trouble Will Save You

ALASKA LITERARY SERIES

Peggy Shumaker, Series Editor

ALASKA
LITERARY
SERIES

The Alaska Literary Series publishes poetry, fiction, and literary nonfiction. Successful manuscripts have a strong connection to Alaska or the circumpolar north, are written by people living in the far north, or both. We prefer writing that makes the northern experience available to the world, and we choose manuscripts that offer compelling literary insights into the human condition.

TROUBLE WILL SAVE YOU

Three Novellas from Interior Alaska

DAVID NIKKI CROUSE

UNIVERSITY OF ALASKA PRESS

Fairbanks

© 2023 by University Press of Colorado

Published by University of Alaska Press
An imprint of University Press of Colorado
1624 Market Street, Suite 226
PMB 39883
Denver, Colorado 80202–1559

 The University Press of Colorado is a proud member of
Association of University Presses.

The University Press of Colorado is a cooperative publishing enterprise supported,
in part, by Adams State University, Colorado State University, Fort Lewis College,
Metropolitan State University of Denver, University of Alaska Fairbanks, University
of Colorado, University of Denver, University of Northern Colorado, University
of Wyoming, Utah State University, and Western Colorado University.

∞ This paper meets the requirements of the ANSI/NISO Z39.48–1992 (Permanence of
Paper).

ISBN: 978-1-64642-488-7 (hardcover)
ISBN: 978-1-64642-397-2 (paperback)
ISBN: 978-1-64642-398-9 (ebook)
https://doi.org/10.5876/9781646423989

Library of Congress Cataloging-in-Publication Data available upon request

Cover art: Glacier Crossing by Jana Latham.

For Frank and R. T.

Contents

Acknowledgments

Any book is more than the product of individual effort; it also reflects the work and support of many people. These stories would not exist without the love and care of my wife, Bonnie Whiting, who inspires me with her devotion to art and life; my children, Dylan, Noah, and Beckett, who have given me more joy than I could have ever imagined; my parents, Alfred and Marie Crouse; my sisters, Jane and Karen; my brother, Michael; and my dear friends Stephanie Clare, Laurie Marhoefer, and Hattie. Thank you to Greg Moutafis and Jon Dembling for unwavering friendship lasting decades and long discussions about art stretching back to our teenage years. Thank you to Chris White for particular help with one of these stories, and to Nicole Stellon O'Donnell for support both spiritual and pragmatic. Thank you also to those I might not have mentioned but who have helped me somewhere along the way. Lastly, thank you to Frank Soos, life-changing teacher and good friend, and to sweet R. T. I miss you both more than I can say.

Trouble Will Save You

MISFORTUNE
AND ITS DOUBLE

PART I

"How many more hours do we have left in us?" Toby asked, because this was what we talked about now: the limits of our resources. Gas and money. Pills and water. We measured the distance in miles when we were looking at a map at night, hours during the day when we were driving.

"A few more," I said.

Just then Toby lifted his eyes to some point over my shoulder and I turned to see a large middle-aged man dressed in a feed cap and a suit jacket thoughtfully scratching his beard. He was the picture that appears in your mind when you hear the word *Montana*. For a moment I thought he was going to push a religious pamphlet at us, but his hands were empty and his face didn't have that used-car salesman look. "Excuse me, sir. Is that your truck out there in the parking lot?" he said to Toby.

"Yeah," I said. "It's ours."

He smiled, looking Toby over, and I looked Toby over too, trying to see him with this guy's eyes—the sling on his right arm, the gash across his nose and the double bruises around his eyes like a mask, the tight black knit cap, dirty army jacket with the florescent orange stripes around the sleeves and the nametag that read *Anderson*. He did not look like such a bad kid. In fact, to this guy he probably looked like any other young person around town, just one with really bad luck.

"Get whatever you want," the guy said, and he flashed a look back at the waitress. "My wife and I are sitting right over there. Tell Cheryl to charge it to us." Toby gazed up at him with that milky I'm-here-but-not-here look in his eyes, so the guy added, more gently this time, "You just seem like some people who could use a kind gesture."

A very specific choreography needed to be worked out here. The waitress was walking over slow so the Good Samaritan could finish what he started. The man couldn't leave until we thanked him, or at least acknowledged what he had done. Maybe a return smile would be enough, so I smiled for Toby and it was enough.

As he walked away I glanced over at the man's table, where his wife was watching all of this unfold. Our eyes met and she opened her hand, moving her fingers like she was tickling the air. I wasn't sure if she was waving to us or to her husband, though, so I didn't wave back. Later in the truck I turned to Toby and said, "Assholes."

But Toby didn't laugh. He didn't agree or disagree or even turn his head in my direction. Somehow his bruises seemed to have grown worse during the walk from the restaurant to the truck, his face cadaver taunt, eyes staring into the space in front of us. The cars streamed ahead in neat rows. To the people behind us our truck was part of that stream, just another set of taillights, but it did not feel that way. We seemed unique. Our adversity made us glow. "I'm fine," he said, because I guess he could tell what I was thinking. He was good at that. He smiled and his face changed again, this time into something beautiful and familiar, hopeful, alive. We were almost there. That's what I told myself.

⚡

That small kindness happened ten days into the trip, when our trouble sometimes seemed like an exotic country we were visiting as wide-eyed tourists. When we had left Fairbanks in those first days of May, the mucky snow was melting and our souls filled with the familiar spirit of that month—a false euphoria that made the winter seem like a onetime thing, a minor tragedy from which you could recover and then forget.

I had been through four springs there and each one affected me more strongly than the one before. Toby said it had taken him six years to get used to that quick shift, that he still wasn't really used to it. I didn't see any signs that it made him feel what I felt though. I was practically vibrating with joy and anxiety.

"This one is coming quick," he said in the middle of April, when things first began to go green, and then he looked out to the long stretch of trees behind our cabin, as if he suspected that the winter would return, and if it did it would be coming from that direction.

I laughed at his seriousness.

That winter had been a difficult one, with an early snowfall and two long stretches of forty below deep into February. Our roof had cracked in the last week of that month and Toby had been forced to repair it himself, scaling a ladder with a hammer, a snow shovel, and a ski mask. It had been a rush job, of course, and come spring the melted snow began dripping down into buckets and open milk jugs we had placed around the floor.

Even that seemed like a gift when I poured it into our plants.

If winter was silent, then spring was the sound of running water. Stuff broke loose, moved around, found its way downhill into gullies and paths. I could waste a morning listening to the trickle from the roof to the floor. Then I'd rush off to work at the Coffee Hut, pedaling my bicycle hard down the long hill to the traffic light intersection where civilization began to make itself known.

Once inside I'd turn the heaters on high, get all four burners going, steam myself up some chocolate milk—always chocolate—and drop in two shots. All this before taking off my parka. Then I'd shed layers—parka first, then the sweatshirt—and stuff it all under the countertop. I'd pull my T-Shirt off, adjust whatever lacy black bra I had decided to wear that day, usually the one with the pink center ribbon, but sometimes the one with green trim. Kick off my boots and tug down my jeans and leave them in a puddle on the floor for most of the morning. As I did all this the coffee came to a boil. I could hear the trucks already coming up alongside the hut. A line of two, three, sometimes four or five. I was in there, but they couldn't see me yet, not until I slid up the window and reached out to open the shutters.

I'd brace myself for the blast of cold, a half second of panic when I was revealed.

"The usual?" I'd ask the repeat customers, and they always said yes unless the weather was making someone feel exuberant and risky, and then they'd sound almost apologetic when they told me they wanted a large instead of a small, or an Americano instead of just a plain coffee, or whatever seemed like a good idea as I looked out at them from my window. And in the spring they talked to me about their lives, about the last few difficult months, as if they had been away, living in a dangerous place, and just returned. But that was just the winter. That was the only place they'd been. And now they were back with all sorts things to tell me, and I had things to tell them too, except I kept most of that to myself.

"Yeah, I'm doing great," I'd say. Or "Thank you very much."

I think it's that spirit of newness that pushed us into leaving as much as the difficulty of the winters. At least that's what we told ourselves, and anyway, how long could we stick with the life we were living? Those were Toby's words, but not too long before he had called friends who had left Alaska wimps and pussies and sell-outs and fakes. And there was nothing worse than that last one. A fake. Better to be an authentic murderer.

And yet he sold all seven of his dogs, the pens and sledding gear too, to a musher from Tok, and then spent a week looking miserable, pining for the lead dog, his favorite and the only one he ever let in the cabin with us. "I shouldn't have taken that offer," he said. "It was insulting." But his grief drove him further down, and he sold off the junk in the yard too, for $5 here, $10 there, car parts and damaged bicycles and things I didn't even recognize. Strangers had always appeared at our back door looking to speak with Toby, but these were different people who came to us now, middle-aged men, sometimes with teenaged sons to help them carry whatever they were carting away. And they looked at me like those people in that Montana restaurant would a month later, like oh, God, what have we stumbled across here? I treated them just like I would any customer, with a sweet-voiced hello.

⁓⁓

In the bird's nest of the truck cab we twitched back into shape, rousing ourselves, *and I thought, I don't want to go outside, I don't want to stop touching you, I don't want to push past the spider web of windshield out into the road.* It was cool and dark inside and it seemed an easy thing—a very important thing—to curl there and hold that good feeling as long as possible. It was a lot like the urge to stay quiet and motionless after sex, listening to birds in the eaves. I swear I could hear water running beneath us, the growling vibration of something deep in the earth. But one person or the other always speaks and breaks the spell, don't they?

And that person was me. I unclipped my seatbelt and found a foothold and settled toward the ground, toward the truck cap's roof, spotted with playing cards and cigarettes. Toby moaned and said my name and I said his and then we caterpillared our way outside the passenger's side window. That was when he found his focus, just for a moment, and he helped me to the side of the road and down into the long, wet grass. He smoothed his hands down my warm face and chest, checking for gashes, teasing them out, but it was his blood covering me. Neither of us knew that then.

Sometimes I place the motorcyclist into that memory and sometimes I don't. Sometimes I don't allow him in at all. But he straddled his bike across the street from us, helmet in his hands, watching through the settling dust. He must have been worried, afraid for us, but when I recall his expression, it's angry and disgusted.

And that's probably why I don't want him there. With his jaw set like that, shoulders back, it seemed as if he might be afraid of us instead of *for* us, as if, even in our state of disarray, we might be dangerous to him. For a moment I thought he might bounce on his throttle, gun the engine, and speed away. I remember his black button-down shirt, a tie thrown around his neck like a scarf. Maybe he was on his way to work. Toby was off picking up pieces of broken furniture that had been thrown from the truck cap. I smiled at the motorcyclist as if to say, *It's okay, it's all under control*, and for a second he seemed like just another customer.

"Look at this," Toby said. "Christ."

He held a brilliant yellow bedsheet in his hand, and as he walked in a circle he trailed the sheet behind him. He had given up on collecting broken table legs and chairs, it seemed, and had taken on a new job. He dropped the sheet and touched his right arm with his left. He walked back to me. The man must have still been watching us. I don't remember him joining us, or even getting off his bike. Maybe he *did* speed away, but I do remember thinking, just for a second, that Toby and I were onstage. We were performing, each in our own way, for that audience of one.

I looked up at Toby and said, "I feel okay. I'm not hurt."

"Same here," he said, although this wasn't true.

All of this took place in a matter of seconds, of course. The patrol cars would arrive, the strobing lights and questions and that soft blanket around my shoulders as they helped me to stand. "I'm fine," I told them. I think I even tried to shrug the blanket off, push the hands away.

The next day the most mundane sights struck me with the clarity of a still life: the empty cigarette machine in the hotel lobby, an old winter coat tossed over it; the blue ink stain I noticed on the side of the desk clerk's hand as he handed us our room key; the oil-dark dirt beneath Toby's fingernails. It seemed like a new talent awakened. I told Toby, "I love you so much," with the sense that love was something I had just noticed too.

But of course I didn't do that, because in the story's mirror I was the only one who crawled from the wreckage. I was the one who bent down and picked up our belongings from the road. I didn't even think of him until they told me the news. Gone, they said, as if he had run away, and it felt like that, like he had done something devilish and unexpected. Sometimes in Fairbanks he would not come home from a night of drinking until the next morning, the dogs barking crazy as he walked up the side of the cabin. It was another night like that.

"But you're okay," someone said. "You're doing well."

Toby's parents were in Chicago and I called them the next morning.

They might have taken it as a validation, a sign that they had been right, that Toby was heading toward doom all along. And who was this crying thing on the other end of the line? they would ask. Hippie wannabe, liar and murderer, lover of our lost son. Why couldn't you have been the one?

"Where are you?" Toby's mother kept asking me, and I kept not telling her. So many other things seemed more important. The life Toby and I had lived together, for instance, the technicalities of the accident, the arrival of the helicopter and the airlifting of the body to Calgary and then to the United States, to this woman on the other end of the line. I knew I wasn't making much sense, but I blundered forward.

She was trying to get me to slow down and take a breath. That's what she kept telling me. Take a breath. Take a breath. It started out as an attempt to comfort and became harder; an irritation, a command. She was used to getting her way.

I was rambling on about the circle of Canadian patrol cars, the motorcyclist, everything but what she wanted to know. She began to cry then and the hardness changed places, from the woman to me. I could keep going and going, but I stopped.

In the motel bathroom I sifted through the pills for the Lorazepam and took two. I took some Sudafed too, crushed into a beer, and some kind of sleeping pill, fat as a button. Her voice was still in my head an hour after the call and TV seemed the only solution. The pills tugged on me slowly and then I was happy and then I was dreaming. That's how it happened. That's another way.

The second week of May and the roof opened as simply as a faucet. Toby set long boards along the side of our cabin so we could walk across the stream that formed there each year, and the buckling of the wood made a clacking sound as he moved from the back door to the truck and back again. We were ready to go and he was packing the truck with garbage bags full of clothes, cardboard boxes of his books, and two pairs of snowshoes: the old ones he used often and the new ones I never used. I was up in the loft, daydreaming, as he slammed the tailgate shut. I palmed my radio close to my ear, listening to tinny country music played out of a station in Anchorage. Country music on a transistor radio was one of the new pleasures I had discovered in Fairbanks, like cross-country skiing, drugs, and reading magazines in the outhouse. In Portland it had just been liquor, rock and roll, and narrow little clubs.

The song was unfamiliar, but a minute in I knew it by heart, and I sang along softly when the chorus rolled around for a third time. The door opened below me but Toby didn't say anything—he just listened to me sing. When I was finished he called out, "There's a lot of stuff left over from the yard sale. Do you want me to just leave it?"

"Yeah," I said. My bare feet were pressed against one of the roof's crossbeams, my butt raised slightly, my weight on my shoulders. I don't know why, but I liked this pose. I felt like I fit tightly into the space when I held my body that way, like I was part of things, hanging there almost, my neck on two or three pillows. I could spend an afternoon up there, reading or just doing nothing, while Toby talked to me from below.

He was doing the dishes now, heating up water on the stove. I heard the burner click, the flame leap and cradle the kettle. It was one of the many things we were going to leave behind, that kettle, and I would miss its weight, its sharp whistle. I had a theory that no two kettles whistled exactly the same and I had told Toby this when he was making up the list of stuff to bring with us. "A kettle is a kettle," he had said, and I knew enough to pick my battles.

"When you get a chance, I need some help with the kitchen table," he said. "I want to slide it in and then pack stuff around it."

"Okay," I said. "Right."

I thought of asking for one more day, but I had asked twice already and he had said yes both times, with an indulgent smile, like I was kid asking for ice cream.

The door opened and closed. He went outside again.

Intensity was what a couple of my co-workers called it, meaning it was a sexy thing, being in love with someone with convictions and drive. Even if those convictions made him a little crazy.

He had escaped, Toby sometimes said, and although he was usually quiet, once he had a few beers in him he would get to talking about the environment, politics, and all the bullshit going on down below. That's what he called it, like he was talking about hell instead of the rest of the country, and when he got to speaking this way he curled inward, shoulders hunched, and his voice dropped lower and quieter than usual, so it seemed like he was speaking secrets—things he had kept coiled in his heart for a long, long time. I would just listen, fascinated not so much by the specifics of what he was saying as by the intensity of his convictions, and I think it was the first time he started talking that way—late one night after a few sweaty line dances at the Blue Loon—that I started to fall for him. It was a pretty easy thing to do.

We had lived together for two years and although I had imagined many scenarios in which I might go back to the Lower 48, Toby had not been in a single one of them. I figured someday he would die here in Alaska, and the United States would be sixty years further down the gutter when he said his good-byes to the few people he knew and loved in Fairbanks. I didn't quite know where I would be by that time, and that made me melancholy when I pictured Toby as a lean old man, living alone, lugging back jugs of water from the Laundromat.

But there was something romantic about that too, and I think I loved that person best, the pure spirit of him I sometimes found in my imagination.

So it was surprising when he brought up the job opportunity *down below*, and even more surprising when he told me exactly where: in his hometown, the town where his parents still lived.

It's hard to admit that the person you love is also the great mystery in your life, although maybe that's usually how it works: the strength of those feelings brings about the mystery. Possibly he had felt that way about me too. I know I must have seemed very remote to him then, up in the loft, listening to my transistor radio. I came downstairs and pushed out into the bright light of the yard. The wooden pallets stacked with buckets, car parts, and salvaged wood scraps, the broken electronics and TV husks—it was all Toby's, at least for the next day or so, and then it would all belong to nobody, or to the person who bought the land. They were knocking over the cabin anyway, and slashing down the trees, because they said only the land was valuable.

I found the plastic bins where Toby kept all the old paint and rummaged through them, trying to find the little plastic packet I had hidden there, but it was gone, probably had been gone for more than a week. My hands came away red and blue and yellow. I wiped them on my jeans.

Over the next two weeks we would be driving more than three thousand miles in his ten-year-old truck to a place he had said he would never return to, so Toby had a lot on his mind. When I came around the cabin he was kneeling by the side of the truck inspecting the tires. "We'll change them in the Lower 48," he said. "I think we can get a few more miles out of them."

"Are you sure?" I said, because the treads looked almost smooth with wear.

"I'm sure," he said. "Don't worry."

Those words again, spoken with such casual conviction that it was easy to obey.

As if he were the one being inconvenienced.

It was the memory of this scene—those two words *Don't worry*—that kept looping through my head after the accident. It was a small pettiness to remember them again, and a larger one not to share them as we walked around Watson Lake. I held a camera, a survivor of the accident and a reminder of our previous obliviousness. It contained seven or eight pictures of our cabin back in Fairbanks, a single shot of Toby with his hand in front of his face, and one of me, naked, trying hard to look as if I didn't know I was being recorded for posterity. Across the lake stood another cabin, a beautiful one with a bright red tin roof angled in a high arch, and I lifted the camera to take a shot. Photographing this new place, recording it next to *our* cabin—what used to be our cabin—on the roll of film, well, there would be something correct about that, something reassuring, like grouping together clusters of the same flower from a field. It was our third day in that little town. We were still waiting for our truck to be repaired.

Later I thought often of the two cabins, the one right side up, the other one reflected on the lake so perfectly that it needed to be preserved in a photograph, and I did preserve it. I snapped a few shots, although it seemed ridiculous to play sightseer after what had happened. When the trip was over I held that picture and I turned it around and upside down. It seemed that both cabins were real, or rather, that both were unreal, each the duplicate. That is this story: a thing and the confusing reflection of that thing, each one casting the other.

PART II

Blood covered my face and chest and he grabbed me and ran his hands along my arms and head and neck, trying to find the cuts. But it was his blood. My knee was scratched, but that was it. I thought, dreamily, *Leave me alone*, because there was something almost sexual about the way he was touching me, something invasive, and even in my dreaminess I was expected to respond. I remember stifling those words and instead trying to just relax into it as he ran his hands from my shoulders to my stomach and up again.

What words to describe the spill of our history around the overturned truck, the strange sight of its undercarriage facing the blue sky? I remember Toby bending and lifting, walking around the wreck in a drunken-looking half circle. Both of his arms were working, and he filled them with debris: a box of cassette tapes, a smashed alarm clock, a dusty flannel shirt.

He must have been embarrassed to have it all on display like that, and the greed I thought I noticed in the way he clutched these things was probably just shame. None of it was worth much, but it was all his, the remnants of his life in Alaska.

"Don't worry about it," I said, or at least thought I said. He was walking away from me, trailing the end of the blanket. I was sitting in the wet grass, the dirt, the mud. It's where he had put me. I managed to rise to my feet and turn in a circle. The truck looked flimsy and toy-like upside down like that, as if someone could walk over to it, lean against it, and upright it with a small grunt. Up ahead, Toby dropped the blanket and picked up a duffle bag, but this time he used only one hand, and by the time the Mounties arrived one of his arms was dark blue and bent, as if he had suffered a stroke. In his other hand he held my stuffed orange crocodile, a thing I used to sleep with when feeling especially sad or stoned. He dropped it on the small pile of stuff he had gathered and turned to the Mounties as they walked over. The air was still filled with dust and dirt and they were both squinting and covering their mouths, as if they were walking through a fire.

"We're alright," he told them. "We don't need you here."

They ignored him and called over to me. "Are you okay?"

"I think so," I said.

"Your husband is in shock," one of them said, as he knelt down in front of me. The other was helping Toby to the patrol car. The lights fanned blue through the dust cloud, and I thought of the ecstasy in the little bottle in his duffle bag. I had to fight the urge to break the Mountie's helpful grip on my hand and run off into the woods. He rested his palm on the top of my head to guide me into the car and I nestled into the seat, staring ahead at the wire mesh separating front from back. For some reason my view of the world from there made me feel strong, distinct. We had moved from the dust cloud into open space. We were heading back where we had just come from, all the scenery—the trees, the hardscrabble bars and hotels—playing out in reverse order.

Up front, the Mounties were talking to each other. I couldn't hear the specifics, but I knew it was about us, and it had none of the friendliness they had used when addressing Toby or me. Then one of them raised his voice so we could hear. "Sorry to put you into a vehicle so soon after your accident," the driver said, "but we need to have your husband looked at. His arm is going a little funny."

I let that mistake stand, allowing Toby to be my husband for at least the time it took us to head down Watson Lake's main drag. I reached across to him, touched the back of his neck and rubbed lightly. He closed his eyes. "How fast do you think you guys were going back there?" one of the Mounties called back to us in the cheeriest of voices. It seemed like he was just curious, that's all, and no answer would have surprised him.

"I don't know," I said. "Not fast. Not fast at all, really."

"Okay," he said.

"Your tires flipped you," the other one explained. "When you went off the road one of them burst, I bet, and then the other one, and they just turned you right over. It happens all the time." He stopped talking, but I wanted to hear him say more about how typical something like this was. The car moved down a narrow dirt road. Grass grew up on either side of us, almost waist high, scratching against the doors as we moved forward.

"Short cut," the Mountie explained.

"What do you recall?" the other asked. Again he assumed that happy tone—he was just making conversation, asking if the food was good on our flight, commenting on the weather. The thing I remembered most was hanging upside down by my seatbelt, my hair in my eyes, and then the sound of the birds, Toby touching me.

"I don't remember much," Toby said, and the Mountie told him not to worry, there would be plenty of time to talk about it later.

The patrol car emerged onto a paved street and took a turn into what looked like the property surrounding some kind of long farm-house. Half a dozen dogs in various shapes and sizes roamed free in the front yard. One passed in front of us and stood there, frozen, in a staring contest, but the car kept moving forward and the dog stepped out the way and vanished into the grass. "He's a rascal, that one," the driver said.

We passed a small corral where a cluster of horses moved around aimlessly, and then we were at the house. When the Mounties opened the doors for us some dogs came toward the car, but one of the Mounties yelled and clapped his hands together above his head and they hung back.

"Our truck," Toby said.

"It's fine," he said. "Don't you worry about that."

"We could have driven you into the hospital in White Horse," the other guy said, "but that's more than an hour away. You need to be looked at soon."

The walls were painted bright white and a series of blue curtains divided the main room into smaller compartments. The place looked pretty clean, considering the outside, but I could still smell dogs and something else, like chlorine. A woman in a white smock stood waiting for us. "Oh, yes," she said when she saw Toby's arm.

They separated us, me to one end of the room, Toby to the other, a Mountie paired with each of us. Every time mine asked me a question—how fast were we driving, where were we headed, how long had I been at the wheel—I answered with a question myself. Was Toby going to be okay? Why was his arm so blue? What was this place?

"Watson Lake," he said, and then again asked a question of his own.

With a sharp swish the curtain parted and the doctor came in. The Mountie stepped to the side to make room for her. She half sat next to me on the medical table, hands folded in her lap, and asked me how I was doing. "Pretty good," I said. "You know, under the circumstances."

I wondered what she was doing in this part of the world, if she was happy here. I had the crazy idea that I'd make her an offer: she could come along with us as long as she made sure Toby was okay. She could even bring a few of the animals. They could ride in the back. It would be like Noah's ark all over again, but without the flood. It was fun to imagine myself as the rescuer and not the rescued.

"Wendy," she said, "I'm a little worried about your boyfriend."

He must have given her my name, the details of our relationship. It felt like a betrayal, but I answered her. "I'm a little worried too."

"His collarbone is broken," she said, putting her balled fist on her own chest to show me the spot. "The seatbelt must have broken it. He was wearing his seatbelt, right?"

It felt like she was trying to trick me, but I couldn't remember the truth of it anyway. I could hide in my own ignorance, at least for a little while.

"Is there someone we should call?" she asked.

"A human doctor," I said, thinking of the dogs and horses outside, the dog dish on the tiled floor just a few feet away. "I mean, a doctor for humans."

"A family member," the Mountie clarified. "Someone like that."

I could see Toby's mother getting that phone call. "No," I said. "Nobody like that. It's just us."

Toby and I were holding hands. I held his up, looking it over as a curiosity, and lowered it again, and then I moved into a slow walk.

The cabin placed as perfectly as in a painting.

The twin scenes—with just the slenderest ripple to indicate the illusionary one—made me think of other not-quite-right doubles, like Toby and me or our twisted upside-down truck and the one that had existed the day before.

Another mirror image: my first trip to Alaska, up through Portland into Anchorage by plane, and my trip out of it, heading east through Canada, mile by mile in an old Toyota truck. That first time—the arrival—I had been nineteen, and although I didn't know what I wanted, my boyfriend at the time was always talking about the summer he had worked in the canneries, and soon the reminisces became a kind of plan. All winter I saved money from the restaurant where I worked, and late at night at the restaurant bar when he came in to walk me home, we talked about the trip we were going to take that summer. The rest of the people in the restaurant—the waitresses and bartenders who were our makeshift friends—kidded us about going there, about the bears, the cold, the usual complaints. "We'll see you in October," they joked, "when the temperature drops and you miss us."

But that didn't happen. We stayed on there, in Anchorage, three or four months, and then we moved to Fairbanks eight hours north, living in a long rectangle of small apartments that had once been air force housing. They had been built poorly, and in cold weather ice came in through the wall outlets and hung in long beautiful strands from the roofs. It was only later that I would recognize these beautiful things as bad signs. Then they just seemed pretty. I spent long stretches of the dark winter afternoons crouched in front of our space heater reading romance paperbacks.

When my boyfriend decided to break up with me late that spring, it hit me so hard I thought about returning—not to Portland but to Appleton, where I was born and where my father and sister still lived. I was waitressing part-time in a place that was not much different than the restaurant I had worked at in Portland, and I figured this was something I could do in Appleton just as easily. I had lived in Alaska for more than a year, but I did not love it yet because I did not understand it. It took meeting Toby to do that.

We had never really talked much about any of that—about my reasons for going to Alaska, about my ex, about my old life, but in the third day of our trip, the boredom and quiet pushed me to talk. I had been thinking about all of this for a long time and I think I wanted to get some of it out of my head. The easiest way to do that was to speak it. "You know," I said, "when I met you, I was this close to leaving Fairbanks. Do you know that?" I held my finger and thumb apart about an inch for him to see the narrow margin, the way luck might rule our lives.

"Oh yeah?" he said.

"Yeah," I said. "I was really a mess. But then we started dating and everything moved so quickly and before I knew it we were living together."

"Well, you had given notice on your apartment," he said.

"That piece of crap," I said.

"Yeah," he said, smiling. "That place."

The bugs were popping against the windshield—big flies and strange awkward beetles. They hit us with comedic force, spraying and twisting and leaving odd death-shapes against the glass. "I remember the first time I saw your cabin," I said. "It was so small and beautiful. And you lit that little candle and set in on the floor and I sat on one side of it and you sat on the other. I loved that."

"I remember," he said.

"I was sad too, though, because I realized what I had been missing."

"You don't sound like yourself," he said.

"What do you mean?"

"I don't know," he said. "Just what I said, I guess."

"Well, I'll stop," I said.

"No, no," he said. "It's interesting. And we have a lot of time to kill, don't we?"

"Some," I said. "But look. We're at the border."

"Yeah," he said, as simple as that, because of course he had no idea what went through my head during those long quiet stretches of the trip. I put my hand on his and asked about the plastic baggie of pills under the seat. I hadn't thought of it before and I assumed he hadn't either. It didn't seem like that big a deal.

I could see the check-in point up ahead: a small booth with a single figure waiting. Not another car in front or behind us. I didn't know if that was a good sign or a bad one. The American flag, I noticed, was flying at half-mast and I regretted not knowing the reason. But I was proud I didn't know too—it showed how separate from things we were. Later, after the accident, I would remember this moment and decide that my only fear had been that Toby and I would be separated and questioned and that I would let him down somehow, that I would be a disappointment. Which is what happened, only much later, and not in the way I had expected.

The vegetation had been cut back a good thirty feet on either side of the road. These were the sickly, thin trees I was used to seeing in interior Alaska, where the permafrost made it difficult for the roots to grow deep. I half expected them to change on the other side of the border crossing, grow larger, darker, like the trees I had grown up with in Wisconsin. Toby tapped the brakes, glanced behind the seat, and said, "Just be chatty. Ask him how far it is to the next town."

"What is the next town?"

"I don't know," he said. He had some papers in his hand—his passport, my birth certificate, folded in three parts and slipped into an envelope. At some point he had gotten them ready, probably at our last stop when I had gone off into the trees to pee and scan the wilderness.

Would the person behind the glass be happy to see us? Was each car an event at this remote station? I often felt bad for strangers, imagining their lives as something they might want to flee. This person was no exception. He nodded hello to us as we pulled up to the window, eyes downcast. He was thin and pale and it seemed like we should just give him a dollar and keep driving, but Toby handed him our papers and the man took them and looked them over. The tape deck was playing a long, grinding psychedelic guitar solo and I turned it down and then clicked it off altogether. "How long are you staying in Canada?" he asked.

"We're just passing through. Going to Montana," Toby said, and then he added, "We're moving. We used to live in Fairbanks."

He asked us if we had any firearms, any alcohol, any animals. No, no, no.

"Well, have a good trip," the man said, and he handed Toby back our documents and made a little motion of his hand for us to proceed. Toby passed the documents to me. I had not seen my birth certificate in a long time, and it reminded me that I had once been a very different person, a girl in the cheap hotel in Anchorage, worried about what might happen if she lost a slip of paper with her name and date of birth on it. Except that maybe I was that same person really, and just wanted to be different.

"Excuse me," I said, leaning across the seat so he could see me through the driver's side window. "What time is it?"

He glanced at his wrist.

⁓⋇⁓

I squared the lake off in the viewfinder of my camera, adjusted the focus, took the shot. Toby said, "What are you doing that for?"

In the late afternoon Toby and I would head down to the lake and walk around it. This was our third time around. He was trying to be a good sport, but it was like walking with my grandfather, stopping and starting, feet sliding like he should be wearing slippers. Finally, after ten minutes of this, he sat down in the grass and said, "I give up. I need to rest."

"Sure," I said, and I collapsed down next to him.

"It doesn't even look like someone lives there," I said, with a glance across the water, and he smiled. He looked his worst, but I told myself that most of it was cosmetic. I thought about that intense look of concentration that hardened his features when he was working on a fishing lure, and I tried to superimpose that look over his slightly drugged, slack-jawed face, but it didn't work. For the first time in the two years we'd known each other I wanted to hug him like a child and tell him that everything was going to be okay. "You know," I said. "We're going to be fine."

He was half asleep already, his good arm folded over his eyes to block out the sun.

"We were lucky," I added. "We *are* lucky." I didn't know if I was lying or not. With the accident the whole idea of luck had passed beyond my understanding. I couldn't tell if he was asleep or not. His breathing was deep and pained. I wanted to stroke his hair but I held back out of some strange politeness, still looking across the water. "Toby," I said. "Are you asleep?"

He didn't answer. An ant crawled across his wrist, winding its way across the bridge of a finger, and I reached out to wipe it away. "Don't," he said. "It feels good. It tickles."

"I can't picture you wearing a suit and tie," I said.

He pulled his arm back from his eyes and looked up at me. "I worked there for a year when I was a teenager and I liked it."

"Stacking boxes," I said, because I had heard some of his stories about the lifers there, like it was a trip Toby had taken to a different planet. Had he forgotten about the vitriol he used to pump into those little tales, the revulsion?

"I won't be lifting boxes there now," he said.

He meant that the new job was better than the old one, but I couldn't help but wonder if he was commenting on the limp arm curled to his chest.

"Yeah," I said. "I know." And then, "Let's just get some plane tickets. Let's get out of here."

A tension entered Toby's features, tightness in his lips and something shining and watery in his eyes. I had never seen it there before and I turned away.

"Wire your parents for money," I said.

"I can't do that," he said. "You don't understand."

"Explain it to me."

"You should know why. How long have we been together?"

"We have to do *something*," I said. I had stopped rubbing his back but my hand was still resting there. It didn't feel like I was talking to Toby at all and I wondered if my hand slid up to his shoulder and turned his face toward me, what would I find there?

I said, "The mechanic, he thought he could do it. He seemed pretty sure." I was beginning to believe it myself. "Let's roll and think about it," I said.

"You know," he said, "I almost died."

"I know," I said. "I know we did. But we didn't."

"No, you don't understand. At the clinic."

"What?"

"I was in real trouble. We didn't tell you anything about it, but they were talking about airlifting me out to Toronto. They were saying I was going to lose my arm."

Where I had been? On the other side of the room answering questions about seatbelts. After a while they had given me an apple and a Hershey bar and I had eaten them both.

He ran his hand through the grass. "Imagine how much money that would have cost? A helicopter?"

He came back to me word by word, but the look on his face, it made me angry. "Toby," I said. "Stop it."

It felt cruel, what he was doing, and he must have known it.

"And anyway," I told him, "it's Canada." We didn't have to pay for any of the medical bills. He knew that. We had reached another gap in the conversation and I looked back out at the lake.

"Toby," I said. "I don't want to walk down to that garage again."

He didn't answer so I repeated the statement, the same flat tone, the exact same words, except with his name placed at the end like a period. I was not trying to make him feel bad, but when I thought of the mechanic with his soft accent and dirty white T-shirt, I imagined all sorts of horribly unlikely things. He probably had a wife, a family, parents and siblings who loved him, but I pictured him pushing me against the wall, running his hand down my body. He would smell like motor oil, of course, and maybe beer, and I would turn my head and twist and choke. But imagining also felt like a comfort. To replace our complicated problems—my complicated problems—with a more immediate one, to shift the menace onto a thing I could kick and claw. It was, after all, a much simpler version of something I had been fighting for a very long time.

"Toby?" I said for the third time, but I was alone. I lifted the camera and took the shot.

~∗~

On the fourth day in Watson Lake I awoke even earlier than usual and walked along the main road, backpack looped over one shoulder. Occasionally a car slowed and then quickened again as it passed. It was a small town and by now most everyone probably knew about the girl on the side of the road. I didn't raise my thumb to hitchhike or even glance in the direction of traffic. I wanted each car to see a certain kind of person, a sight that would stick with them as they rushed past.

Each day I had to pass the spot where we had overturned. I recognized it by the shattered tree off the side of the road, the glass and plastic bits the size of teeth in the dirt.

There the truck was, up on the lift, as I entered the garage. Its undercarriage seemed fine, but really, what did I know? I stood in plain sight, waiting for someone to notice me. The mechanic had explained—giving the truck a hardy double pat with his palm—that the engine was solid, that he could get the body into shape with some work. "I'll take care of you," he said. "Tell your mother not to worry." So each day I walked to his shop to check on its progress, and each day he told me that it was coming along, that there was a lot of work that had to be done. His tow truck was always coming and going—I sometimes sat drinking coffee and watching the goings-on—and occasionally it returned from one of its trips dragging an expensive car that looked like it had no business in that landscape. These cars always ended up in the back, the surrounding fence topped with loops of barbed wire. It was, I decided, the absolute busiest place in town.

Occasionally the Mounties showed up and chatted with me about the weather. They were friendly—they sat down next to me on the bench and seemed genuinely interested in my answers—but they did not ask me how I had arrived at the shop or how I was going to get back. Maybe they just assumed that was all taken care of, that there were people who knew every inch of my recent experience.

I could hear old-time country music from the back of the garage, the same music I had listened to on my radio, possibly the same station. The mechanic was sitting at a folding table eating his breakfast. I stood watching him for a moment, and although he must have known I was there, he decided to let me play the spy. He pushed his toast under his eggs and lifted them, using the bread as a scoop; he cupped his other hand beneath as a safety net should the whole mess fall.

Finally, I walked over to him. "Hello," I said. "I don't mean to interrupt."

I had already gotten off on the wrong foot. My voice was meek, apologetic, and I was still standing a few feet away, as if I suspected he might reach out and grab me. If he had told me to shoo I probably would have stepped back wordlessly into the outside world. Instead he smiled and motioned me closer, his mouth stuffed with food. "Do you want anything?" he asked. The table was littered with cans of orange soda and small bags of potato chips.

"I'm okay," I said. "Thanks."

"We fixed the windshield," he explained. "I'm trying to get you out of here soon, so I didn't order a new one. It would take a week to have it shipped in. We cut out some heavy plastic and fastened it in place. That should get you into Calgary at least. I'd have it replaced once you get to civilization." As he talked, still chewing, he stood, wiped his hands on his jeans, and stepped over to the back window. "See?" he said. He indicated the truck, like it was something I wouldn't have noticed otherwise. It looked fine other than the truck cap, which was crushed to half its height, and the flattened, torn tires. "That was Sam's idea," he said. I had no idea who Sam was, but I guess I should have. I wondered if I had met him at some point during that first day when everything was a mad blur.

"What was?" I said.

"The windshield," he said, and then, "We had to do some work on the engine too, and we're going to put four new tires on there. That'll make it very safe for you. Are you going to have your parents wire you some money?" He pushed the back of his hand across his mouth like a napkin. "We don't take credit cards."

"I'll have the money," I said. "We'll have it."

"Okay," he said. "That's fine," and he walked me to the door and opened it for me like a gentleman.

"Tomorrow?" I said.

"I think so," he said. "We're just waiting on the tires." He twisted the doorknob in his hand—back and forth, back and forth, like he was unscrewing it—and it made a distressed squeaking sound. He seemed to want to tell me something else. He was smiling again, and there was something almost dirty about the way he twisted the doorknob around. I stepped outside sideways. He said, "I'm not saying this is a dangerous place, but these highways, you should be careful. Did you take the Richardson or the Glenn in?"

"The Glenn," I said.

He frowned like this was the wrong answer. "Okay," he said.

On the walk down the road I thought about his question and my answer. Toby had chosen the Glenn Highway, had mapped a route through the Kluane National Park, where we had stayed up late eating cheese sandwiches in the glow of a flashlight. He seemed full of innocence and conviction, and so did I, although even then I think I knew enough to know that these things are often a temporary condition, a state that can come and go like weather.

In the lobby of the little hotel two men were talking by the cigarette machine. They said hello to me and I turned my head away and muttered hello back, moving past them as quickly as I could without breaking into a jog.

Somehow I got turned around and I had to come back down one corridor and up another before finding the door with the right number. The windows in our room were open and the flower-print curtains were blowing in a light breeze. The sheets were bunched up at the bottom of the bed. I couldn't stand it and I headed out into the hall again to take my chances in the lounge. One of the two men at the cigarette machine said, "I don't mean to intrude, young ma'am. I'm just letting you know how sorry I am."

The second man's body formed a pose of disinterest, leaning against the machine, but his voice was kind. "Really unfortunate," he said. "I saw the helicopter come in. Did you see that? It was only here for a couple of hours."

"Yeah, I saw," said the first. "All those kids came running like it was the ice cream truck. And then waving good-bye like they knew him."

The first seemed disgusted by this, the second amused, but they were content to let that difference stand.

One of the two men at the cigarette machine said, "He's in the lounge."

I had been there five days now and I didn't even know there *was* a lounge. But there was: a room with low ceilings, a small bar, and five or six tables, each one with its salt and pepper shakers, its ketchup and mustard. Toby sat at one of them, talking to a man I presumed to be the bartender. I stood by the bar—almost behind the bar—while Toby lifted a beer and nodded his head. "Toby," I said. "Hey."

"Hey, hey," he said, and I walked over to him, pulled out a chair. "This is Stanley," he said. "Stanley, this is my girlfriend. The tough one."

"I've heard a lot about you," he said, and he shook my hand tight.

"I was just telling him that we're heading out tomorrow."

"Hopefully," I said. We were spending $70 a night on the room and we had an $800 limit on my credit card. Toby didn't have a credit card. Capitalism, he said, was a trap.

I held out my hand and Toby passed me his beer. I had a little swig and handed it back. Stanley seemed to like this exchange because he smiled. He seemed to think that we were a cute couple. He folded his arms and said, "What's Fairbanks like?"

"You've never been there?"

"Nah," he said. "I don't travel much. Been to Nova Scotia once when my dad died."

He must have been in his early fifties, with a big belly straining against his T-shirt and big hands that seemed like they should have been lifting heavy things at a construction site. They dwarfed the beer he held. I wanted to ask him how he had ended up stranded in Watson Lake. The story promised to be at least as interesting as ours. Maybe it could match it pound for pound, make me feel better about our misadventure.

"My mom still lives out there," he said. "In this gigantic house on a cliff. Sometimes it's the saddest place in the world, but I'm always wanting to go back."

"Home is like that," Toby said. He was passing into one of his philosophical moods.

What about this place? I wanted to ask. *Isn't this the saddest place in the world sometimes?*

"She's eighty-one years old last week," the man continued, "and she still walks to the store."

It seemed odd that the first piece of information I would get from a man that age would be something about his mother, but for some reason that made me more comfortable around him, and I said, "I like Fairbanks a lot. I miss it already."

"Me too," Toby said. He finished the beer and asked the man for another. "Do you want one?" he said to me.

"Do you think you should be drinking on your meds?" I asked, and I realized I was playing a role too. If Toby was the adventurer, the risk taker, then I would be the doting girlfriend, not the tough one but the cautious one.

"I've only had one," he said.

I didn't know if he meant the beer or the pills.

"How long ago were you back there?" Toby asked the bartender.

"Gosh," he said, and I liked him even more for using that word. "That was almost twenty years ago. For my dad's funeral. He was pretty young when he passed. A mining accident. The mines took a lot of people early."

I noticed the wallpaper for the first time: blue and red flowers, the kind you might find in someone's living room.

"I'll cook you up some burgers too," the man said, although he didn't move. "What's so funny?"

I was laughing, snickering, and I didn't really know why. "I'm just happy," I said, and I was—deliriously so—although I knew it wouldn't last for more than a minute. Knowing that made it more precious and I luxuriated in it like a bath of warm water. "I didn't know this back room existed until just now," I said.

The man laughed along, and Toby too, and I realized he had come here before, possibly several times, to have talks a lot like this one. The happiness vanished—just like that—although I was still laughing, my body stuck in that place my mind had occupied a second before. I said, "You've been having a lot of fun, Toby. I didn't know."

"I was bored in the room," he said.

"I can imagine," I said. "Just lying there on all those pillows."

"I broke my neck," he said.

"Collarbone," I said.

"Same difference."

I thought of the car accident, except this time remembering was a small, decisive gesture, like reaching out and taking Toby's beer and swigging it down. During the last few days the memory would sneak in and surprise me when my guard was down. This time it was my decision. I stepped there in my own head and looked over the truck again, felt Toby's hands sliding down my body to check for wounds. And this time—it was another small act of will—I imagined that I was the one who was injured, that glass had cut my face and stomach and chest and legs, that Toby's hands found gashes and broken bones and he was so afraid he began to mutter nonsense, as if his words could call me back. And although I was punishing myself by imagining this, it was also punishment for Toby because in the dream sequence running through my head Toby's mad panic stretched on and on.

In that spray of imagination, I discovered something. I wasn't sure what, but I brought it into our little scene. I sat there with cuts crisscrossing my face, a broken hand, bruised ribs, but I'm not sure if it made me understand Toby, or myself, any better. It was a form of play, but the serious kind. He said, "She almost died." He said, "Are you sure you should drink on your meds? Because that's powerful stuff."

We were all laughing because we were all alive. The man from Nova Scotia he understood, he recognized love when he saw it. He seemed to feel the same thing for his mother, at least, and maybe the place where he had been born.

"I'm going to get her home," Toby said. "I would, anyway, if she had a home. I guess I'll get her somewhere." He went on, "Let's get a little drunk."

"We can't afford it," I said, although I liked the idea. There were more open beers on the table. Where had they come from?

"I'll get you drunk," the man said. "Don't worry about that. You have bigger things to worry about."

Later, sprawled on the bed, my hands in Toby's hair, I would tell him, "Eighty-one years. I can't even imagine it."

"Alone in that house," he said. "On a cliff."

"We should have told him what happened to us," I said. "Our story."

He was trying to take off his shoes by rubbing his feet together, catching one, and sort of popping it off. After a short struggle one fell to the carpet, then the other. "I wouldn't have known where to start," he said, "and anyway, he knows. Everybody here knows."

But I promised I would sometime the next day, when I was sober and clear-headed and the events had lined themselves up in an order that made sense. My hand was throbbing, but my spirit felt as light and focused as an arrow. Everything in the world felt like a target. "Listen," I said. "Ravens."

"Nearly morning," he said.

And then the pain was gone, my face clean and unmarked, and Toby was gone too, gone to the same place as my injuries. Had it all just been dress-up? In my head I walked into the bathroom to find him in the shower, head buried under the blast of hot water, and I sat on the toilet, legs spread. For a moment we were like an old married couple, side by side but each oblivious to the other. The room full of steam and heat, or just the sound of my own motion, my footsteps and the click of the light switch, the clatter of the toilet seat and my shallow breathing.

⁓⁂⁓

Maybe I am discovering my life. Maybe I am losing myself. A strange surprise after all these years. The other stories, the versions told to the person across from me at a bar, in a therapist's office, repeated in my own head, what do they matter except that they've led me here, to the hotel room in Watson Lake, the day after the accident, alone with a phone in my hand? I was calling back to Fairbanks, listening to the ringing and anticipating my voice making the joke I had rehearsed in my head. Finally, someone picked up on the other end, my boss at the coffee house. He owned four of the huts, two bars, and a revolver he liked to keep strapped to his belt. I could tell he was at one of the bars now and I could tell it was a busy night from the pulse of voice noise in the background. He sounded harried. I could tell from just one word, hello.

"Gerry," I said. "I'm in trouble," and I'm sure he thought, *Why me?* I had instantly forgotten the joke.

"Oh, there you are," he said. "How you doing?"

As if he hadn't quite heard. "I'm in trouble," I said again, and I remembered how he had always promised to kick the ass of any guy who was rude to us at the huts, how he'd drive from one to the other, dropping compliments, asking if everything was okay, if we were cold. He was always asking me that—Are you cold, honey?—in a way that seemed almost fatherly. Then he'd drive off to the next.

"What kind of trouble?" he asked. He was probably assuming that Toby had done something to me, and was ratcheting his anger up to a higher pitch. I could hear it.

So I told him. I told him where it had happened and how and I told him I missed Fairbanks already and then I told him about Toby. I knew I didn't make any sense but that was how it came out of my mouth.

He asked me if I was high and I said yes, but it didn't matter, I was telling him exactly what happened and it was the truth down to the last detail. I said I was sorry for calling, but I had always liked him and I knew he liked Toby and Toby had always liked him too. *All of us like all the others*, I wanted to say.

"That's true," he said. "Hold on. I'm shutting a door."

"Okay."

For a moment I thought he had hung up, but then his voice came back on the line, thicker and heavier. The noise in the background was gone. He said, "I can't believe it."

"They were trying to airlift him out to Toronto. Not Toronto. Edmonton. I guess that's where it is. I don't know. I think that must be it."

I sounded like an idiot, but I felt imperial. Something had happened and now life would be different.

He said, "I need you to focus, okay? What do you need?"

"I'm focused," I said. "And I'm fine."

"Okay. I suppose I have to believe you."

"It was stupid of me to call anyway. You're not even my boss anymore." I could feel myself getting angry and I didn't know why. Yes, I sounded like an idiot, but so did he, for listening attentively, for being so helpless in the face of my tragedy. I remembered him smiling at me from behind the bar, making jokes about the repeat customers. I would sometimes get angry then too, because he seemed so happy to be there every single day.

"So much for our big plans," I said.

"I didn't mean it," he said.

"What?"

"When you left. I told you you'd fail. In the Lower 48. That was a bad thing to say."

"I don't even remember that," I said.

"Come back," he said.

"No," I said. "I'm going to keep going."

I hoped he would just shut up, that obligations would call him back to his real life, but he kept talking, because I guess he was trying hard to make it all better. He was trying to coax me back too, because it was crazy to do otherwise, and I did wonder if he was right. But I told him, "I need to sleep. I'm going to go to sleep."

"Right," he said. "I should go too."

I listened to him breathing and then I killed the connection with my index finger. The bed was all torn up and the floor was covered with my clothes and the TV was on low. My savings were in an envelope in one of my sneakers and the rest of the drugs arranged on the side table. This was my situation and it was important to recognize it. Tomorrow I would see the mechanic.

⁓ฝ฿⁓

The day we left Watson Lake we discovered a playground in a small town, and while I climbed to the top of a metal jungle gym, Toby sat in the sand below, talking to me as I perched above his head. Across the street an old man in a suit and tie was sweeping the sidewalk in front of his business. He was a lawyer—the small sign in the window proclaimed his name and the half dozen mundane problems he specialized in fixing. I said, "He looks peaceful, doing that."

"We do too," Toby said. "Doing this."

Annoyed he had to make such an obvious point.

"I wonder if he noticed us," I said.

I had plucked a lilac from a bush and I dropped the petals into Toby's face while he talked. He didn't make a move to brush them away. We had only driven three hours, but it felt much longer. The truck rattled whenever we hit thirty and the plastic they had cut into a makeshift windshield buckled and bowed. Occasionally Toby's good arm pushed it back into place. At fifty the wind made a threatening sound through my damaged door, but we didn't go that fast too often on the narrow, unpaved roads, so the finding of the town had been a reprieve, a blessing. We had turned off into the parking lot without even having to discuss it.

"He probably thinks we're up to no good," I said.

But for some reason that made me sad. I wanted this man—this man I didn't know—to think well of us. I wanted him to notice the way I dropped the petals down, the way Toby lifted his chin and accepted them. I wanted all of it to be real in the eyes of another.

"When I first met you I thought you were a little crazy," Toby said. "Do you know that?"

"No," I said, and then, "maybe."

And just when I was about to ask him why, he said, "When I first went to Fairbanks I had wanted to meander, go down south, down through Texas, and then up. I had a checklist of states I had never been to and a whole month to kill."

His eyes were closed and he was speaking softly. "I owned a beat-up Chevy Impala from the dark ages of American glut. I had bought it for cash from a guy with an eye patch. Like a pirate. I'm serious. He had it parked on his front lawn. It seemed like it was a thousand years old. The seatbelts had been chewed off by his Doberman. I loved that. I loved the eye patch and the list of states. I loved the way the car swam all over the road. It prowled, that's what it did."

He paused a beat, blinked open his sunken eyes. "I had read the usual books. I don't even have to say their names. You know the ones I mean."

He chuckled and turned his head to the side. His voice was so low I thought he might be falling asleep. "The Impala broke down five hours into the trip. Smoke came pouring out from under the hood and that was it. I hitchhiked back home and spent a couple of weeks in my parents' basement watching the NHL playoffs. They ended up helping me buy a plane ticket. I think they thought that once I got there, I'd turn around again."

"Okay," I said.

"My father never once raised his voice to me, but I knew what he was thinking. That label. Being someone who doesn't complete things."

"Well, you got there," I said.

"And now I'm leaving. I don't know if they'll see that as me completing what I set out to do."

"But it's been years."

"That's my family." His voice grew to almost a shout. "I don't know when something is complete," he said. "When is it? How do you know?"

"Are you tripping?" I asked.

"Yes," he said, "but it's a serious question I just asked."

"I asked a serious one too," I said. His answer had tilted our entire talk, sent it spinning at an odd angle. I thought of the man across the street again, assessing us, but when I glanced over he was no longer there. It was like Toby was in one place and I was in another. I made a raspy sound with both my throat and nose and dropped down to the ground, crouching for a moment before straightening up, moving from animal to human.

Toby lifted himself up on one arm. "How far was that walk?" he asked.

"Two miles maybe," I said.

"And nobody gave you a ride?"

"I didn't really ask," I said.

"Why?"

"I didn't want to," I said. "Let's get going. I want to get more driving in."

"Two miles," he said.

"It wasn't so bad," I said, which was especially true now that I didn't have to do it anymore. The walk had truncated in my mind, become a series of small signposts and images. I wondered if our drive would shrink that small someday; it seemed a shame, even if it might spare me the worst parts of the journey.

I was figuring that out about myself. I wanted it all. I was greedy for it.

After a brief inspection of the truck—it was a nervous habit that would continue through the whole trip—we climbed inside and drove back out onto the main road. While my hands did the work of driving, my mind did the work—the intricate work—of remembering what had happened. It picked apart the accident again and again, imagined ways that it could have been avoided, offering them up as some kind of punishment. I didn't know then that I had started a process that would last years, that would become habitual and strange. But it was like scratching at acne. There was so much dreamy pleasure in it.

"I feel great," Toby said after a while. He drummed his good hand on the dashboard. This was the person who all the Fairbanks dropouts loved, the hero of the transfer station, dumpster diver and armchair philosopher. I remembered him smoking dope openly as he moved through the debris looking for bicycle frames and kitchenware and anything else. "What was the best thing you ever found?" I asked him.

He said, "There were so many things. Toys. A box of Playboys from the '70s. Remember that remote-controlled car? It still worked."

That answer didn't satisfy me, and I was thinking about his last question, the one about distance. Why did it matter to him how long the walk had been? Was a mile and a half different than two? If I had answered three would that have changed everything? Distance,

I decided, had become as arcane as astrology. A whole etiquette had already developed around watching the odometer. The key was to glance at it without letting the other person know you were keeping track. It was the invisible thing that united us. "What else?" I asked. "What other things?"

It was not, though, a measure of progress. The accident had changed that. We were counting down, not up. I was anyway.

⁓⁓

Although I had left Watson Lake in broad daylight, slowly passing the spot where the tires had blown out and the truck spun over, the departure felt like an escape. I didn't turn on the radio until I was far out of town, and when I did, I discovered that the tape player was broken.

That morning when the mechanic had appeared in his tow truck, knocking up dust, I had waved to him like a friend. I had arrived before him, and he found me with my fingers interlaced through the chain link, watching the building on the other side. That's when I turned and raised my hand and smiled. I wasn't sure myself if I was being sarcastic or desperate to please. The gesture surprised me, and so did the hot-faced shame following it. I tried to shape my expression into nothing in particular.

Somebody new stepped from the truck's passenger's side. Judging from the shape of the head, the flat curve of the nose, it was his son. The boy, about sixteen, had his head lowered apelike, listening to headphones. He walked around the back of the building while his father came over to me. "Early bird," he said, a wide ring of keys in his hand.

"I haven't gone to bed," I said, which was close enough to true that it didn't feel like deception. I watched his face for some sign of surprise, but he was twisting the key in the lock and pushing inside.

The bill was three pages long, written in scrawled handwriting, stapled at the corner. I went through it slowly, asking him what the words said, and he was patient, leaning in close as he talked. $1,081. I said, "I'm going to need a little time to get this cash together."

He said, "You can have money wired in down at the post office, you know."

"Is this an estimate? Could it turn out to be a little lower?"

"This is what it is," he said.

His son was back, standing next to our truck, when I left, headphones still plugged into his ears. He noticed me now that his father wasn't there—our eyes locked and I saw his hand move upward just slightly, as if he was ready to unplug himself if I opened my mouth—but I wasn't going to give him the satisfaction. I kept walking. Ten steps later I turned around and said, "Can you give me a ride?"

"I don't know," he said. "How far?"

"Not far," I said.

I told myself he wasn't used to seeing people like me. I smiled at him and asked him what was in his head. He looked confused for a moment and then answered, "Aerosmith."

"Cool," I said.

And just like that we were in his truck and he was asking me what kind of music I liked. "All kinds," I said. "What's your name?"

"John," he said.

"Mine's Wendy," I said, when he didn't ask. "Would your dad get angry if he knew you were giving me a ride, John?"

He shifted up, glanced in the rearview. "I don't know," he said.

He handled the truck like he had been driving it since he was ten. It surprised me how short the road was when I didn't have to walk it, and I didn't know whether to be happy for the ride or annoyed that I hadn't asked sooner. I asked him, "Do you like to get high?"

"I think so," he said.

We were parked in the hotel parking lot. He turned off the engine while I rolled a joint. "Is there a better place around here?"

He shifted the truck and we began to move. He seemed like a smaller version of his father physically—the same thick neck, already the beginning of a hard belly hanging out over his belt—but there was something soft to his personality. I felt like I could say, *Take me here, take me there*, and he would obey. Instead, I told him more about the accident, about what Toby and I were doing in Fairbanks and where we were headed. I was trying to color in the lines, make myself a real person. "I should be going soon," he said, after I had rolled the joint and taken a hit. I handed it to him and he held it for a long time before inhaling. He coughed thickly, head turned away from me toward the driver's side window.

"It'll make the music sound better," I said.

"Your boyfriend didn't die in the accident?" he asked.

"No," I said. "Of course not."

"Somebody, a friend of mine, he said your boyfriend died."

"You should have given me a ride earlier. Especially if you thought my boyfriend was dead. That would have been the polite thing to do, don't you think?"

"I'm a pretty shy person," he said.

"You're a pretty stoned person," I said.

"Yeah, I guess," he said. His nose reminded me of a piece of clay stuck there as an afterthought.

"Where's your mom?" I said.

"At home."

I was looking for a connection, or I was simply probing for some sensitive spot I could dig at. I didn't know what I was feeling, what I was doing really, except that I was in a good mood. The weather was beautiful and I considered myself good company. We handed the joint back and forth, working it down to a nub, which I then smudged out and handed to him. I said, "You're a lucky boy."

He didn't say anything. His whole body was tense. I wondered if he would head back home or straight to the garage, if his father would smell it on him. "And I am too," I added. "My boyfriend is alive."

I couldn't help myself.

"I can wait if you need me to," he said.

"It's going to take a while," I said.

"Okay," he said. "See you later."

I climbed out of the truck and walked around the front toward the hotel. He was backing away when I turned and looked over my shoulder.

Inside our room Toby was awake and watching TV. He said, "That was quick," and pushed his thumb down on the remote. The TV clicked off and the room went dark except for a sliver of light coming through the shade.

"How much money do we have?" I asked.

He stood up and began fumbling around for his jeans. He was dressed in nothing but his boxer shorts and socks and he looked a little foolish—gangly and boyish, like he had magically grown younger in the time I had been away. "You know how much we have," he said.

"Nothing extra?"

"I gave you the extra," he said.

"No *extra* extra then?" I said.

He was pulling on his jeans, hopping slightly, first on his left leg, then his right. I looked away from him at the TV, although it was nothing but an empty dark screen.

I said, "You need to make that call."

"I can't," he said. "We'll find a way."

"How?"

"Talk them down."

I turned that scenario around in my head, looking at it from all angles, trying to make it a real possibility. And then I called the shop and told the mechanic it would take us an extra day to get the money together, that I would see him tomorrow.

Toby was tucking in his shirt, pulling out his jeans and stuffing it down in a violent motion of his hand. He was moving with such conviction and speed that it seemed like he was getting ready to go visit the mechanic himself. "Some kid thought you had died in the accident," I told him.

He seemed to consider this. "That would have been interesting," he said.

〜〜〜

Or this: I left the mechanic's son and walked into my room to find the unmade bed empty, my clothes scattered everywhere. I clicked the TV on and let the stream of stupid images console me.

The next day I rose early and stepped outside into the light rain coming off the mountains, cold as any rain I've ever felt. I pulled my hoodie up and lit my cigarette and considered what I was going to do next.

I saw him before he saw me but I didn't act like it. It was the mechanic's son, parked directly in front of the motel, engine idling. He was staring ahead, both hands on the wheel. He closed his eyes and leaned his head back and then turned, which is when he saw me.

"Hey," he called out. "I thought you could use a ride."

I walked over to him, rested both hands on his half-open window. "Well, thanks a lot," I said. "I hope you haven't been waiting long."

"Nah," he said, and he scrunched up his face.

"Should I get another blunt?" I asked.

"I guess, sure," he said.

"You know," I said, "I can sell you some."

He ran his tongue along his top teeth. I guess it was something he did when he was thinking. "Okay," he said. "Sure." Not *How much?* or *Maybe*, which is how I knew he had been thinking about this all night.

"I'm a little insulted," I said with a smile. "I thought you came here to see me."

"I did," he said.

"But you don't get this opportunity that often?"

"That's right."

"Hold on," I said, and I headed back inside the motel. "There," I said, when I climbed into the truck. I showed him the little Ziplock bag with the debris inside.

"Cool," he said.

We talked about death for a little while, and about the places he wanted to see. Disney World. Hawaii. It was like listening to a paraplegic talk about walking.

"Drive around back," I said, and he did, and then I laid it out on the seat, the pills and the plastic baggies. I said, "Let's do this quick." I told myself that if he touched so much as my hand I would make a grab at my stuff and push myself back out of the truck. I had left the car door unlocked.

But he didn't. He really did seem shy. "It's like in the movies," he said.

"Not really," I said.

And then when we were done and he handed me the money— $130—he pushed the stuff under the seat and turned the truck around. I put the cash in my other pocket. There was a song on the radio, something languid and syrupy, and I wanted to ask him if he had good friends around here, people he could share his chemicals with tonight. I closed my eyes and asked him the question in my head, gave myself the answer I wanted. *Sure I do. We're going to have a party.*

He started laughing. I said, "What's so funny?"

"Nothing," he said. "I just don't know if you ripped me off or not."

He left me at the front of the garage and I said good-bye to him.

"Not coming in?" I asked.

"No," he said.

"Don't drink with those pills," I said.

"I don't drink," he said. "I don't like how beer tastes."

"Wow," I said. "You're an interesting specimen."

The door was open, but the mechanic wasn't there. Then I saw his legs emerging from beneath an old truck. "I'll be done in a second," he said.

It was the same truck he had been working on the day before. An American flag filled the back window. I walked over to his workbench and found the bill there. He came up behind me, wiping his hands on a cloth.

"I don't have that much," I said, and I told him a number: $50 less than what I did have in both pockets.

"This is a business," he said.

"I know," I said. "But I don't have more."

Jesus, he knew what had happened and there he was wiping his hands and considering me like I was some stupid little girl. Maybe he was expecting my eyes to well up, and maybe if they did I would get what I wanted, but I didn't feel like crying.

I don't know how I knew what I knew, but I could tell from the way he was standing that he was thinking hard. Saying anything at that moment would have reminded him that I was there so I tried to be as invisible as possible—hands folded in front of me—so that he could come to a decision on his own. "Fine," he said. "Give me the money."

But it would take some acrobatics to remove the money from my pockets, peel off the right amount, return two twenties and a ten. "Do you have a bathroom?" I asked.

He gave me a dirty look, but he pointed in the right direction. Later I was sure he'd turn this into a story around the dinner table, or at the bar with his buddies. He had helped out that poor girl, you know the one, and then they'd tell other stories about other idiots, because the Yukon was a big place. It had a way of swallowing people like that right up.

There were several stories he could tell, though, and in one of them he was a fool and so was his son. The horrible fool and the sad fool, smoking dope with the girl with the truck. In this story I am sitting in the passenger's seat of his son's vehicle, and his son's eyelids are heavy and I am asking him questions about his life.

"Let's go inside," I would eventually tell him.

The boy fiddled around with the padlock on the gate in the dark while I watched the sky. I told him to hurry up, I was cold. He was used to commands, so he didn't talk back, and when the gates opened he turned to me for approval.

Inside we moved around the garage floor, talking about the cars and about his life. He said he had ambitions, he really did, but he was the only boy in the family, and he had obligations too. I told him to sit on the desk and when he moved to kiss me I tilted my lips to one side so his mouth found my neck. That seemed more acceptable.

Then I reached down and fumbled with his zipper just as he had fumbled with the lock outside. We were both desperate and I was hoping he thought that desperation had the same origin. I held him with one loose fist and looked hard into his face and I felt bad for him and I felt bad for myself too but that didn't stop me from jerking my hand up and down and telling him I liked his ambitions. It was important to look him right in the face. I wanted to make sure I knew at all times who he was and who he wasn't. He made a little groaning sound that wasn't exactly unpleasant.

When I was done and he was wiping himself with a paper towel he began motor-mouthing about his dreams, about how maybe it would be cool if he came with me. Was that a crazy idea or what? He laughed but he was serious and I told him that maybe that would be nice. I asked him if I could start the truck. I wanted to see how it was running.

We listened to the engine idle and I said, "It sounds good."

"My dad is a good mechanic," he said.

"Let's drive it around town," I said.

"We shouldn't."

"Please?"

We headed down the strip kind of slow and he began talking again about getting out of this town. I was content to half listen. Sure, there were so many places better than here. You wouldn't believe what's out there. We did the loop down to the edge of the place and then back and when I pulled into the garage I stopped short of the gate. "I think I'm going to go tonight," I said. "I just want to get out of here."

"Fuck," he said. He was looking at his knees move up and down.

"I'm just trying to be okay," I said.

"Yeah," he said, "I know," and then I wondered if maybe everything I had done wasn't even necessary. Maybe all I needed to do was tell my story in the same way he had told his. Show him some vulnerability. It would have been an act too, but a different kind of act.

I pushed that regret to one side and said something about driving at night being romantic. He climbed from the truck and moved around to me, but he didn't come close enough to touch me. He was stoned enough that maybe all he wanted to do was sleep. I needed some other ingredient to make everything possible though.

"You don't have to be like your father," I said.

"Yeah," he said, and that was enough.

When I nudged the truck into motion he was content to watch and by the time I had turned it around he was already gone, slipped back inside the garage. I would drive six, seven hours that night and he would go to bed and I would become something else: the girl who had tricked them, the bitch probably, but also the smart one, the strong one, the one who had done what was necessary.

Six days in Watson Lake. I had climbed from the truck through the splintered windshield, but I think even then I was looking past that moment to the moment when everything would be okay. What else can you do? The truck drove well and I traveled with the window down, enjoying the cold on my face. It would keep me sharp.

Just thinking about that now, remembering it, imagining it, is enough to bring me out of whatever moment I'm trapped in: washing the dishes, scolding the kids, stuffing grocery bags into my hatchback, or studying too hard for my night classes. It is as real as anything I might hold in my hand. It is always me escaping.

PART III

A few hours outside of Calgary, two days until the U.S. border, and strings of motels began to appear on the side of the road, squat little buildings with brightly painted doors and empty parking spaces out front. A giant orange dinosaur standing in the middle of a mini-golf course, overlooking the windmills and waterfalls, and then I was there, in the center of the city. As soon as I checked into the room, I made a beeline to the shower. The water was weak, but it was warm, and I let it trickle down between my shoulder blades, head tilted back and eyes closed. That evening, after dosing myself on television, I slipped into my jeans and out of the room, walking up the boulevard. People nodded hello to me as we passed each other. There were teenagers in a parking lot sitting on the hood of their car smoking cigarettes.

"Hi there," I said, to the first one, but he wasn't a kid, he was a grown man, about forty, dressed in a baseball jacket and a baseball hat, a fan searching for a team. His face was sunburned from hard work.

"Hey, you," he said, flirty right out of the box. He gave me a once-over with his eyes, a half second up and down, which probably revealed more to me than to him.

"Do you like to get high?" I asked him.

"Sure," he said. "Of course."

I would let him think whatever he wanted to think, then let him buy what I'm really selling. I would give him a bargain though. "Ten bucks each," I tell him.

"What are they?" he said.

"E," I said. I looked up past him but there was nobody there, just a public phone I thought was a person. The streets, in fact, seemed completely free of mystery. The idea made me happy-giddy for some reason, and when he looked hesitant, I decided to open up to him. "This stuff is for personal use," I said. "But I need the money. I'm in a little trouble."

"Everybody's in a little trouble," he said, and just like that something switched off in my heart. I didn't like him anymore. He was trying to come across as jaded and wise but it seemed silly, and if I had been a prostitute—I allowed myself that thought for a few amusing seconds—I would have charged the guy double out of spite.

"This is a good thing," I said, and I didn't like how my voice sounded. He was already skeptical. How could the stuff be any good if I looked so bad, if my voice cracked like that? I said, "Just buy a couple. I'll give you one for free. I really need the cash. We really need it." And then I was begging, my fist down the side of my body, the pills heading into my pocket. I said, "Look, don't take the pills. That's fine. But maybe you have a few dollars to give me? All I need is a few bucks."

I had somehow become a beggar.

He stepped away from me and headed toward the crosswalk. I threw the pills at his back. "Take them," I yelled after him. He was almost jogging across the street. I threw them and then I considered scurrying after him, after *them*, bending to find them on the road. But instead I threw a few more and that's when it turned from humiliation to fun. I began to yell, to scream, and I became the mystery on that safe little street.

On the way back to the room I stopped and looked at the truck for a long time. The cap was pretty much destroyed, a mass of rippled plastic and metal, but the most interesting thing about it was that one side, the side facing me, looked almost new. I had parked in such a way that in the morning as I came out of the hotel I would see the good side.

In the dark of the room I reached out and found a bag of potato chips, opening it slowly to avoid making noise. "What were you doing out there?" Toby spoke into the dark. It was just his voice, a hint of him.

"Nothing," I said. "Just wandering around."

"I need to buy postcards tomorrow," he said.

"Why?"

"To send to my family."

I put a few chips in my mouth but didn't chew. I let the salt melt on my tongue. "Remember the Boatel?" I asked.

He laughed. The Boatel was one of our favorite bars, a little shack built on the river that ran through town. In the summer people would drive their boats up to it and order beer to be passed down to the docks. In the winter they closed for one hour, around three in the morning, and a few of the regulars sometimes hung around in the parking lot in the dark, talking and running their heat off their car batteries, then headed back inside to order another Bud. "I love the Boatel," he said. "I wish we were there."

I thought of the shapes our breath made in the air in winter, the way our eyelashes would tip with frost, the muffled crunch of the snow underneath our boots. There were trails just behind the cabin and we usually walked them in silence, carrying our laundry. Then we'd emerge out behind the Sunshine Laundromat, lifting our boots high over a small wire fence, Toby pausing to make sure I had made it. "I miss the winter," I said, because it would have been too hard to put my thoughts into words.

"The winter," Toby said. "Very funny."

His voice was so quiet and then nothing. I thought he had gone. But he spoke up again. "What's-his-name," he said. "The taxi driver. The guy with the dirty jokes. Remember him?"

"We're talking about things we miss, not things I'm disgusted by," I said. But I missed him too. I missed all of it, missed it and hated it for missing it, because I knew if I was there it would not be anything special. It would be dirty dishes and cold and Toby sullen in the corner talking about the vanishing of the frontier while he took a drag. I wanted to tell him this, but my imagination wasn't strong enough to call up that scene. Disasters, fine, but not that little intimacy. I could not think of how he might react if I said those words. He slipped from me and then I was alone. Or he was right there in front of me and all I had to do was say the stupid words and he'd listen.

"Once when I was eight or nine," I said, "my mother came home and told me we were moving. She started pulling clothes out of the closet and throwing them in trash bags. Those were our suitcases. She told me just to take the things I really needed so that's what I did. I started putting my toys into a cardboard box. I was excited. I didn't like our apartment or our neighborhood and when she said the word *California* I pictured the movies I had seen with blond-haired kids surfing. I figured she had it all worked out. But the stuff didn't even make it to the car, of course. It was just like the time she said we were going to my grandparents' house in Florida for Christmas. The trash bags sat there in the living room all week and finally she unpacked them again and we didn't say anything about it. No, that's not right. She said one thing. She said that men were full of lies." I grinned and slanted in Toby's direction. "Are you full of lies, Toby?"

"I'm so full of lies," he said.

"Me too," I said. "I'm full of lies." I said, "I was sad about California for a long time. But now I think, well, what would it have changed? The weather would have been better. That's about it."

Toby tilted to the window, rested his head there, and closed his eyes, and for a second I thought he had escaped into sleep. But then he said, "I don't know. It could have changed everything."

"True," I said, and then he was gone again.

—※—

Watson Lake fell further and further behind us, behind me, White Horse further behind that even, and Fairbanks still further.

Fort Nelson, British Columbia and a narrow road so cracked and curved with frost heaves that I had to slow down to half the speed limit. Then Medicine Hat, Alberta, where the barns slumped to one side like trees in the wind, and an old man stood at the side of the road, staring off into the horizon while he ate peanuts from a paper bag. His face bent like a peanut too, curving at the middle, and he dropped the shells to the side of the road as he watched the sky. He waved like we were old friends returning for a visit.

The towns became one town with slight variations, a post office here or there, a gas station, but each one played a trick on me. Each one seemingly indelible, as if I would remember it forever, but then quickly replaced by the next. "Toby," I said. "Wake up."

"What?" he said, but his eyes were still closed, his cap tilted forward. He had been moving in his sleep for the last hour, his body trying to find a perfect painless position.

"Talk to me," I said. "I'm nodding off."

"What should we talk about?"

"Anything," I said. "I don't care."

It was two in afternoon and the sun had been warming my face for hours. The road was clear of traffic. It felt like we were the only two people in the world, really, but there was no romance in the thought, or darkness either, just a kind of stark boredom.

Toby rested his good hand on the makeshift windshield to stop it from curving inward from the force of our progress. It was probably his way to help me, to assuage the guilt for not being able to drive, but the more I drove the more I liked it. Because the wipers were almost useless, we tried our best to outrun the dark clouds, making a game of it. That's what we were doing—flying away from the dark stretch of sky—when Toby said, "How much money did they wire you?"

He was talking about his parents, and specifically his father, who had sighed with resignation when I had brought up the accident on the phone. "More than I asked for," I said, "but wow, he had some stories to tell about you."

"The overdose," he said.

"That one. And law school."

Something rattled above our heads—a loose scrap of metal—but quietly enough that it seemed like background music. I was feeling generous so I said, "You didn't ask me to get in touch with my family. I shouldn't have asked you."

"I know your situation with your mom," he said.

You know some of it, I wanted to tell him. I turned the wheel and let the truck slope into another dilapidated town. I tapped the brake at a stop sign. A procession of children walked by the side of the road holding brightly colored knapsacks, but there was no school bus to be seen. A few of them waved to us as we drove by. All the boys had the same close-cropped haircut. "They looked like one family," I said.

"She's not as bad as you might think," I said, spinning us back to our first subject. "It's a two-way street, me and her."

"Present tense," he said.

"What?"

"You're talking about her in the present tense, like she's still alive."

"Well, maybe she is," I said, and I smiled.

"Maybe," he said. I had always thought we had been more or less honest with each other, but we had never talked like this before. Maybe it was the accident itself—it had jostled something loose inside us. Maybe it was just the boredom. What were we looking at? The occasional wind-blasted building, tilted like it had been stopped in mid-fall. Other than a sleepy gas station attendant, the children had been the first people we had seen all day.

"You know what?" I said. "I bet she's probably dead. I'm sure of it. Stupid alcoholic."

The edge in my voice surprised me. It must have surprised Toby too, because he turned away from the road, to me, and said, "Don't wish that."

"I didn't wish it. I just said it. I didn't wish for anything."

I felt like I could drive through the night, drive us straight down into the Lower 48, hard and precise, like a needle sliding under skin. Toby was still looking at me. "You've been taking a lot of stuff," he said. "Speaking of your mother."

When another car came into view—growing larger and larger in the cracked rearview mirror—I savored it like good food in small portions.

"I don't think the windshield is holding," he said.

"We'll buy more electrical tape in the next town."

"It was a bad idea," he said.

"It seemed strong," I said, although I remembered pushing the plastic outward at the garage and stopping myself because I was afraid I might break it. But the mechanic's idea had become my idea, and it needed to be defended. This was something new for me and I could tell Toby didn't like it. We were making a lot of decisions in silence now, without talk or even real thought. This is how we arrived at the next hotel. "It's not bad," Toby said as he clicked on the TV. "Better than the other one."

It was too early to stop driving. The sun was still high in the sky and we'd only gone two-thirds of the way through a tank. I closed the curtains and sat on the edge of the bed.

On the news, a black-and-white photograph of a smiling guy holding a basketball. Some sports hero in Boston had died from overdosing on crack cocaine. He was younger than Toby and I, even, and was set to make millions of dollars the next year when he entered the NBA. In fact, he had been celebrating his future when he overdosed. His mother's voice spoke over the photograph, but I wasn't listening anymore. It seemed wrong that he should be on the news and we should be here, unknown to anyone but ourselves. I felt bad about not having any sympathy for the dead millionaire on TV, but that was the way it was, and then I was alone and Toby was dead too, and instead of being stoned I was as sober as I had ever been. I sat on the edge of the bed and let the room shift around me, because driving always carried through to the next still moment, performed magic on it, and made it shake with motion.

And then Toby was back with me, holding my shoulders, and I pulled away from him. I dug deep into the backpack, found the plastic bag inside the paper bag. There were thirty-something small pills in there, mixed in with another hundred vitamin C. I spilled some out on the bed and separated four of the smaller circular pills out, put three on the hotel room dresser, a fourth in my pocket. I took a vitamin C, moved my tongue around to get some saliva up, swallowed it down, and then followed it with one and a half X.

The celebratory mood was long gone. It felt more like maintenance —like taking vitamins. "You should have one," I said. "It'll make you feel better."

"The painkillers are supposed to make me feel better," he said.

That was part of the gulf between us—his pain, my unbroken bones.

I felt that about the driving too, that I was discovering things nobody had ever seen before: the particular forlorn shape a grain silo made against the sky or the sight of small rabbits standing at attention and then scrambling into underbrush. It was, I suppose, a way of being trapped in myself—behind the screen of my own vision—and it had been happening for a while, even before the accident.

I could still feel the motion of the road when I flopped on the bed and closed my eyes. My hand slid across Toby's chest. His forehead was still sprayed with small cuts, but they were beginning to crust over, and I kissed him there, lightly, as if I were checking his temperature by touch. "I wonder if they're talking about us in Watson Lake," he said.

"Probably," I said. "I bet they're sorry to see us gone. We're the most exciting thing that's happened to them in years."

"Especially since I died. They're going to be talking about that forever."

"The Mounties were nice," I said. I had intended it as a joke but it came out as heartfelt.

"Yeah," he said.

"Did it hurt?" I asked. "Dying, I mean?"

I wasn't really smiling. I wanted to hear his answer.

I was interrogating myself.

"I wouldn't describe it as painful," he explained, as he pulled his arm across his eyes. "It was interesting. I got to see what goes on when I'm not around."

"And what was that?"

"You moved on," he said, "without me."

He was mumbling. I wondered if he was stoned, but we hadn't been separated all day. I put my hand on his belly and began to rub in slow circles.

"I was going for help," I said. "I wasn't moving on."

"I rescued you," he said. "You should have at least rescued me."

"I don't want to play this game anymore," I said.

"I'm just talking," he said.

"Let's stop talking."

He placed his hand on mine and stopped its spiraling motion. "I used to think I was going to be something special," he said. "Not financially. I wasn't going to buy into any of that. I was going to carve a path, though. I was going to go all over the world. But I haven't even left the country. Canada doesn't count, of course. I got as far as Alaska. That's it."

I had the sense of watching someone fall in slow motion, down into someplace deep and dark. "You're talking like an old man," I said.

"I'm talking like a dead person," he said, and he laughed. "It's just talk. We're talking. Talk talk talk."

"You're stoned," I said.

"I'm clear as a cucumber." And then, "At least I bringing some of Alaska with me."

"What do you mean?" I was thinking of our stuff strewn across the road.

"You," he said.

I had always considered Toby to be the Alaskan, me the outsider. Had he always viewed it in reverse? "We'll talk in the morning," I said.

"I want to talk now," he said, and then nothing. I pulled my hand from his.

Asleep, I realized, and then he was gone again and I was alone and cold sober. The TV played soundlessly in the background, meditating on the face of tragedy. A woman mourning her stupid boy.

Two guys and a girl were standing by the ice machine and when the girl leaned back and stretched with catlike tedium an idea occurred to me. I approached them, walking slow, letting them look me over while trying to pretend I was oblivious to them. One of the boys removed his glasses and rubbed them clean with his T-shirt as I moved up close. "The bugs are nuts," I said, because a storm of midges floated around the light above our heads. He nodded and replaced his glasses on his face. "Hey," I said. "Do you guys like to get high?"

⁓

We had salvaged things from the accident, but none of it mattered much anymore. We left the damaged bookcase in the breakdown lane a few hours outside Watson Lake on the side of the road when we stopped to pee in the woods. We left the black plastic bag full of hats and scarves and raincoats in a campground the next day. The electric mixer stayed behind in a diner parking lot just before we hit Montana. Toby dropped a squashed box of old photographs and love letters behind a gas station while I talked to the attendant about the best route to take through Glacier National Park. We left our snowshoes—one pair splintered into shards, one pair perfectly whole—outside another diner where the food had been almost inedible. We left the broken dishes and the unbroken dishes and we left a box of mystery novels we shouldn't have brought along in the first place. I got rid of the ski mask and the heavy boots and then I got rid of the cracked lamps.

Most of it was useless anyway. I left Toby's clothes, stuffed deep into a green army bag, outside a Montana Salvation Army, and no sooner had I dropped them in front of the bright yellow dumpster than a man approached them. He began pulling them out and looking them over while I stood there watching. He held up the shirts to his chest to see if they could fit. I told him, "Hey, that's stealing," but it was like I wasn't even there. I told him again. I swore at him and told him to get out of there like he was a little dog sniffing at poop. He finally looked at me and said something about finders keepers, losers weepers.

I stepped close and punched his arm and shoulder and I'd like to say he gave out a howl of surprise and dropped the clothes. His face was sunburned to the texture of old wood with loose skin around the bridge of his nose and there was something crazy in his eyes. He swore and swore and even then it was like I was the one who was at fault. He looked at me like I was the crazy one, but it was his face that was nuts, with his gray beard stubble and wide fish eyes. He backed off but I kept at it, socking him in the chest. I wanted to see him turn and try to run and then I was going to hit him again. Except that maybe it wasn't him at all. It was Toby, and we were just outside Milwaukee, and we were fighting hard. He raised his good arm to block my slaps and cars slowed down to watch the battle. "You idiot," I said. "You prick." I aimed for that sharp point on his shoulder but he turned sideways, using his good side as a shield. "So this is it, huh?" I said. "After everything you break up with me four hours from your parents' house."

We paused and stood facing one another. I could feel the cars coming at my back, the surge of force and then release when they passed me. "I wouldn't use that term," he said, and I stepped forward to hit him again. He backpedaled, still talking, and again I felt like I was the one who was at fault. Just moving that quickly was still enough to hurt him. "Don't you think it's possible to know a person too well?" he asked.

I pictured one good punch finding that weak spot and then the shock of pain. Our radiator had overheated and his father was coming to pick us up. His older brother too. They would probably bring sandwiches and cans of soda and we'd eat while we rode back. Toby took deep breaths. He could see the cars and I could tell from his expression that he was afraid for me because I was standing on the white line. "You can stay at my parents' place as long as you like. You know that."

"I saved you," I said. "I saved you."

I knew what he had done. He had called them the day before or even the day before that, spoken with his mother and then his father, and made a plan. They'd meet an hour or so from their house in a restaurant parking lot. His family would stand around staring at the truck and make the expected sounds of amazement and respect, but there would also be the slightest rebuke in the way his father shook his head and touched the destroyed thing. Yes, it was real, and it had brought his child all this way to him. And then he'd remember the boy and hug him and they'd go inside. I'd trail behind them or maybe I'd just drive away, leaving him there like we had left the coffee maker, the broken dishes, and snowshoes.

"I saved you," I said again, and I jumped forward and hit his good shoulder. He danced away into the weeds and a passing eighteen-wheeler shook our truck. "This is what you want," I said, and he said, yes, yes, this is what I want. "Fine," I said, but I gave him one more punch to let him know my feelings.

You don't have to go looking for the conventional life. It will find you. Even if you run the opposite way.

~ ～ ～

I was sitting in another restaurant on the edge of the expressway when he said, "Excuse me, ma'am?" A man dressed in a feed cap and a suit jacket, scratching his beard thoughtfully. For a moment I thought he was going to push a religious pamphlet at me, but his hands were empty and the waitress was looking at him from across the counter like she knew him. He was middle-aged, but his face was open and boyish, hopeful. "Is that your truck out there in the parking lot?" he said.

"Yeah," I said.

"You shouldn't be driving that thing," the guy said. "It's not safe."

"Safe enough to bring me this far," I said.

He nodded at this. It was hard to argue with the evidence, after all. I thought of telling him how far I had come, but instead I rearranged the food on my plate. He said, "Well, we'd like to help."

"I don't need any help," I said, and my voice had an edge to it. As he walked away I glanced over at his table where his wife was watching all of this unfold. She looked down as soon as I glanced over, contrite. Maybe she was the one who had put him up to it. The waitress was part of the whole deal too. She edged away toward another table.

Later in the truck, I felt the weight of the keys in my right hand, let my head roll back as I took a deep breath. There he was, at the center of my mind, and I considered him for a moment and then sequestered him in his proper place, a secret I was keeping even from myself. The tires made their thumping music as I sped out onto the highway. I remember the cuts on my forearms, now healed into small red freckles, the speedometer shaking around forty-five, and then the shudder of an eighteen-wheeler passing me at eighty. In this moment Toby's death is real and his life—his survival in that other story—is a stupid trick, a child's way of dealing with grief. But minutes later, when the truck is out of view and Toby is riding beside me, eyes closed and talking about the future, it's his death that is the trick, the romantic little-girl fantasy. He's smiling despite the lingering pain because he's just seen a deer hurdle the road in two jumps. No fear of a collision with the leaping, beautiful thing, because just getting to the United States has made us feel safer. He talks about his parents and about forgiveness and about how a person can expect too much from life. The road's supposed to impart new insights, but these? Toby's letting me down. My imagination is letting me down.

So I spin back to the accident, the motorcyclist watching us through the dust storm, Toby's left arm dragging a sheet along the road, and me so bloody it's as if I've just been born, and crying, because of course I must have been crying. In this version, the best version, the motorcyclist watches with the detachment of a man looking at a television, but it's because he's in shock too. We're contagious in that way, Toby and I. What is there to see through the haze but the shape of a man dragging *something*, another shape huddled on the ground making mewing noises? Shadows without people to throw them. Finally, he calls out to us and I swear he says, "Nobody wants to hurt you." Toby is moving down the embankment, still dragging the blanket, stumbling and falling. He's heading to the tree line. The man on the motorcycle calls out again and this is when he sounds angry, or maybe it's just that I'm angry. Toby stands again, climbs out of the ditch, makes a break to the woods. He's walking but it's a fast walk and I'm thinking,

Hey, what about me? I stand and that's when the motorcyclist notices me for the first time. He yells, "Stay where you are," but what else am I going to do? Obviously, I'm hurt. It's the cyclist who runs his hands over me, takes my head in his hands and stares into my face, and then Toby is turning and yelling, "Leave her alone, leave her alone." I'm fine with these unfamiliar hands until I hear Toby's voice and then I'm kicking and punching, but all that does is drive away the thing trying to help. I fall over and it's Toby who picks me up. The motorcyclist is gone. Colored lights strobe through the dust cloud.

Toby's arm is blue and twisted but the sheet is still is in his clutched hand. He has to open his gnarled fingers with his other hand, his good hand, to let it go and then I pick it up and ball it into a bundle, like it's just dirty laundry in need of a hamper. Soon we're on our way to the vet's office, up the dirt road past the long horse fence. The faces of the animals—there are three of them, standing at the fence at attention—look at us if this is all routine, so serene as to be alien, but one's head is shaved and bandaged. The doctor covers my arms with small band-aids and I wonder if Toby is going to die. It seems possible because now almost anything seems possible. The place smells of cats and horseshit but the floors are polished clean. I smell lemon too. The doctor says, "Are you stoned right now?"

"No," I tell her. "I was just in a car accident."

That's enough to quiet her.

When I see Toby again he raises his arm, the twisted arm, and opens and closes his fingers. The skin is still dark, but he's grinning, and he says, "It just got better. I don't know how."

The doctor explains that the circulation had been blocked. Toby willed the blockage away by raising his arm up and down, up and down. His hair is wet with sweat and a sharp triangle of bone has risen beneath the skin of shoulder, as if something man-made and metallic has been lodged there. Only something man-made would have that perfect sharp-edged shape, but no, it's just the bone cracked in half almost penetrating the surface of his body. Behind him there are diagrams of a dog's digestive track posted on the wall. "Christ," Toby says. "Miracles do happen," and he laughs and looks down at his sneakers.

Imagine everything else as a kind of daydream and this is where I make a choice. It's the only thing to do, and Toby agrees. After all, it's only fifteen hours back to Fairbanks if we turn around, more than a week ahead of us if we keep going. I put my hands on his thighs and fall into a crouch and say, "Maybe we can get the cabin back. We could call from here."

And Toby says, "Maybe we can hire a ride. People are going through here all the time."

"The truck could be okay," I tell him.

Imagine that is no argument, and nothing held back either. We're just glad to be alive. We have friends in that cold city, people who love us and will be waiting for us, right? Imagine I'm here in Alaska, and Toby is here too, fifteen years later, with two children and a house now instead of our cabin, a new car with monthly payments and neighbors with children who knock on our door in the early evening to see if ours have finished their homework. I have homework too because I'm going to night school. A delicately calibrated life.

It's as if the accident never existed, scrubbed from our lives the way I scrub out a blueberry stain from our child's shirt. The same with much of the past. My work, my mother. Actually, it's taken much less effort than that. The kids speak about Grandma, but that's our friend down the road who brings us cookies and pies and sometimes even smoked salmon in long, perfectly cut strips. When I talk about my past it begins when Toby and I met. Toby's parents send money on birthdays and holidays and ask when we are coming for a visit. Toby goes moose hunting in the fall with friends and they're always successful. I walk the road with the girls riding their bicycles ahead of me on Farmer's Loop and sometimes a strange truck passes with out-of-state plates. The girls are far enough ahead that I feel alone for the first time in days, just a middle-aged woman walking, unhinged from anybody or anything. I wonder what the people in that truck make of me before they've rushed onto the next thing. Then the girls turn and race back to me and I'm their finish line, the thing they need to reach, so I raise my arms in the air.

Toby comes home from teaching at the middle school dog-tired and sometimes when the kids are asleep we smoke a joint and talk about the old days, the things we did and didn't do. He laughs at himself, the person he was then, with all that junk in the yard, all that ridiculous anger. Maybe it's the same heavy lamp casting light, the one that I left broken by the side of the road. Toby reaches across me and clicks it on, and our bodies touch and then recede. This is who he is, and who I am, and we are happy in the way that most people are happy.

⫸

Ten minutes before the border we took four of the last ten pills with a bottle of gas station Gatorade. It was a nice little gamble—more play than anything else—because as long as they didn't ask us too many questions at the crossing we wouldn't be peaking until the station had disappeared from the rearview. It turned out that the border guard asked us three. "What were you doing in Canada?" "How do you know each other?" And then, in a more conversational way, with his head leaning close to our window, "Did you have a nice time?" He did not even ask us about the truck.

"That was easy," Toby said, but saying anything else seemed like bad luck.

We seemed to be standing still no matter how fast we drove. The land was that flat, the horizon that distant. I began to push the truck over seventy and the frame shook and the windshield bowed inward so much that Toby couldn't hold it. Other trucks passed us as if we were standing still. "Here we go," Toby said.

"Let's not stop until we need to fill the tank again," I said.

"We'll need money to do that," he said.

"It swallows you," I said, meaning the sky, the land, the driving, the talk and the non-talk, the drugs and the now the non-drugs, and the money too, the hope for it. I didn't really know what I meant. But Toby nodded and agreed. The land sprawled worn and open and it occurred to me that maybe I understood time better from looking at that dusty landscape for so long. But outside Great Falls all of this twisted into strip malls and brightly colored buildings advertising fireworks. It was nice to be in civilization, such as it was, but I immediately missed all that unmarked land. There's a kind of amnesia when you're driving through land like that, a suspension not just between places but everything else too. It's as if anything might happen. In a way you are nowhere at all.

Toby and I were smiling and talking about our favorite board games, our least favorite ones, the ones that made us cry when we were kids.

I said mine smelled like damp from the basement. His favorite was one I had never heard of, some kind of military game. He was trying to explain the complex way he would maneuver the pieces and capture his opponent when I laughed from pure joy. We hadn't eaten since the night before but we were so close. His family was waiting, and there would be a big meal, terse conversation but comfortable beds. This is what he promised. I imagine myself alone, traveling through Indiana, all cornfields and farmhouses, and into Ohio, with the truck shuddering, one hand on the wheel and one on the windshield. Just the slight pressure of my hand seems necessary. The whole thing seems ready to fall apart: this small space I live in.

It's not ridiculous to say that I'm full of joy in this moment too, joy and loneliness, yes, but joy. Am I the same person in those two scenes? I break through Ohio and into Pennsylvania, where the lakes are as dark as the ocean, and I see the signs for Buffalo, New York and I am running out of country. I am running out of imagination. I'm exhausted—the children have exhausted me—and in New Hampshire the next day the truck dies, or maybe it's Maine, right at the border, and even then, that strange joy doesn't leave me. It will always be there, even when I am thinking about what might have been. Especially then. I pour in a quart of oil, duct-tape a water hose, and the truck sputters back into motion.

If you are lucky, then trouble will save you from your life.

The money is gone and the truck is shaking, but the weather is good and it's easy to keep going.

A ROUGH MAP OF THE INTERIOR

I

FAIRBANKS MOVING AND STORAGE

The woman on the phone said to hold on, that help was on the way, and Sarah told her, "Okay, sure, that's fine, but all I need is a human voice."

"There are protocols," the woman said.

She sounded miserable, more miserable than Sarah, who just a few minutes before had seriously considered hanging herself from one of the crossbeams of the storage locker, and certainly more miserable than any young person had a right to sound. What was the expression? World-weary. She sounded as if she had received dozens of calls just like this one and it wasn't Sarah's story that was getting to her, but the slow accumulation of *all* these stories, all of them dreary, all so much the same. It wasn't difficult to imagine. Harder for Sarah to envision her own life: her future and her past and even the small pocket of her present, engine idling in this no-man's-land between home and town. The girl's voice—her miserable human voice—was explaining the protocols step by laborious step and Sarah wanted to tell her about those summers in Homer on the *Lazy Bones*, the nets flashing silver with Pacific cod. But the largeness of those days did not fit properly into the cramped space of her truck, her left hand on the steering wheel, the heater fan clicking like a cheap clock. To talk about those times would have been like sharing them with her sullen shaven-headed nephews, their eyes on the TV. The cold, Sarah had told them, the cold. She would pull off her gloves and flex her hands and gradually they would return to her and then she'd tug on fresh gloves and get back to it, rolling the netting into the boat, cod tails fluttering and bright as the brightest joy a person could imagine. She thought of the thousand bodies as one pulsing thing, the way you might think of the sun, the ocean that had hidden their writhing shapes until that moment they were pulled free. Dangerous, she wanted to tell the voice on the phone, because she had once seen someone drown, a teenager not much older than her nephews, not much older than this girl listing protocols. The memory found her then, in her idling truck, as if it had been searching for her these past months, these many, many years, building speed and purpose until it arrived at the center of her body.

She had not talked about it since that time at her sister's house two years ago and then only to say, "It was cold enough to kill a full-grown man. That's why so few of them bothered to learn to swim. What would be the point? You'd freeze before drowning. Although technically that's drowning." She had been boasting, and she was boasting now too, in a way, as she told the girl on the phone about her racing heart, the mess she had made of her life. But everything was going to be fine, right? That's what the miserable other voice kept saying. Across the parking lot ravens laid claim to a dumpster, swaggered around it in circles. Some flew away and were replaced by others. The voice enumerated the steps she should take to ensure her safety. *Turn off the ignition. Remain calm. Stay on the phone until assistance arrives.*

⋙

It was his carelessness, of course. That's what the small crew had talked about afterward, when they were ready to talk, which was not for a long time—another day and night of fishing, of making good money. Those were prosperous times then, in the late '70s and early '80s. Money was everywhere. Twenty-four years old and she kept a bankroll in her jeans pocket wrapped in a red rubber band.

She remembered looking at the water and thinking, *Him, not me,* with a kind of terrible elation, except now it *was* her. The girl on the phone was still running through the list of what to do and not do and the ravens were wrestling with a bag of scraps, but Sarah was there now, in the past, watching the sunrise from the bow the morning after their crew had been reduced from four to three. Years later and it felt as solid—more solid—than her cold hands on the wheel, the voice giving her assurance. The deck had been pink with watered-down fish blood. She remembered the smell of her peanut butter and jelly sandwich, the shame of finding pleasure in it.

They sat and ate and she knew that each of them felt the same: proud to be alive, to not be the idiot in the water. And as she finished her sandwich she brought up the kid's girlfriend, who everybody knew and liked, and who had a baby by another man and a part-time job at the local Safeway. People made noises of agreement, small acknowledgments that the worst was to come. The shore was coming into sharper view, rising and falling with the bow, and the girlfriend was probably not even awake yet, and they didn't even have a body to share with her. It was Reggie or maybe Harris, the oldest one, who said, "I knew it was coming. I knew when we hired him in March."

Sarah had understood this to mean several things: that it was their fault for letting him get on the boat in the first place, that it was the kid's fault too, for being so stupid, and that they needed to do a better job in the future. That was the lesson of accidents small and large and Sarah felt herself recede from the two men because she was the other exception, the other break from normality, the only woman ever on that boat, and young too, more than a year younger than the one they had lost. Her pride in that was always turning into embarrassment and then back again and she refused to dwell on it. The thing to dwell on was the dead boy himself, his face, which was fat but handsome, at least to the girl on shore, and his body, which was strong, much stronger than Sarah's. Maybe that bull strength made him overconfident. She remembered it now as if it was happening again, his boot on the side of the boat and then his arms reaching out. Then he was falling sideways and his face didn't even have time to register his fear.

He had hit the water at the stern and disappeared beneath the surface near the churn of the double engines. Everybody ran back there screaming to kill it, kill it, kill the motor. With the engines dead, they could hear their breathing and the gulls and even the fish twisting in the hold. Someone threw a lifeline out and they stood and watched it flip around in the surf. Sarah finally thought to ask if they had immersion suits, but nobody answered, and she knew not to ask again. They huddled close, waiting for him to surface, each one expecting a miracle. She was expecting one now. She wanted to remember the kid's name, but it had followed him, very slowly, to that deep place where his body had gone, as if pulled behind him on a very long line. Ten years ago, she had still held it in her mind, maybe even five, but somehow recently it had escaped her and it seemed as if that too was a form of carelessness. And carelessness on the *Lazy Bones* had moral value. To be careless was to be a thief, a liar, a coward, and she felt the justice of each one of those judgments as she tried to remember the kid's name so she could tell it to this young woman on the other end of the phone, who didn't know any of that story at all and probably would have just been confused to hear it ass-backwards like that. Instead Sarah said, "Do you have a script that you follow? Like right now, are you reading to me from a list they give you or something?"

"Let's focus on you," the girl said, "on how you're feeling."

"That's probably a good idea," Sarah said, "but I want to know I'm not talking to a robot."

The girl's laughter was world-weary too. She said, "I can assure you that I'm not a robot. I do this because I want to do it. I feel like I'm helping people." Sarah moved her hand from the wheel to the heat switches and even though they were already pushed full to the right she nudged them again. The defrost was finally working and she had a clear view of the storage unit, still wide open, with her bureau and her two La-Z-Boy recliners, one upside down on top of the other like they were spooning lovers, a few lamps wrapped in blankets and placed on the sofa. The garbage bags of summer clothes and boxes of tools and the dip net she had been planning to repair for two years. Why had she saved any of it? The couch was torn along the back and smelled of dogs and cigarettes. In trying to save it all Sarah had saved none of it—it had all ended up piled here, and if just this second she were to decide to leave the warmth of the truck to search through it all in a quest to find that single important thing it would take her hours and even then she might not find it.

So yeah, that was pretty much like not having a thing at all, wasn't it? "Let's focus on me then," she said, and she shifted the phone from one ear to the other. "I'm here at a storage locker. I came to get something for my daughter. The snow is falling, but not that bad really, and

I feel like I'm having a heart attack. Well, not exactly like that. It's in my head. Like a heart attack in my head."

She meant this to be a joke. It was funny, right?

"Right," the girl said. "It's good you called then."

Sarah thought of the line again, the invisible one connecting the boy to his name, and then of another. When Sarah had first pulled out her cell and punched the three little numbers she imagined a similar thing stretching all the way from some big city, Los Angeles maybe, or Seattle, all the way to Fairbanks, Alaska. The line was so slender as to be almost nonexistent, a strand of a web trailing behind a spider. "So you think you're good at your job then?" Sarah said. "You don't lose people?"

"Again, I think we should really talk about you," the girl said. Was that annoyance she heard in her voice? She imagined her using this tone with a little brother, the mother who didn't know how to use the internet. "Do you have a plan?" she asked, and Sarah said sure, she had lots of plans. Ambitions, she said. "A plan to kill yourself," the girl corrected, and there was the sadness again, and Sarah considered those other people who had called for help, maybe one sitting at a kitchen table covered with sections of an open newspaper, dirty dishes in the sink; another shaking apart in a narrow stairway, her boyfriend in the next room. They'd become a blur, wouldn't they? You'd lose them all.

She remembered then how he had returned to them, six days later, washed up on the beach. Solid as a block of ice, they said. She didn't want to think about it then, but now the memory—the story—had become something else. She held it at arm's length and turned it around to see each new facet. For some reason this seemed to be the most important thing to share, everything else an avoidance, a kind of falsehood. She said, "When do you think they're going to get here? Because I'm not doing so well." She was only dimly aware of her own strange body. She was breathing with difficulty, as if she were running, but she was sitting still. She wondered if the girl could even hear her correctly.

"Soon," the girl said. "Very soon. Don't worry."

"I'm not worried," Sarah said. "Not about me."

She didn't know if that was a lie or not.

"Do you have a gun with you?" the girl asked.

"I own guns," Sarah said, "but they're not with me."

"Are you sure?"

Did the girl think she was an idiot? Sarah didn't even bother to answer that one, but then the girl asked again, are you sure, more forcefully, and Sarah said that yes, she was very sure, and she was also very sure about what city she was in, what time of day it was, and her own name. She was sure of a lot of things. "Okay," the girl said. "When the police get there, they're going to ask you that same question. It's probably going to be the first thing they ask you. Just so you know."

"And I'll tell them what I told you."

"Great."

If someone asked her who she was, she'd tell them that she was a tough customer, a character, a survivor. Her sister Beth called her that sometimes, *a real character*. She was pretty sure about all of that. She wasn't sure about this phone call though. Maybe she had made a mistake. It wouldn't be her first. "When?" she asked. "When will they be here?" Soon. Soon. Soon.

She jumped from the bow to the dock, rope in hand, and even though there was more work to do, the second her boots hit the wood and the rope tightened in her grip she knew she was home. But home always seemed a bit off after days at sea, or home was the same and *she* was off, and she needed something to bring her back all the way. So she spent some money and drank some beers and swaggered and joked and laughed when someone got so drunk or high they walked into a wall.

Nothing about this ritual changed when they returned after the accident, except in degree. They blew money on steaks flown in from Anchorage and hard liquor. The older men told stories of close calls and they managed some laughing fits later on in the early morning and they didn't say another word about the drowned boy until a week later when he washed up. That itself was unusual and miraculous. Sarah heard the news through one of the other crew members. He came to her at her cabin in the early morning and banged on the door. The banging was needlessly urgent and her first thought, waking up, was that she had forgotten to turn off the stove burner and the place was on fire. She was surprised to emerge from the bedroom to find the room peaceful, dishes stacked in the sink and sunlight falling through the window.

But there it was: the smashing at the door, the yelling of her name. The night before she had smoked dope and slept with one of the locals and she imagined him returning, angry for some reason she could not identify. In the time it took her to pull on a shirt she had dismissed the idea, but the shame remained—a sharp sense that she had done wrong and the banging on the door was her accounting. The man standing there when she opened it was not the man she had slept with, the young man with the hooknose and curious way of whispering her name over and over while stroking her. It was someone she knew much better, a person she had gone to sea with, and even when he said, "He's down at the beach," the sight of him made her happy. She had not seen anyone from the boat since the first night back, when they had done shots until three in the morning. She stepped outside to talk.

He was almost unrecognizable, soft-spoken and humble, victim of a shave and a new haircut, and the news came out slow, as if he were making it up as he went along. Hearing about it, he had thought of her, joined her to the chain he was making. "I wish he had just stayed out there," he said. "It just feels weird." His truck was still running and he said he had to go because he was heading to the east side to make more stops. "Nobody is going to like this," he said, and he seemed to want to say something else. They hung there for a moment and finally she put her shoes on, steadying herself in the doorframe. Was he expecting her to go with him? She had not been up this early all week and her body was greedy for coffee and a big breakfast and maybe good conversation. Her mother had called three times in three days from Seattle and each call went unanswered.

She imagined the boy washed up on the beach but could only get as far as the general shape of him, the general shape of the crowd, the curl of the tide against his boots. She couldn't decide—if that was the right word; it felt like a decision—whether he was face up or face down, how his body might be decorated with seaweed, exactly what she should feel about any of this. "Thanks for telling me," she said. She realized that she was still a little stoned, a little queasy too.

"This kind of thing happens," the man said. "I'm not saying it's not a big deal, you know, but don't make too much of it." Except that he himself was making a lot of it with his grim messenger expression and nervous speech. The night they had returned he had been the drunkest of all of them.

It sounded like good advice, but the more she thought about it after he had driven away, the less sense it made. How much was too much then? What was the exact right proportion of responsibility, shame, and indifference? She heated water, poured some in the basin, and washed her face as she thought about telling her mother this story when she finally called her back. It would be an act of revenge.

Because, of course, it could have been her. Her mother would not see the luck in that, just the potential for further disasters. Her voice would get that strained quality it had when talking about money or politics, and then she'd say, "I want you back on the first plane. I don't know why you ever decided to even go to that crazy place."

More revenge?

"You wouldn't believe the money I'm making," she'd tell her, although that was not the real reason, and anyway, a lot of that money was spent foolishly, on the things you had to buy if you were to keep pace with all those men and their appetites.

She came as close as resting her hand on the receiver. The talk would escalate into near argument, become just another version of their other talks, and every minute of it would cost big money. Why had she come to Alaska like a runway, without even telling her family, and what about her friends? Everybody was worried about her. Her father was fighting an ulcer because of all of this.

She rubbed that imagined conversation out and tried to come up with a different one. What she wanted to tell her mother was not that it could have been her. That was obvious. But that it *should* have been her. She should have been the one on the beach, face down or face up, the story carried from one person to the next. Bad luck had found her, out there at sea, and only just missed. It was learning to find its target.

When she finally did call her mother, a few days later, it was to leave a message saying, "It's beautiful here. I'm doing well. No need to send any rescue missions or anything."

"I never believed in zodiac signs or any of that bullshit," she was saying, and she knew she sounded crazy because it didn't make sense without the rest. She touched the keys in the ignition but didn't kill the engine.

The girl said, "I don't believe in them either. Have you had experiences like this before? Feelings like this?"

"Not exactly," Sarah said. She could hear the sounds of cars passing from the road that ran behind the storage facility. Soon one of them would be the police car. It would cut through the dirt road, slide behind the metal buildings, and then come up behind her, just as the memory of the boy had done. She'd see the flashing lights in the rearview mirror and then she'd say good-bye to the girl on the phone and get out of the car. Except the girl explained that she should stay in the car and keep her hands where the police could see them. They would probably draw their weapons, but Sarah shouldn't be nervous. She asked Sarah to tell her more about her plan. Sarah said, "Hanging."

Was this a kind of boast too?

"Right," the girl said. "Tell me more." What else was there to say? She was embarrassed by the melodrama of her choice and wanted to defend it as pragmatic. The nylon rope had been waiting right there in her truck, after all, curled up next to her tool box and old paint cans, convenient and comforting as the radio, the cup holder, the heat switches. "But you don't really want to do that, do you?" the girl asked.

"Not really," she said.

The iron crossbeams running across the ceiling of the storage locker had looked sturdy enough to support a person. She had once used the rope to pull a car from a gully so it was definitely strong enough. Even now as she sat in the comfort of her truck it seemed a possibility. All she had to do was click her phone off, turn her head to the front, and it would be there, waiting for her to enter like an elevator. Going up, she thought. Or down. She thought again of last year's trip to Seattle and then the drive to her sister's house in Port Orchard, the entire adventure of her life squeezed into that freshly vacuumed suburban space as she spoke to those staring children. She had wanted to boast then too, but it had come out all wrong, and the worst part of it was her own daughter, Celine, staring at the TV too. She had heard these stories a million times before, after all, in many variations depending on Sarah's mood and whims. Of course, the drowning had never been one of them. She kept that for herself.

"She's so proud of being normal," Sarah said. "It makes me sick."

"Who is that?" the girl on the phone asked.

"Everybody," Sarah said. Yes, the girl was definitely from somewhere else, not even in the state, let alone the city. You, she wanted to say, but she held it back. This call had connected her to a vast network, a whole system designed to catch her and safely return her. To where? To the normal. Finally, she turned her head to the storage locker door. There it was, dangling, ridiculous. "You have a very nice voice," she told the operator. "What's your name? I mean, what's your first name? I know you can't give me your full name. Hell, you can give me a fake one if you want. I don't care. I just want to attach a name to your voice."

"Sure," she said. "It's Carol."

She tried again to think of the long-ago boy's name. His head had vanished beneath the waves instantly, an arm raised up and then covered in an arching whitecap. The speed of his disappearance had seemed almost willful. She said, "Is that made up? Because it sounds like a made-up name."

She couldn't resist. Even under the circumstances.

The girl laughed a little. It sounded like a laugh. "No, that's my real name. I don't care if you know it. But it does sound a bit generic, doesn't it?"

"Mine too," Sarah said, although she liked the name and its implications. She could tell from Carol's voice that she was a nonsmoker and that she cared about her work. "I was afraid I might end up talking to someone with job burnout," Sarah explained, "but I can see that's not the case."

"The police should be there by now," Carol said.

"They're not," Sarah said, and she thought of the beach as seen from a distance, the ring of a dozen or so people. The cops had driven right up in the mud in their truck. She had decided there was something rude about that. Not just rude but cruel, and stupid just as the crew had been stupid. *Careless, careless*, she thought. Would it have hurt them to just walk some?

She wondered what Carol looked like, and then, as if she had clicked a switch, she knew that the name *was* fake. It seemed obvious now, and her grip tightened on the phone. "I don't have any weapons," she said, but then she thought of the crowbar under the passenger's seat, the knife in the glove compartment, two-by-fours in the truck bed. It felt good to be lying too, and she let the withholding stand for a moment before she added, "I guess a lot of things could count as weapons." Carol read Sarah a list. No handguns, no rifles? No knives? No blunt objects? "I have a knife," Sarah said, "but I can put it on the dash."

"Why don't you do that? That would be great. Thank you."

"Sure," Sarah said, but she didn't move. A complex array of forces held her in position, one hand to her ear, the other on the wheel. Inside some unidentifiable part of her was still shaking. "Okay," she said. "There you go." Except that she felt like she was being watched by someone with a telescope. Not moving was a form of rebellion, but it was also pretty stupid, wasn't it? Carol asked about guns again, and Sarah said, "No, no, definitely no guns. I own a couple, but they aren't with me."

"When they get there the police will ask you to get out of the truck and put your hands in the air. They'll frisk you, but don't worry, you're not under arrest. They just want to make sure you're okay."

"I'm not a violent person," she said, but maybe that was a lie too. Just like there were all kinds of weapons, there were all kinds of violence.

"They should be there," Carol said. "Do you see them?"

"The help," Sarah said.

"Yes," she said. "The help."

And there they were, in Sarah's rearview mirror: two patrol cars, one with its driver's side door open. They were parked a good hundred feet away across an open expanse of snow and ice, and it took Sarah a moment to understand that they were there *for her*, because they seemed to be investigating something else going on over there by the entrance, something much more important. Two of the cops had already climbed from their car but they weren't even looking in her direction. Sarah happened to be part of something completely different, another story that did not require two cop cars and four cops and the bullhorn that began calling out instructions to her from across the lot. The bullhorn transformed the voice, made it louder and deeper, like some kind of macho cartoon. They were asking her if she had any weapons and she didn't know who she should talk to anymore. She told the girl on the phone, "I see them. They're here. Behind me."

Except she was back on the beach with those other cops, looking at the dead boy's open hands, and then she could see the second cop's face as he came up behind the first and told her to back off. She was a stranger there, after all, and she should know her place. "Mind your own business," he said. But he wasn't angry. He looked sad with his big black moustache and curly hair graying at the temples, and ridiculous too—like a walrus, like someone's impotent dad. "I knew him," she said. "I knew him better than anybody here."

"You still need to step away."

She did, but she made a point of pushing against the younger cop, shoulder to shoulder in a gesture that was half flirtation and half bullish anger. She had slept with him a couple of times and he had thought something more might come of it until she had told him she wasn't interested. She pushed through the small crowd and out the other side and sat on one of the water-polished logs scattered on the sand. The cop, the one she had slept with, was still looking at her. They had made love without tenderness or patience the first time and the second. Which was fine, sometimes sex was like that between two people, especially when they had been drinking. But this time, the time she was imagining as she waited in her truck, the hypothetical third time, would have been different. And anyway, she wasn't really yearning for the cop. He had been an awkward lover and had left in the middle of the night. She yearned for the drowned boy, who she had slept with as well, just once, on one of those nights after drinking too much. Just for fun, she had told him when she pulled her sweatshirt over her head, and they had both laughed.

She called up the boy again, the living version of him, and thought of his body against hers. They had matched each other's desperation like athletes in competition and then they fell away and he grew silent until he told her about his girlfriend and the kid. He said something about being a horrible person. He had never done anything like this before, he explained, and she believed him. She put the kettle on the burner and teabags in two cups. Still naked, she talked to him and tried to make him feel better. She was very good at keeping a secret, she told him. She smiled and the shame vanished from his face. He wanted her again, and she said, "Don't think with your prick now, okay?"

The town had not decided she was a whore yet. That came weeks later, after she screamed at the cops on the beach. She remembered now that she had screamed. Not just at them but at the others, the crew of the *Lazy Bones*, all of them, because none of this should have happened. Someone was responsible. Years later, listening to the voices calling for her to step out of the vehicle, she decided that she had loved him, not in some star-crossed fashion—not any of that trash—but in a small way, the way you love a certain coffee cup or a time of day when the light falls just right. And the feeling had grown over time, hidden to her. She had waited all this time to receive it, and the cops in the rearview could wait a little longer for her. Carol and the four men in uniform and Beth with her lawn and extra room and clothes with the price tags left on in case they didn't fit.

She kept her eyes shut and allowed the boy to just stay there on the beach. Her will held him there, in her memory, with a compassion that wasn't exactly unexpected. Only its intensity was surprising. But that might have been the panic, the weight of the cold. Why was a thing never just simply what it was? She pulled the phone back from her ear and set it on the passenger's seat. What was the word she had used back then? *Pricks.* That was what she had called them from the log, not just the two police officers but the whole circle of bystanders, her face hot, almost burning, and then she had wandered up the beach, kicking up sand. She'd take the long way around, head back into town and hit the bars, find someone to talk to and then bring back home. It had seemed a moment of triumph, but she remembered also thinking, stupid, stupid, about herself, about the boy with sand in his hands and in his mouth and washed across his legs. They were both so stupid. And she was thinking it now, stupid, so stupid, as she leaned forward and almost touched the steering wheel with her forehead.

"You live in a beautiful part of the world," Carol said. "You were smart enough to make this phone call. You have lot to be happy about at a basic level. Sometimes people don't make this call and they leave behind some very sad people."

She fumbled for the phone, lifted it again, and placed it to her ear. "I'm not a violent person."

"Then you should get out of the car. But do it slowly."

"I don't have gloves," Sarah said, because it was twenty below. She could picture them on the kitchen table right where she had left them, and for a second she was there again, at home, pulling on her boots and screaming back at Beth, "You're not my sister. You think you are, but you aren't. You're something else." The terror had started then, she decided, in the kitchen as the talking turned to yelling, and then followed her to the truck, but she knew that was another kind of lie, like the girl's name, like her setting the knife on the dashboard. Maybe it had started twenty-five years ago on the *Lazy Bones*, or before then even, back in Seattle. *So senseless*, she thought, and yet there it was, that same victorious elation. She would show them. She was a tough customer.

⁓⁓⁓

She had come to this place when she was twenty-one, hitchhiking up the ALCAN with a backpack dangling from one shoulder. Men pulled over and gave her a look like, what the hell? But then they offered her rides, told her their stories, shared food. Simply being there was a sign you belonged, proof that you were tenacious and maybe a little bit crazy. The word *crazy* was always being used as a compliment, certainly not how her father used it when she told him what she had planned. Twenty-five years later and she was sitting in her truck—the best thing she owned—and missing him. Not missing him, not really, but yearning to speak to him in the same way that she was speaking to the girl. Except she would tell it all. The stuff in her head would make it into the air: who she had become, what she believed in. Except she would lie then too, right? Because how could she tell him about what was happening now and what would happen soon? "It's going to be okay," the woman on the phone said, and for the second time that afternoon Sarah didn't believe her.

After all, her sister had said the exact same words.

So she would speak to her the way she had spoken to her sister in the beginning: with patience and a generous spirit. She told her that she understood that certain protocols had to be followed, but she was feeling much, much better. She was thinking of just driving herself home. In fact, people were there waiting for her. Celine would be sitting on the couch reading one of her horror novels, listening for the truck. They'd meet at the door and share apologies, Sarah first, like always, and then her daughter's voice a reluctant echo.

The police said, "Come out of the truck and we can talk." Two of them had moved closer, halfway between her truck and the patrol cars. This seemed like a compromise on their part and maybe they weren't happy about it.

"My hands aren't shaking anymore," Sarah said, and the lies balanced again, two and two. "I'm heading home."

"You can't do that," Carol said. "What are the police telling you to do?"

"They're saying I should get out of the car with my arms raised."

"Then that's what you should do. You did the right thing when you called. Now you have to do the next right thing. Step out of the truck. There's only so much we can accomplish talking like this."

"I feel like we're accomplishing a lot," Sarah said.

"Thank you," Carol said, and Sarah imagined her smiling, reaching for a Styrofoam cup of coffee. She was starting to like her again.

"Let me tell you about where I live," Sarah said. "It's a very interesting place."

"What do you do there?"

"That doesn't matter," Sarah said, because it didn't, or at least she didn't want her to think that it mattered. Instead she told her about the salmon runs, the fish shimmering silver-pink, and about the light in the summer, strong enough to convince you that winter never happened and *would* never happen. She told her about the drowned boy, the string of boys in that fishing town years ago, and that day on the beach when she realized that some of them wished it had been her who had drowned. Better the stranger, the whore, than a man with a girlfriend, a child, someone they had known since grade school. Her thoughts were racing so far ahead of her words that they had lost each other, so she told her about the birch trees, straight as rails, and about her favorite restaurant, where they knew her by name. They knew her daughter's name too, and would ask about her when she was gone. How to explain that to an elderly waitress serving you an omelet? *She's in Seattle now with my sister* when just weeks before they had eaten enough pancakes there to make their stomachs hurt.

Although she didn't speak any of this except in her mind, and only for a moment as she shifted the phone from ear to ear. Instead she said, "I work at the grocery store here in town." That was all, and even that spoken in a raspy whisper. Three lies now because she had been fired from that job last week for swearing at her boss.

Carol said, "Think about a miracle day. The best day of your life. What would it look like? What would happen?"

"I still have family, you know," Sarah said. "I don't need help from people who don't even tell me their real names."

Carol said, "You can tell this to a doctor, you know. The hospital is just two miles away. The police can take you there."

"Sure," she said, but she didn't move. She glanced up at the cops in the rearview. They had nudged a little closer, although one had hung back. The doors of one of the patrol cars were open and he stood behind one like it was a shield. "I come from a good family," she said. She felt the phone's weight in her palm and then against her ear again. Then she remembered that her father was sort of a drunk, actually, and the kind of person who thought talking was for women and her leaving for Alaska a sign of colossal ingratitude. She pulled those stories into the frame of her mind and let them sit alongside the other images of him, the ones she had sort of just made up over the years, or exaggerated at least, and then she thought of what she had told her sister just a few hours before: that people could change. If Beth gave her a chance, only one more summer, by August she would understand just how amazing and unpredictable a person's life could be. Sarah's coming here to Alaska years ago was incontrovertible proof of that. Her friends and family had told her she wouldn't last a month. Only the men who had helped her out on the ALCAN had seemed to believe in her, and the crew of the *Lazy Bones* before all that went wrong. Sarah made a sound, deep and painful, as she adjusted herself in her seat. "My older sister—her name is Beth—she came up here with her husband last week. You wouldn't believe those two."

"Something to tell the doctor?" Carol asked.

"I'm telling it to you," Sarah said. "Right now."

"The police are going to wait a little longer and then they're going to approach the vehicle, but what they'd really like is to have you step out with your hands up, so they can tell that you don't have any weapons. None of us really know what you have, right? You have to understand, it's a very dangerous job for them, and sometimes people call and lie, and then take potshots at them."

"You don't believe me," Sarah said.

But Carol didn't seem to hear. She kept going. "And you're in a very remote area. It's the kind of area where cops get ambushed."

"I don't have a gun," Sarah told her, and then she remembered the crowbar again, the knife, and also the pot in the plastic baggie in the glove compartment. The image of the knife had led her there, to that other thing she should have remembered when all of this started. It was a lot of pot and she certainly didn't want them to find it. "Will they search the car?" she asked.

Sarah could hear Carol breathing, once, twice, like she was getting ready to exert herself, lift something heavy or make a long jump. "Should they?"

"No," she said. "I'll get out."

"Good."

So she got out. She opened the door and it all changed. The world grew bigger. Her boots crunched on the snow when she took a step. Away from the vehicle, the cops told her, and she noticed that they had drawn their guns. The sight almost made her laugh. Her hands rose above her head, but it didn't feel like a decision. They rose as simply and steadily as balloons—they were that weightless and distinct from her—and then she walked forward without knowing why. The cold felt good and seemed to sharpen her mind: she wondered if she should have killed the engine, but it was too late now. And where had her cell phone gone? On the passenger seat, still connected to the operator? No, it was in her hand, raised above her head, and she could swear she heard the voice still talking, asking questions, holding onto one end of the long line.

She had left something else in the truck: the boy, the image of his face. She couldn't recall it now, either in life or death, and as she tried the shadows across it deepened until she couldn't be bothered. She felt that loss the way she did the first time and so she called out, the anger in her voice surprising her, "Four of you for an old lady, huh? I should be honored."

She held both hands above her head, her cell phone in her closed right fist, and of course she could not hear Carol's calm voice. That was just her remembering. *Ah*, she thought, *so you've crossed over into the past with the rest of them. Or maybe it's me, going down, down, down.* She had wanted to explain the weather on the coast to her, and the sight of the fish in the nets and then sliding into the hold, moving like the ocean from which they'd just been liberated. But she couldn't do that and a light crossed the truck, along the ground, and hit her in the chest. It hovered there for a moment and then scanned up her body, her arms, her hands, then down again to her face. She tried to smile into the glare.

All she could see was the light and as she took another step she imagined her fifty-two-year-old face squinting into the dark. Were the guns tilted in her direction? What would it take for the cops to squeeze just a little harder? A voice spoke and told her to drop the thing in her hand and she told them it was just a cell phone, and they said, okay, set it back in the truck then, and that's what she did, moving sideways like she was sliding along a ledge. Her hands were cold and she wanted this to be done. The light followed her, bobbing around her head and shoulders. Four o'clock and it was dark as hell.

"There's a crowbar," she said, because she didn't want them to look in that other place, where the knife and pot were, the license and registration and expired coupons and wide-faced doll with a pink dress. All that junk.

My face, she thought, and maybe because the boy's face was lost to her she thought of her own. She could see it well. She imagined it how the police must have seen it, pinched hard from the light, her lips pale, hair falling around her forehead in a mad mess. Behind her stood the storage compartments, each with their orange door, each packed with things important enough to save but not important enough to use. Her fishing nets and rods and her tools and one paint-spattered hammer she had used when shingling roofs in Anchorage one summer. She tried to think of herself as a photograph—something she could take out in a few years and look at with a fresh perspective—but it didn't work. The shadow had fallen across the future too, and three of the four cops loomed around her, speaking to her in normal voices. The fourth was the one with the light. "We're sorry about this," one of the police said. "You're not under arrest."

His hands were sliding up and down her body, patting the pockets of her coat, and she remembered the other knife, the jackknife, in her breast pocket. He found it, took it out, made it vanish along with a screwdriver. Then he turned her around—she felt like she might spin around completely, then twice, three times, like it was all some kind of game designed to confuse and amuse her—and told her it was okay, she could lower her arms.

It was a relief not to have the light shining in her face, and maybe it was just the spots in her eyes or the adrenaline, but the storage units beyond the fence held her attention like a good mystery. Several bags held clothes from Celine's childhood: the bright green sweatshirt she liked to wear at Christmas, a succession of winter hats; the one she'd worn as a toddler, a kindergartener, a middle schooler. Sarah could imagine the clothes, the plastic bins, the furniture left behind by dead grandmothers—and the place struck her as a kind of purgatory where objects waited around to be delivered to a new home or a junk heap. She wished that this insight had occurred to her ten minutes earlier, so she could have shared it with the girl on the phone.

Carol, she thought, and decided that this *was* the operator's name.

The cop was putting the handcuffs on, explaining again that she was not under arrest, but that they would be bringing her to the hospital. He was the oldest of the three, heavyset, with a kind voice. "Fucking cold day to kill yourself," another cop said under his breath. He was talking to his partner, not to Sarah, but she heard him clearly, and it seemed like such an odd thing to say that she turned to look at him. The youngest, he was tall, muscled, probably an athlete, and she supposed that he was handsome. She looked him over with real scrutiny, but it was hard to know what to make of him, and he looked back with disinterest. I'm something he has to do, she decided. She might as well be a criminal. That's how he was looking at her, as if she had done something wrong. The other cop was explaining that they needed to shut up the locker, turn off the truck, put her in the patrol car. Was her heart still racing?

"I really didn't expect any of this," she said.

"Don't worry," he said.

"I want to get a book," she explained. "It's right in there in a box. I can practically reach out and touch it. I'd like to have it at the hospital, is what I'm saying." She twisted her shoulder toward the open space in as close to a pointing gesture as she could manage and the cop steadied her with an open hand. It was easy for the shoulder roll to turn into something else, another pointing motion with her head, and then something else again: she was stepping toward the open space now, head bowed, lifting her legs high through the snow. She could practically see the book: in a stack of boxed books at the front of the locker. And even when she realized she had forgotten the title of the book itself her desire to get it grew. If anything, the simple fact that the book had become vague to her made her want it even more. She'd know it when she saw it. She really would.

The older cop steadied her, said, "Hey, hey there. Careful," and then he tugged her backward, but the tug made her want to push forward more. That was just natural, wasn't it? It was animal nature and it was human nature too and she tugged back, found herself trudging forward again. She felt free despite her handcuffed wrists and it seemed for a second that the police had decided, hey, sure, let her get her book.

Except that the third cop, the one who hadn't spoken, said, "It's never easy."

It was funny because it was true. She fell into the snow and called them names. She cursed her sister and her husband and her father and all the people who had not believed in her. At that moment this lack of faith seemed like the worst of all possible sins and those people were all guilty of it. She rolled like a dog and kicked her legs and then the fight bled from her and she lay still without feeling cold or angry or anything. "Lift her up," one of the cops said, and then she was warm again, beginning to get warm. Her Carhartts were covered with snow, and so were her hair and face. She had wanted to tell them about the summers and about the boy, of course, but he was gone. She had not escaped but he had, down into the water and into the past. Her elbow hurt and so did her knee and she was sorry to cause such a fuss.

They made a long, slow loop around the parking lot before heading back onto the main road. The handcuffs pinched her wrists and she shifted around, trying to find a position that didn't hurt, while the cop in the passenger's seat talked to her. "I've been through two divorces, ma'am," he said. "I've been shot in the stomach and I've had a knee replaced. Things have a way of getting better. Believe me."

"You're still young," the other cop said, which was obviously not true, but she liked the way he drove, slow, his fingers guiding the wheel with relaxed authority. Occasionally the radio made noises or spat out sentences, orders that weren't meant for them. There were other cars out there roving around. She decided that she did not feel bad at all. "I'm fifty-two," she said.

"Young," the driver said, with a force that surprised her. "I'm fifty-six. I retire next year."

She wasn't ungrateful. But she kept thinking about Carol and the things she must have been talking about in those last few moments. Maybe there was another important part of the protocol she had wanted to share, something about the way Sarah should hold her body as the police approached. Next would come the doctors and medications, the observation in the small room, all there before her, like sleep waiting for a person in bed. "We're almost there," the cop said, and then they both fell silent, and the car eased up to a red light. The snow blew across the road sideways and then a man crossed, walking fast, looking front and center, hands shoved down in the pockets of his coat. He looked like he might be up to no good, but he passed like a ghost.

They moved onto the main street now, down under the highway overpass and through the gauntlet of signs advertising fast food and liquor and tattoos. Cars idled in parking lots. People conducted their small transactions. She had come this way a billion times, but the route passed before her eyes in slow motion and she couldn't stop and become a part of any of it. It was a film playing before her and that made her want to notice all of it, every speck of activity. Was it weird to think of it all as entertainment?

She *was* entertained. But she also wanted to throw her face against the cage and tell them to stop the car, rewind it all. She had more to say to the girl on the phone. One of the most important things being an apology for not listening, because Sarah could have made it all so much easier if she had just listened. But she had been too busy talking,

talking in her own head, the boy spiraling away from her into that deep place beyond her reach. She had wanted to join him there. In a way she was going there now, wasn't she? Kicking at the wire cage with her feet would not solve a thing, but it seemed like this might be the only way to get them to stop, the only choice between doing nothing and accomplishing something. It was all she could do to just rest her forehead against it, taking deep rasping breaths. "I need to call someone," she whispered.

But they didn't speak to her, and she realized she had been talking to herself, mumbling, this whole time, like the fragmented messages on the car radio. They had simply tuned her out.

They were taking the turn into the hospital parking lot, up to the emergency entrance, and Sarah still hadn't let Carol go. She should have told her about Celine: the adventures down south, skipping school so they could see autumn leaves, listening to rain falling on the tent and then the surprise of the rain turning to hail, sweeping in off the mountains and all they could do was laugh. That more than balanced the rest of it, the screaming as she left the house, Beth's comfortable living room. More time and she could have put it into some kind of shape that made sense.

The whole episode now seemed shrunken, merely the latest in a series of small failures. Beth had pointed out each one for her that morning at the cabin while Celine stared at the floor, wearing new clothes brought from Seattle. "This is a hard thing to do," Beth had said, "but I think we should do it," as if they were collaborators. And then Sarah heard a different kind of boasting as Beth talked about her well-adjusted husband, the good schools, and the extra room Celine could make her own. They had worked this out beforehand.

"I need her," Sarah said through the wire.

The driver put his fingers on the keys but didn't kill the ignition, and the cop in the passenger's seat said, "This is all we can do for you, ma'am. We're just the delivery boys. But you're going to be in good hands. These people know what they're doing." She sobbed against the wire, but when they opened the back door for her she was able to change her face as easily as an actor. She stood and set her shoulders, trying to find the position of most dignity, and then she allowed it to happen: the next step. But she was still speaking to Carol in her head, trying to hold on, because there was the other time when they drove ten hours through the ice eating peanuts off the dashboard and the miracle of sleeping almost until noon and seeing your own breath because the fire had died in the night. Ice more intricate than flowers at the corners of each window and Celine in her sock feet and crazy hair, eight years old, a hot animal against her chest. What was the rest of it but hallucination?

"Tomorrow is a new day," the other cop added, but he was looking sideways out at the snow, as if he wasn't quite convinced by his own words.

How high was the ceiling? The walls rose up around her, each one white and blank, and it was the emptiness she found comforting. It reminded her of images of heaven bubbling up from her childhood, things she had imagined in church or that one time, sick with pneumonia, when she had envisioned her own death, had even longed for it the way she might a slice of her mother's cranberry upside-down cake: as a little treat. She curled on the metal table, blanket kicked to her feet, and she tasted blood in her mouth. She sucked her tongue and the taste grew stronger, but that was comforting too. It gave her something to do.

Slowly she let small things into her mind, arranged them, silverware and glasses and plates on a table. The world of objects. Book first. She remembered it now, not just the title but its particular weight, the envelope she had used as a bookmark, graffiti-scrawled with phone numbers and little cartoons. *The Old Man and the Sea*, a book she had stolen from her father's library, oversized, with reproduced paintings every few pages. It was right there and she could have held it if they had let her. Oh, well. She curled on her side and after a long while—it could have been hours—she heard the door open and someone tell her, "Your family is here."

"I don't want to see them," she said. She felt like a kid pretending to be sick. But she was sick, wasn't she? She added, "Are they going to take me home?"

"No," the man said. "They can't do that. You have to stay here for at least three days. But they want to visit with you."

"Who?" she asked.

"Your sister. And your daughter."

"Celine," she said. "Beth."

"Yes. That's right." The man stepped around her. She could hear his plastic shoes scuffing on the floor and decided that he could do what he liked except touch her. His hand on her shoulder or head—that would be the most horrible thing. He seemed to think about something for a long time and then he said, "Are you sure about that? They've driven a long way in bad weather. And they both really do want to see you. Your girl, she's a real firecracker. I can tell. I have a girl that age. Maybe younger."

"I'm very sure," she said. "Send them away."

"Okay," the man said after a long while, and when she thought he was gone she opened his eyes. But he hadn't left. He had just moved to the door but he was still standing there, watching her, and when she opened her eyes he said, "Do you need anything? Would you like some apple juice?"

She didn't even bother answering that one, and then he closed the door and she closed her eyes and the other things appeared again—the book and then the rest of the storage locker, and then all those complicated people, and then Celine's toys scattered in the front room of the house, her homework scattered in much the same way on the kitchen table. Dishes in the sink. Stations of small messes. Her sister had most likely eradicated each one by now, consolidated and stacked and ordered by category.

Later when they talked about the drowning it was to say not just *What a shame, what a shame*, but also *How stupid*. The two of them. The boy. Her too. They had become a story—the dead boy and the whore from the Lower 48—so she quit and headed deeper into the state, away from the coast. Her yelling had helped him lose the glossy shine he had gained in death. She might as well have killed him a second time. The crazy girl, the whore girl. What had she wanted to tell her sister? That she wouldn't be that story again, the story of her yelling and screaming and then losing her daughter anyway. But here she was, neatly categorized as well.

The girl on the phone had moved on to someone else by now. That was her job. To save people, and the only way to do that was for each to have their turn. What did someone get paid for that kind of thing? Less than a plumber or electrician, but probably a little more than McDonald's.

Sarah remembered her fake name and then she didn't. She was asleep, just for a moment, and then she wasn't. *Apple juice*, she thought, and she had to laugh.

II

FAIRBANKS MUNICIPAL HOSPITAL

The fall of '82 and a city full of generous men. They'd buy you a drink and then another in one of the boxy downtown bars and not even expect anything in return, or they *did* expect something, but it was so small as to be nothing: just a smile at one of their dirty jokes or a wide-eyed look as they explained their work on the pipeline.

Everybody was from somewhere else and everybody was looking for a good time, so it was easy to feel at home. Sometimes she stood on tables in her muddy sneakers and danced and they all called out for her to keep going, keep going, and she could have too, forever, except that she had found within herself a sliver of restraint she was trying to nurture. So she held both arms aloft and said *that's enough, you idiots*, and somebody always held out a hand to help her climb down. She walked home alone as often as not and made herself tea and read from books she had pulled from the library stacks, big piles of them she flipped through, considered, dismissed, returned. They made a nest in her big queen bed, the single extravagance in her place, paid for with fish money.

She had found a new way of living, days full of miraculous habits. Strong, black coffee in the morning and then to work on the road crews, holding signs and grading pavement. The sun sat on the horizon for hours. Dusk seemed to take over the entire evening. At night she threw herself on the bed and felt her blood throb. Sometimes she dozed off still wearing her boots.

Her father finally wrote to her. He had tried many times before, he said. A series of letters. Maybe they had made it through and maybe they hadn't, but here he was, trying again. Mostly he wrote about her younger brother. Baseball had taken over his life. He could strike out any high school team's three best hitters. It was the fastball that did it. He could place it on the outside corner of the plate as easily as setting it on a table. But he was still shy, held doors open for his mother, had few friends but at least no enemies. Her sister, she was enjoying college. She had a boyfriend a few years older than her. He had been to Alaska once, with his family one summer, and told them some stories.

The writing grew smaller as it reached for the bottom of the page, like a man crouching to step through a narrow space. He was trying to fit everything in. *We cannot be truly happy without you*, he said, and then, *but we hope you are well. We truly believe that you are, but we would like to hear it in your own words.* She imagined him working hard on a letter like this, in the same way that he might work on the engine of their Impala, hood open, brow furrowed, sizing up each part and then the whole. Did they still own that crazy car? She remembered falling asleep in the back seat, the rush of air from the half-open window and the stereo playing news stories. The memories seemed to come from some other world where bad things happened.

The letter had eventually fallen into a trunk and the trunk had made its way into the storage unit, but maybe the letter was no longer there. It was hard to place a finger on its exact location and it did not matter much except that she liked the idea of touching it, opening it, and verifying that the picture in her head matched the object. In this place she seemed shorn of the clutter of memories: no books, no truck or house keys, no clothes except the red hospital V-neck and pocketless pants, no baseball cap to tuck her hair under. No boots with the stink of sweat inside and no knives and pills. She drank water from a plastic cup and crushed it. She stood at the windows and scrutinized the snow-covered parking lot eight floors down, the business of life down there as some people left and others arrived. She watched a little TV for the first time in more than a decade. All the people on the shows were worse than morons. They were smug about it too. Somehow what was supposed to be seclusion had brought her closer to what people thought of as the world outside.

She brushed her teeth whenever she could. Four or five times before lunch. She told herself, *This is useless*, but she did it anyway. She liked to look at her face, gargle, spit, then do it all again. She didn't know if she was being vain or monkish and she didn't care. She stepped from the bathroom and became part of the crowd again. "Hello," the girl said. How strange. You run a few thousand miles and almost thirty years away from your childhood only to find a teenaged version of you sitting on the other side of the hospital common room at ten-thirty on a Sunday morning. She radiated hostility and poison and a familiar measured discipline, all black sweatshirt, legs up and knees tucked inside. Always with the hoodie raised, her face turtled half inside, her hands up the sleeves, body pushed into a corner, her back to the wall and taking it all in: the milling patients with their paper slippers and ice creams in little plastic cups. She was trying to turn herself into a ball, something inert and inconsequential, but all this did was draw attention to herself.

Why was hoodie girl allowed to wear street clothes and nobody else? Wearing the sweatshirt—being allowed to wear it—seemed the height of arrogance. The others revolved around her, gauged their own well-being by hers. If she was agitated—if her foot began to tap, if she began to talk a mile a minute—then they grew agitated too. But when she was happy, wow, the place was not a bad place to be.

The hoodie girl didn't look anything like Sarah had at that age. She didn't even have the same hair color. But she could pull that switch just like Sarah, from innocent excitement to badass disgust and then back again. Earlier she had been talking about how beautiful the snow was outside, how it looked totally different from this high up, on the fifth floor of the hospital, but an invisible string had been pulled and she had collapsed into herself. "What's her name?" Sarah asked the befuddled-looking guy with the spaghetti hair, and he said that he thought it was Estrella and she had tried to kill herself. This was not a surprise. Most of them had tried to kill themselves. The befuddled guy was one. *A funny story*, he said, when he introduced himself at breakfast.

Sarah said, "I hate the paper shoes."

The befuddled guy looked down as if he had only realized, just then, that yes, he was wearing paper shoes too. He laughed a little—it was a sort of high giggle on the edge of hysteria—and moved off to a different wall.

Her first full day and Sarah had refused visitors again. She sat on the other side of the public room, letting her vision slide back and forth between the girl in the hoodie and the pamphlet on her lap. She couldn't concentrate on either, or rather, she had to concentrate on both: the clip art expression and then the girl's pouting statue face. The trick was to make them the same thing. Neither seemed particularly genuine. The nurse came in and began passing around forms to fill out. She was one of the comedians, but she had decided not to be funny this time. "Describe how you're feeling," she said. "Be as descriptive as possible." She smiled and glanced at the befuddled guy against the wall. "Don't just use words like 'good' or 'bad.'"

What words should she use then? She thumbed her pen and meditated on this little puzzle. Each word she came up with seemed worse than the last and after a minute of swirling around in all that language she wrote, "Bad" in small letters on the first line. Then she wrote, "But not always." Then she raised her hand because that was what she was taught to do in school and said, "Excuse me. I think I need another form. I've made a mistake."

"Just cross it out, honey," the nurse said. "It's okay."

So she did, but she didn't feel right about it.

The girl said, "I'm not doing this," but a few seconds later she was writing along with the rest of them. She scratched and scratched and when she was done, far ahead of anybody else, she said, "I don't know what the point of that was. I have to get out of here. I've been telling you that and you don't listen. I have dogs to feed. If they're in trouble then it's on your head, not mine, you know?"

The nurse took all of this in as she collected the sheets and pens. Obviously, she had heard all of this before. "Your dogs are going to be fine."

"Except that they're not," the girl said. "Except that they're starving."

"Keely," the nurse said, "you and I know that's not true. You've been talking to your mother every day."

"To death," the hoodie girl said. "To death. To death."

"Not true," the nurse said. "Remember your mother. You talked to her yesterday."

"She can hardly feed herself."

This whole conversation conducted without eye contact while smiling, as if each was not even talking to the other, but the girl's knee was bouncing hard. She seemed ready to leap into action at a moment's notice. When the nurse had gone Sarah shimmied over and said, "You have dogs." But the girl didn't respond except to grunt and shake her head. Was she saying no?

Food arrived on a wheeled tray. Some people were eager. They stood almost immediately. Others played it aloof, acted like they didn't even notice that the cart had teetered in. The meals were not bad: ham or roast chicken, mashed potatoes and gravy, usually a soft dinner roll, fruit, and then there was ice cream, vanilla or chocolate or a combination of the two. The best part of that was pulling the lid off by the little paper tab. It was a gesture that sent her on a straight line right back to her childhood. She thought of the girl's dogs starving in their kennels, raging to break out. She said to the girl, "Why are you here?" and she couldn't help herself. She let the boy in again, his body slowly spiraling as it sank. She couldn't help but imagine it like that, and the beauty of it made her angry with herself. She said, "I can tell you if you want."

"I'm here because of my boyfriend," the girl said. "Because he's a giant dick."

"I guess a lot of us are here because of someone else," Sarah said.

"Lady," the girl said, "you're so wrong that you're right," and she let loose with a little doggy bark bark bark. It was a parody of laughter, a mockery of the very idea of human communication, and it was funny and scary and stupid. She bared her teeth and said, "I tried to kill myself."

"Me too." Sarah was trying to sound adult. She was trying to sound calm and wise. A good thirty years separated them, after all. "I didn't really try," she explained. "I just thought about it."

That same bark. "Well, good," she said. "That's smart of you. What were you thinking about? What was your method of choice?"

A nurse appeared in the doorway, friendly and good-looking. His graying hair was cut short and stylish like a movie actor's, a particular one, but Sarah couldn't remember the actor's name or his films, just his general persona. He was from a long time ago, had starred in movies when they were still in black-and-white. He said, "Don't let it get cold," and then he stepped out of the door frame and was gone. The girl said,

"Let me guess. Can you let me guess? I bet you were going to do something really intense. You were going to swallow Drano. Or use a gun."

"Hanging," Sarah said, and she considered the shock of someone finding a body like that days later when you roll up the metal door to get your things. In her imagination she was the limp body and also the person finding the body and it wasn't an unpleasant feeling—like being the killer and the victim in a film. She remembered that the actor, the one from long ago, had a played a killer once, or at least a man accused of being a killer. At the end of the movie he had been declared innocent, been reunited with his wife. The clock had spun backward and everything was normal. She wondered if the girl was thinking the same kind of thoughts, but her face was a blank thing, like the table surface, the floor. Sarah wanted to change the shape of that thing, to get it to smile or frown, so she said, "I've seen your way with the nurses. I'm not one of them. It won't work on me."

The girl puckered her lips slightly. Which seemed a kind of a victory?

"Hanging," the girl said. "Me too."

Was she mocking her or was the lie designed to bring them closer? She remembered telling these kinds of lies herself. Some had been to the boy who fell overboard. Her father had transformed from a lawyer to an electrician and her feelings—the words themselves—had been made to match what she received from him. She tried her mashed potatoes, but they just tasted like salt and she drove the spoon into the middle of them and let it stick there at attention.

It was nice of them to give you metal silverware, to trust you with knives and forks and frank talk about the future. The kindness was overwhelming, really, and she had done nothing to deserve it except to fall apart in the face of crisis.

The girl was eating too, gobbling up her applesauce, taking big bites of her flank of ham. She occasionally picked raisins off the meat, placing them to one side in a small pile. Not on the tray, on the table. "They remind me of bugs," she said, but she was smiling.

The same meal, but it looked more delicious—more *possible*. Her own tray was a mountain face she had to climb and she decided to ignore it completely. Ignoring things. That was the kind of lying she did now, right?

"At the barn," the girl said, "on the hill."

"At a storage locker." Sarah laughed. The story seemed so incomplete, but where could she start? She imagined the boy again, his innocent, stupid face, but she was quick to replace it with her own face, the face the police must have seen as she climbed from the truck. The girl had cleaned her plate and Sarah nudged her food across the table to her. The girl began picking raisins off the second slice of ham but this time she flicked them, one at a time, like little footballs. They seemed to not travel so much as completely disappear. Nobody else seemed to notice.

"My dogs are starving and here I am eating two meals," the hoodie girl said.

"They'd still be hungry if you were hungry," Sarah said. "You should eat."

But all the hoodie girl did was flick the raisins with her finger and thumb, using them as ammunition against some unseen enemy.

Celine entered Sarah's mind, a memory of her at nine, refusing to eat broccoli, picking it apart with a look of real hatred. But she rejected the memory, sent it back where it had come from, and it spun downward into that dark place where it had hidden for years. Something hard and sharp came into her throat and she said, "I don't know why I'm here. I just called to talk to someone. I didn't want any of this."

The girl continued setting up the raisins and launching them into oblivion. In fact, she seemed more interested in the activity than ever—her face had become a mask of concentration, her eyebrows pulled together, a little snarl in the corner of her mouth—but she did say, "There are probably good reasons." She moved to the small pile gathered from her first meal and began launching those too. Sarah considered reaching out and grabbing her wrist. Stop it, stop it. But she just began to ramble even as she pushed her chair back further, about the book in the storage locker and the ropes and fishing supplies, half of them useless, and her truck, which had been moved, of course, but in her mind it still sat there, door open, engine running, waiting for her to return.

"My dogs are part of me," the girl said. "You don't understand how something like that can feel. You're just talking about objects. Who cares about a book? What does it matter? There are books here. Magazines. Go read *People* or whatever-the-fuck. My dogs are my dear ones. They're out there hungry for their kibble. They're wondering where their Alpha has gone, you know, and you're telling me about *things*."

It took her more than two decades to write to her father: a postcard with a photograph of the Denali mountain range, on the back scribbled a summary of her life, and even then, she didn't fill the white space. She received a call months later from Beth telling her that their parents were dead, just two years ago, three months apart, Mother at the beginning of the summer and Dad at the end. The house she had grown up in was still on the market. The town had dwindled in size when the Gillette factory moved to Mexico and nobody was buying. Questions about why it had taken so long to send the card, and why now, and who are you anyway? Their grieving was all finished, put into tidy order, but Sarah had to steady herself against the news. Of course they were dead, she told herself, what had she expected?

"We moved south," Beth said. "Remember that boy I fell in love with in college? He's a lawyer now."

Sarah said, "Fantastic. Fantastic."

Celine was listening from the other room. Sarah could tell because she had turned down her music. When the call ended the music swelled again into a euphoric rush of guitars and drums emanating from behind a closed door.

The postcard had been a whim, a thing she had bought because it reminded her of the trips she had taken with Celine. She had used it as bookmark for weeks and weeks before finally fastening a stamp to it. She had not expected it to call back the past in this way. How could such a small thing, a stupid thing, have such power? Beth's voice went on. Their brother had played Triple A baseball for a couple of years, had two children and a lovely wife and lived on the East Coast. She spoke to him every week. Their father had found religion later in life, and it had ennobled him. He grew softer, gentle. He talked about traveling to Italy, the land of his grandparents, but he was infirm by then and everybody knew it would never happen.

"I have a daughter," Sarah said, "but she's also my best friend."

"Incredible," Beth said. "Well, you and your husband and daughter need to visit. You can stay in the old house. It's only an hour away from us. It's just like they left it."

"I would like that," she said, because she would, but Celine threw a fit when she explained it to her afterward. She didn't even know these people and she had never been on an airplane and weren't they supposed to decide everything together as partners? "This is important to me," Sarah said. "It really is. I'm asking you to consider it."

But why was it important? They arrived without resolving that question, exchanged hugs with strangers at the airport, and then pushed themselves into the car. It smelled of fake pine trees.

They sat around that suburban living room talking about fishing trips, the northern lights, the dark and stillness of winter. Just a couple of months later everything had flip-flopped and Beth and her husband were visiting *her*. Except that there was nowhere to put them, and they couldn't believe the lack of running water, the tightness of the space, the state of the truck. They appeared one afternoon with a couple hundred dollars' worth of supplies from the Fred Meyer, bags and bags of stuff, but there was no space to put it all. "You just sleep in the one bed," Beth said. "Doesn't she want her own room?" When the aurora appeared above her head one night on a trip to the outhouse Sarah called out to them, *Look, look*, but nobody appeared on the path, not even Celine, and when it split into purple and green Sarah thought, *Okay, all of this is mine. They can have comfort and I'll have beauty.*

⁓

"You're shaking," the night nurse told her. "Are you cold? Do you need anything?"

She wanted to stand watching a pallet fire drinking from a can and eating a stick of beef jerky. She wanted to fall asleep in her own musty bed up in the loft listening to the sound of Celine's breathing. "Yeah," she said. "I want a beer."

"You can't have a beer," the nurse said. "You know that?" and she laughed. What a character. What a tough customer.

Sarah sat small and tightly wound as a curled cat.

The nurse poured a glass of water into a paper cup and handed it to her. Sarah held it with both hands, lifted it to her mouth. The water tasted metallic, but cold and good and she finished it, feeling like a fool for holding the empty cup. "They really want to see you," the nurse said. "They're downstairs again and they're eating dinner from the vending machines. Why don't you just say yes?"

Her *no* took a strange new form: she closed her hand into a fist and placed the crushed cup on the bedside tray. She tilted her chin to the window, where the wind threw itself against the glass in slow, rolling waves. She heard the nurse step back, her footsteps across the floor and then out to the hall. The lights in the rooms were going out one by one. Sarah let her daughter inside, only for a second, and then shut her out again. Or rather she replaced her with another face, a few faces, revealing themselves like flipped playing cards, and it *was* a kind of game. The officer from yesterday and then the officer from years ago and then, of course, the boy staring at the sky, lungs full of water. Everything strung along that long rope, the knotted string that connected her to the hotline operator, who sat at attention, headset on, waiting for something horrible to happen somewhere, anywhere.

"Hey, pretty lady," came the whispered voice. It was the hoodie girl, the liar, the one who cared so much for animals. She certainly wasn't supposed to be out of her room at this hour. Nine-thirty. But there she was in the doorway, her hair wet from a shower. "You look like you're scared of me," she added. "Am I a ghost?"

"I was just thinking," Sarah said.

A rare storm. Usually those happened down south nearer the coast, but this one was genuine, and Sarah hoped for ball lightning. She had seen it a couple of times before in the southeast and it had made her think of the Bible. It seemed to come right from that old place, where seas parted and bushes burned. Both of them looked out the window and then the girl said, "You look like a man. I mean that as a compliment. You look like you could really kick my ass. Which is why I'm being rude to you. Maybe I need my ass kicked and I figured you might be the one to do it."

More performance. More lies. The hoodie smelled of wood smoke. Sarah smelled it all the way across the room and even stronger when the girl came over and sat at the foot of the bed, the pose of someone visiting Grandma in the hospital after a bladder operation. She even looked a little concerned. *Do not touch me*, Sarah thought. She sent it out like a command and then, because she couldn't quite control herself, she said,

"Your dogs. I love dogs too, sure, of course, who doesn't? But you don't know me. I could tell you a thing or two. I've done amazing stuff."

She imagined the thick wet rope, the heavy iron wheel. All she had to do was twist it and let the memories sluice out. She had done cocaine in the back rooms of every downtown bar. Some of them didn't even exist anymore. Some of the men had ceased to exist too. She rode on the back of a Harley to British Columbia, had sex in a tent with a man twice her age and then in the morning smoked cigarettes while watching moose down by the stream. The rocks were as white as children's teeth and the man told her, this is the prettiest little place in the world, meaning not the province or the campsite but the very spot where they stood. The moose raised their heads in the direction of the voice but didn't move away. She remembered every bit.

"You were born here," Sarah said. "I can tell. But I had to earn it. I had to make a place for myself."

What place was that? This place right here? The girl was probably thinking, *Good job. Nice effort.*

So Sarah told her about that older man and the night in the tent and then the other man, years later, who reminded her enough of that other one that she opened herself to him like they were old lovers reunited. Except they were the same age now. Years had passed and she was thirty-nine and had not been with someone in two years, was living in a junky apartment on the avenues within walking distance of the Midnight Mine. They coupled at his place, out on the outskirts of town, a log house with a big black stove at its center, and when they were done the man said, "Have to see to the fire," and slipped from inside her and then from bed in a motion that seemed like one long reverse dive. She began to shake inside because he wasn't that other man, the one from British Columbia, or the drowned boy, or any of the ones in between. He was his own thing and there was no knowing him. She could hear him moving around, the sound of running water, a door opening and closing, and she stopped her crying with a little internal snarl. *So stupid*, she thought. But she didn't know just how stupid. She found that out later. Thirty-nine years old and when the man had said, I don't have condoms, she had said, whatever, that's okay, just come here. She thought of the other man in British Columbia saying almost the same thing. They had been lucky then, and in the morning they had watched animals and felt like the only two people in the world. At least that's how *she* had felt, and he had allowed her to feel it, had said nothing to break the spell. She appreciated that, even years later, remembering. It was an act of mercy.

She recalled the three moose, the mother and two calves, their hooves tentatively finding purchase in the river silt. They seemed to be explorers. That's exactly what they were, lifting their dancers' legs. Sarah told the girl all of this, or rather she would have, if the girl hadn't been talking herself. "I don't believe in gray areas," she was saying. "You're either a hero or a motherfucker in my book and that's how it is. I'm on your side or you're my worst enemy."

The girl paused as a word occurred to her. "Nemesis," she said, "my nemesis," and Sarah thought it would make a good name for a ship, something sleek and military moving underwater. A submarine. The girl was talking about her ex-boyfriend, who had crossed over from hero into the world of motherfuckers, as simply as if a light switch had been slapped off. He'd never return from that place now, and when she got out—which would hopefully be tomorrow—she had a little plan she was going to set in motion. First the dogs, of course, but she had friends, big friends, and they were going to do some damage. "He's going to wish he was never born," she said. "He'll be the one with regrets, right?"

It was impossible to fit words into the spaces of this other story, which sat between them as tight and confusing as a ball of rubber bands. Alone and thirty-nine, living in one room, and she could feel the baby kicking inside her. The father had vanished, possibly to Canada, possibly further, and the bartender at the Midnight Mine told her she was better off without him. Bad news, that one. Not once during that difficult time did she come close to sending a postcard or phone call to the Lower 48, so why years later? She had wanted to tell her dad how it had all turned out.

She said to the hoodie girl, "It's a different city now."

"Meaning what?" the girl asked, but she was smiling. "Meaning that I shouldn't stand by my convictions? That a person can't do what they want in Fairbanks anymore?"

All Sarah wanted to do was describe the room: the lamp in the corner with its dented shade, the coffee table covered with dirty glasses. "I'd be careful," she said.

The girl laughed at that. "Oh," she said. "Why should I be careful?"

"It's just a good idea to be careful," Sarah said.

"I'm not just some dumb white girl you can give advice to, lady. I'm not going to lap up everything you say," the girl said. But wasn't she a white girl too? Her hair was dark, but her face—maybe it was better not to even think about it? Sarah said, "Well, I'm not going to apologize to you."

The girl moved her hand across the air in a motion that took in everything before her. The smile came and went in random flashes. She seemed happy again. "No apology necessary," she said, and then the girl told her about her boyfriend's car and about how he cared for it more than he cared for anything else, including her, and it spent most of the winter in a garage because otherwise it would just end up in a ditch. Who was stupid enough to own a Corvette in Fairbanks, Alaska? And what kind of man spent that much time in front of the mirror in the morning? It was like he thought if he kept looking at his face long enough it would turn into a more handsome one. That's what he was trying to do, actually: put the nose and eyes and forehead into just the right positions so he could be the person he wanted to be. "That first glance in the morning must be rough for him," she said.

"Just forget him," Sarah said.

The girl was going to say something else but the night nurse was there, pissed off but trying to be friendly. Words were exchanged. Then they were both gone and Sarah sat rigid and straight and she knew sleep was going to come on slowly if at all. The wind made its clattering noise against the window and she turned the heavy wheel. Her sister's words came back to her. *Everything is going to be okay. This is what she wants.* And Celine sitting in the big chair with her head down, nodding ever so slightly. Once Sarah had strapped her to her back and hiked through the southeast alpines until her left heel bled, finally appearing at a circle of public-use cabins with a sleeping two-year-old and a limp. On the beach in Homer they had slept in a single sleeping bag, chest to chest, face against shoulder. They had shouted down bears.

The hoodie had been pulled back, her face open to view. So much to say that she had run straight from the shower, creeping down the hall, checking each room to see which one contained the lady who looked like a man.

Day 2 and the handsome nurse handed them lined paper and pens. They sat five to a side at the long table and wrote down their thoughts. What were their short-term goals? Their long-term goals? How had they come to be here? They bowed their heads and worked at their words. At lunch the nurse told Sarah, "Your visitors are here again."

"No, they're not," Sarah said. It was meant to sound tough but it came out as borderline nonsense. "No," she added as an afterthought, to make sure the nurse understood what she meant. And even then, she had to follow that up with a dismissive wave of her hand.

Three o'clock and the dark came across the parking lot and even into the building like it was searching for something inside. The lights dimmed and people napped. Ham sandwiches and a banana and the hoodie girl didn't appear. She had been absent all day. "What makes her so special?" someone said.

At the nurses' station the big woman with dyed blond hair stared at her computer screen. Sarah's mouth still tasted like toothpaste. She played solitaire, moving the cards into neat columns. The woman across from her watched as the red eights moved over the black nines, queens onto the kings. Her face was all twisted up. She seemed disgusted by the proceedings, but she kept watching, four, five, six games, and still the girl wasn't there. Maybe she was gone, back to her dogs, or they had moved her to someplace else.

"What's the deal?" the twisted-face woman asked.

Sarah didn't answer.

"Snob," she said. "I'm just asking a question."

The girl finally appeared at dinner. Her hoodie was gone, but she had wrapped a red blanket around her shoulders, a superhero with her cape, a fairytale character wandering through the dense woods. She was biting her thumbnail, working it down to the quick. "I had an episode," she said to one of the men, and he nodded from across the room.

"It's going to be okay," he said. "You can book it."

"Right," she said from around her thumb.

"And the weather is getting better. It's ten degrees warmer."

"And dolphins eat rainbows," the girl said.

"What?" he asked.

"Never mind."

"They're not leaving," the nurse said to Sarah. She whispered it from behind her shoulder. "They've been here for almost an hour."

"I'm busy," Sarah said.

"Are you sure?"

"She said no visitors," the hoodie girl said, and her voice cracked. She stood up and looked ready to fly across the room, up to the ceiling and out the window.

The nurse said, "You should sit down. You're having your conversation and we're having ours."

"It's okay," Sarah said. She was talking to everybody. But she also felt that she should add that, no, it wasn't getting warmer outside. She had checked and it was still hovering around negative twenty-five. The blond nurse at the front desk had told her so, glancing up from her screen with a flicker of a smile. And why was it so important to know what it was like outside anyway? It could be sunny and eighty-two and what difference would that make?

A nurse was explaining to Sarah that her sister would be returning tomorrow morning, and would she please consider seeing her then? They were so patient. All they wanted to do was visit her.

The hoodie girl circled around the room, sat down, stood up, paced to the window, and then turned away from the weather. She seemed to act on Sarah's thoughts, and the more Sarah's thoughts jumped the quicker the girl moved, until she was standing an arm's length from the nurse, yelling, screaming, pulling at her hair. What was she yelling? Noise mostly, high pitched and keening, but also *No visitors, no visitors, and don't you ever listen? Listen to her. Listen to her.* And the nurse was saying, very calmly, "We can go to the four-point restraints again, you know. We can do that." It was like she was trying to talk over the television, and Sarah decided to turn the telescope around and look through the big end so that everything shrank and became far away. She tried hard to do this, to put herself at a distance, but it only worked halfway because the girl was yelling and a second nurse had entered holding padded wristbands.

"You don't want to do that," the girl said. "You know what a pain filling out those incident reports are. Let me talk."

"You can talk," the nurse said. "You just can't yell."

Just like that she stopped and the rest of the patients pulled back down deep into themselves, each one an island of their own troubles, and the second nurse looked at the first. Some silent transmission signaled to the second one that it was okay to leave, that things were better, except that now Sarah had to start from the beginning again and say, "I don't want to see anybody," as flat as she could make it, and the girl repeated the words, *She doesn't want to see anybody*, not yelling but quiet now, almost like an echo. In the hall the sound of the food trolley. For the first time that day Sarah wished she had a couple Vicodin and maybe a shot to chase it down.

They ate, or rather the girl ate and Sarah slid her plate over to her, bolstered by a mix of generosity and exhaustion. She saved the chocolate chip cookie for herself, to eat at bedtime. "It's like being on an airplane except you never arrive," the girl said, as she tugged at the plastic lid of the applesauce, but she didn't laugh.

And then she said, "I talked to him this morning."

"Your boyfriend," Sarah said.

"Yes," she said. "I called him and we talked."

"What did you talk about?"

"About what a dick he is," she said, "and how he needs to get up there to Murphy Dome and feed my dogs. Some other stuff."

Sarah imagined driving Sheep Creek with her window down in summer, turning up Murphy Dome Road and feeling a tug in her stomach as she sped up into the incline. Near the top a person could see forever. She knew that area by instinct, all of it right there in front of her even though she was sitting in a chair holding a chocolate chip cookie. She considered tearing open the package.

"The thing about him," the girl said, "is that I need to say I'm wrong about what I told you last night. If anybody ever deserved to look into a mirror that long it's him. I'm serious about that. He's beautiful. Not the way that a person is beautiful either. He's beautiful the way, I don't know, a piece of art is beautiful. Just his face. And I want to put my fist right into it over and over again."

"I've never known anybody like that," Sarah said, but she thought of the boy on the boat and decided that just maybe he had a face similar to what the hoodie girl was describing, and if the face was art then memory was the artist. She measured the distance of herself from him and made another decision too: she decided that she could have reached out and saved him. *Everything would have been different*, she thought. But that would have meant being different herself—the kind of person to react in that split second, to grab out of instinct and then pull back and in. It was like at the house: she should have looked her sister in the face, tilted her head, just a little, and made a joke, and Celine would have laughed. The husband was trying to chop wood—he said he wanted to help out—and the irregular thump, thump from outside was funny enough. She could tell just from the silences between the thumps that he was having a tough time. A joke would have pushed it all over the edge into absurdity. His offer to help out and Beth's offer too. Celine would have seen them as the same thing, and would never have agreed to go.

Sarah looked up from her cards and tried to think of what it would take to help this red-caped girl. The blanket had come loose in the commotion and what she thought was a lie wasn't a lie at all. The ring bruising her skin was brown at its middle, red at the ridge. The color reminded Sarah of a bruised apple, but it was shaped like fine jewelry, simple and elegant. It circled the slender neck just below the chin, deepest brown at the larynx and then mottled as it moved to the nape. A miracle, then, that such a simple thing—a neck—had not been broken. The girl spoke about her boyfriend's face, the high cheekbones and the sad eyes and the ears, the ears were the best part, and as she spoke she bent down and pulled the blanket up around her shoulders again, sliding back into her costume. A smile and an insult or two and the disguise would be complete. It was almost reassuring when she said, "You look like you're going to start blubbering. What's the matter with you?"

⁓

The third day and Sarah said, no, no, no, she didn't want to see anybody. And she didn't want to eat French fries and cheeseburgers or even a fruit cup and cottage cheese. She wanted to talk to the hoodie girl. That was all. But the girl was in her room again and would probably not be out for a while. That's what the handsome nurse told her.

"She's having some problems," he said. "She needs some time alone."

"Like me," Sarah said, because they were downstairs again, waiting to be let up. That's what the nurse had come to talk to her about. "They brought you something too. A gift," he said.

"Flowers," she decided.

"No," he said. "Not that."

"Something else."

"I'm not going to tell you. You'll have to see them to find out."

He took the chance to sit down across from her and watch her play, two to the three, king of spades revealed, a run of queen, jack, ten, nine, and then nothing. She gathered the cards together and shuffled. "It's relaxing to watch someone who knows how to shuffle a deck of cards properly," he said, because she split them, then sent them against each other with a satisfying snapping sound. It was something she didn't have to think about. It just happened, and then she arranged them on the table in a row of seven.

"You should eat more," the nurse said.

"I know," she said, and for the first time she pulled the tray closer instead of pushing it away. *A defeat*, she decided, but then, barking right at the heels of that conclusion, *a victory*, because she was starving. She began eating French fries with her fork, stabbing at them.

He smiled and said, "They're not so bad, see?" But of course they were. They were horrible. It was just that she was ravenous.

The eating seemed to make her hungrier. She ate quickly, without really tasting, and then moved onto the fruit cup. She lifted it to her mouth and drank the thick syrup and then she arranged the dirty dishes in a stack to make it easier for the people in the kitchen.

After lunch the girl was back and so was her hoodie and she said, "Here's the thing. A person, a person you're in bed with, say you're waking up from a dream, that person will kiss your ear and whisper that you're the special one." And at this she widened her eyes, leaned in a little. "But a dog. A dog will lick your foot."

"True," Sarah said, but she wanted to add something to that. She had licked a man's thighs, his privates. Where did that fit into the equation, and what the hell were they talking about anyway?

"You're waking up and you're not sure what's real and your lover, he's all turned away from you. His back is a wall and he's snoring. But your dog, your dog is at attention at the side of the bed. At the foot of the bed. In the bed right next to you."

Not always, Sarah answered, but that was only in her head, because she had lost another game and she was pulling the cards back together into a stack. "If it could pull you out of bed and into the world it would," the girl said. "If it could yell your name it would."

"You've been to college," Sarah said.

"Yeah," the hoodie girl said, and it came out embarrassed. Maybe she had dropped out or maybe college graduates shouldn't end up doing what she was doing now or maybe the whole idea of college was stupid in her mind. Sarah had never had those ambitions except in a fleeting moment after the baby was born and everything seemed possible. She held its hot weight against her chest and the future was like a thing she could take apart and put back together. My best choice, she had thought, and in a way her only one. That and going to Alaska in the first place. Those two, but this one the most important, the most difficult.

"Not me," Sarah said. "My sister did, but I didn't." She put the cards in their order, seven across, and saw that it was good luck, a nice mix of reds and blacks, spades and diamonds, but she didn't make a move.

"The soap here makes me smell like the inside of a dishwasher. You know, when you first open it up and everything is hot and steamy? But I don't like that smell. It's such a horrible smell, don't you think, because it's just not natural. And that's how my hair smells now." She turtled her head down into her sweatshirt and breathed in, as if for some relief. "The other smell I don't like here is that big orange couch. It smells like everybody who's ever been here. You sit on it and it's like you smell every single one of them, back into the '70s or something."

That didn't sound so bad. The thought was somehow comforting, but the girl wouldn't stop about the couch. She was describing it in minute detail, as if Sarah couldn't just turn her head and look at it. It was right there. "Listen," she said. "This isn't a theater. I'm not your audience."

"I don't know what you mean," the girl said, but all of sudden she was like one of the dogs she loved if you had smacked it with your hand.

"When I was your age I was working on fishing boats," she said, and then, because she finally had the girl's attention, she went on. "The fish. That was a smell. So don't talk to me about smells. And I saved someone's life. There was this kid. An idiot. But a good kid. And he almost fell overboard."

"Listen," the hoodie girl said, but Sarah had found a crack and she was wedging it open, getting her shoulder in there, her whole body.

"This is real," she said, meaning all the things around them, "and that was real too. He did fall into the water and I had to go after him. I didn't even think about it. I remember throwing myself over the side from a sitting position and there I was and I put my arm around him. But what then? We were both in danger." She let that sink in: the fact that they had moved into even deeper trouble, and then she said, "But before I knew it we were back in the boat. I pulled him to the side and the crew, they yanked us up. It hurt, I remember that. We fell back into the boat and they started pulling off our clothes. It was crazy. It felt like they were attacking me."

She considered this turn in the story, the wet clothes, the naked bodies, and then what? The blankets, the hot coffee? The swearing at the boy for being so careless and then, only after the danger had truly passed, the talk about what might have been. "I was shaking," she said. "I was shaking so hard I felt like I would fall apart and they were asking me if I was okay."

"Right," the girl said.

"So in a way, everybody else, they saved the two of us. And we were shaking. I'm shaking now remembering how we were shaking."

And she was shaking. She might fall apart. She was laughing and shaking.

"They wrapped blankets around us and I could feel my teeth smashing into each other and we drank coffee and the kid, he kept talking. He was talking about his parents. He was talking about how sad they would be if he had died and how thankful he was that I had saved him. Like I had loaned him $20. That's how he was talking about it, like it was just this easy thing. But also, he knew it was bad. Because as soon as he hit the water he thought he was dead. That was the thought he had and that's what he told me."

"He would have been dead," the girl said. "In water that cold." But her skeptical look shifted to something more hopeful. She wanted more.

Except Sarah had nothing else. The moment had burned itself out and the next part of the story didn't exist. The boy, he was back in the water, twisting downward into the black, and that wasn't something she could share, not now. And then it was four and then five and the trolley wheels clicked in the hall. Macaroni and cheese, and then it was it was six and then seven and the doctor told her, "You can't say no forever," and she said that she wasn't planning on that. She wasn't thinking about forever or even next week. That's how she had thought about the baby too in those early days, and it had preserved her and ruined her. She asked if she could have an extra ice cream.

"You okay?" he asked.

"Yes," she said, and then, almost by accident, "Tell them sure."

So the faces appeared from behind the door frame, the one she knew well and the other one, the person she hardly knew, and Sarah thought, *I've made a mistake.* They didn't belong here because *she* didn't belong here. But they *were* here and so was she and they moved closer and held her—they enclosed her without saying a word as she rose from the side of the bed to meet them—and Sarah screwed her face into something hard and cold, something you might find at the back of the freezer.

Her sister was shorter, svelte, and her daughter too. Sarah segregated their names to some remote part of her brain and tried to think of them as simple bodies, sources of warmth and bulk. And because they were smaller she felt like she enclosed them. She was a tree and they were animals sliding up the trunk, and she was also the stupid woman who would think of herself as a tree and her family as animals. She knew it didn't work. She wasn't that strong. But the thought didn't leave her and the more she thought of the tree the more it became a true thing and the more it became a lie too. She divided into two opposites just like the boy had divided into the dead one and the rescued one, and when Celine tightened her grip pain had to be part of this configuration. She said, "Jesus Christ, Jesus Christ, Mom. What were you thinking?"

"Getting help," she said. "All I did was call a number."

And now the grip loosened. The bodies made space and fell away from one another. It was time for her sister to look around the room, to look hard into Sarah's face and say, "We can get you out of here now. Are you ready to go? Pack your things."

"Where's my truck?"

"Jesus Christ, Mom," Celine said, still holding her hand. "Your truck."

"It's at the house," Beth said.

Celine's dyed hair splayed in a million directions, blond pocked by pink and purple. She was not so traumatized that she couldn't find time to mousse and style it, apply a light shade of pink to her lips, put on heavy mascara and a tight black T-shirt. Sarah pushed the judgment aside and just squeezed her hand. Good to touch her. "I'll get your things together," Beth said. She was opening drawers now, and Sarah noticed she had a leather travel bag in her hand. She had been holding it while they had been hugging, when Sarah had thought the stupid thing about trees, and now she was looking around for clothes to pack inside. But the drawers were empty. Her wallet and keys were in storage behind the front desk, her single pair of jeans and her top in the bathroom. Celine squeezed back and the geography of their bodies changed: the mother and daughter as a neat pair, the sister orbiting them.

_____

Sarah knew what she would find at home: the cracked ceramic cup full of dirty spoons and soapy water; the sugar bowl from that yard sale in North Pole, sugar hard as brick; the kitchen drawer full of dead pens and paperclips and aged business cards. The old board games and spatulas and grocery lists from two years ago. The pieces of bone and antler on the windowsills arrayed in lines. Twelve years' worth. Thirteen. Some green with moss. They had left all of this for her, and the shoeboxes of receipts and pennies and orphaned socks, all of it left as a concession. The stacks of newspapers in the arctic entryway piled outside now, or in the back of the truck, or gone altogether; the dishes washed and the floor swept; the garbage bags full of clothes taken from the back hall and folded and stacked; and the long piles of two-by-fours in the loft thrown behind the house, maybe, or gone too, over to the storage locker or maybe even the dump, where someone else would find them. Would they have found the emergency pack of cigarettes at the back of the cupboard, the marijuana in the empty cereal box?

Beth drove the rental car slowly. She was not from here, of course, and was nervous behind the wheel. Celine sat in back and occasionally leaned forward to speak about the storm. Sarah glanced out to her right at the snow, the trees heavy with it, so they didn't seem like trees at all, just excuses for the snow to hang on. "You've never seen anything like this before, have you, Auntie Beth?" Celine asked. Weather, no matter what kind, could be comforting, because it came from outside of you and eventually it would pass.

The buildings in town were blasted white. They passed through downtown and across the bridge and back into trees again. They were heading down the long stretch of unpaved road to the cabin where she had lived for thirteen years. Her best splitting maul still angled into the same stump. The snow had covered it but there it was, rising like an arm in salute.

The bumps of half logs were still scattered in a rough circle at the front of the place. Sarah thought of them breaking into two and flying apart, the sharp crack. An act of pure pleasure, really. Those were *her* logs, she thought, the good ones. She had been cutting wood for almost an hour when Beth's husband said he could take over, Beth wanted to talk to her about something important. She raised the maul above her head. The wood opened to the wedge and flew and he waited for the noise to settle before adding, "About Celine's future." But still Sarah had made them wait, the maul hanging still for one sweet second, two. She could have just let it stay there, held the moment still for days. She knew what was coming. All of it had been arranged.

The next time it came down he added, "It's important, Sarah. Please. We want to help."

III

MURPHY DOME ROAD

Always the cart with the wobbly wheel, but there was satisfaction in seeing heads turn in the direction of the squeaking as she moved up and down the aisles, piling in milk and eggs and pasta and bread and expensive slices of chocolate with the faintest taste of orange. She was starving and there it was: all the food she could eat. All she had to do was buy it.

Celine lingered behind or ran up ahead, coming back with even more. "I think we have enough," Sarah said, but she was caught up in the mood too—a milder form of the same illness. She cradled a couple boxes of cereal, granola bars, a can of tomato juice. The cart made a flapping, creaking sound. The place was crowded. The aisles were narrow. Families asked, *What's that coming?*

Where were the potato chips? They were next on Sarah's list.

"Mom," Celine said.

"Don't worry," she said.

"It's just a lot of stuff."

"Well, you and your aunt threw everything out. We need more."

"We *had* to, Mom. We were cleaning."

"Perfectly good salmon. Perfectly good rice."

"We were trying to make the place nicer."

Sarah listed a few other things lost in the purge, but by the fifth one she was making shit up. As she said them she felt her grudge gathering force, settling for a difficult battle. But it was kind of funny: the theater of it. The grudge could shift its focus any second, turn around, transform into self-recrimination. "Mom," Celine said again. She had a way of tightening her face that made her look, well, old. Not fifteen but thirty, and weighed down with responsibilities. One of which was her mother, of course, sliding down the bread aisle to the rear of the Safeway. That would be Carol's face too: that tight expression, the kind of face that came from juggling all those phone calls. The thought hit her with the force of a discovery just as she wheeled her way up to the deli counter. Provolone cheese and ham and turkey. She pulled a paper number from the dispenser while Celine talked at her back.

The guy behind the counter called out, "Eleven!"

"You should be resting," Celine told her.

"And you should be at school," Sarah said. Bringing that up silenced her daughter. Celine hated school—the bullies, the cliques, the rich kids complaining about how tough they had it, the jocks and their stupid girlfriends. They returned to being co-conspirators.

"I only have $40," Celine said.

"I have 20." Sarah reached into her pocket, found something else. "No, 25."

It was their turn. She pointed her finger at blocks of meat in the case and the butcher moved them through the slicer. He did not seem to remember her from when she worked here—at least he gave no sign—but she remembered him. He would sit in the break room and read the newspaper, his face close to the page, and sometimes tell the room about what was happening in the world, voice touched by amusement. And he smiled at the customers, of which she was one. "Thank you," she told him, and everything in her life seemed normal.

"No problem," he said. "You two have a fantastic day."

When he smiled at her his face changed and she didn't recognize him anymore.

"Ready?" Celine asked.

But after they moved past the desiccated oranges and sad lettuces, Sarah began gripping and inspecting apples. "In a minute," she said.

Celine's hair was spiked in a different direction than it had been yesterday at the hospital and her lips were dark blue. She looked like she should be dancing on the television, singing some dumb song about love or sex, except that she wore a heavy parka with duct tape holding the shoulder seams together. That and the tightness in her face. Sarah remembered coming home from the Boatel or the Midnight Mine to find that exact same expression worn by a nine-year-old Celine standing in the doorway of the cabin.

Am I so bad? Sarah wanted to ask her.

They found four good apples and put them in the cart. A cucumber and some hard tomatoes. Too much, Sarah decided. They pushed it all to the front of the store. It came out to twice their cash and Sarah's credit card was maxed out so she wrote a check that had a fifty-fifty chance of bouncing. It was the most complicated thing she had done since getting out and the line behind her was three deep, all women with young kids, all military wives, from the look of them. They acted like they didn't notice anything, but their skulls were full of meanness, and when Sarah took too much time signing her name the one directly behind her watched every motion of her hand. Celine did too.

"The root of all evil," Sarah said, as she handed over the check.

In the truck Celine blasted the heater and the radio both. They hunched forward toward the warmth and waited. "Unplug us," Sarah finally said.

"You," Celine said, but a second later she was climbing out of the truck, pulling the cord from the front and coiling it around her arm. Sarah watched her through the ice of the windshield and now she looked very young indeed and a little foolish without a hat to protect her head. So cold out there. Sarah told herself, *You should have gone. A small thing, but that's what you should have done*, and for a moment she felt like she had three days ago, staring down her belongings at the storage unit. *Come back*, she wanted to say.

"God, it's cold out there," Celine said when she climbed inside and threw the cord on the floor by her feet.

"Wear a hat next time," Sarah said, except there wouldn't be a next time.

Celine was fiddling with the radio, trying to find the perfect level of bass and treble. Sarah put the truck into reverse and backed out of the parking lot. She took the long way, the difficult way, but Celine didn't seem to care. She was watching too. The trees here were large, but they had been abused by the storm, and some were twisted into strange shapes, broken at the middle and bowed into arches. Everything had been assaulted by the ice: the forest on both sides, the cracked road, the occasional cabin decorated with icicles. She shifted into low gear when they hit the hill. Soon the ski trails were gone and then the power lines. Celine said, "Why are you going up here?"

"It's beautiful," Sarah said, but that was only half the truth. Celine nodded, looking to her right out the frosted window. She seemed content. Maybe she thought it was all beautiful too.

⁎

Sarah had been adamant. "No hospitals," she had said. "That's where people go to die," so instead Celine had been born at her neighbor's house. Sarah had appeared at her door as an apparition, still dressed in a bathrobe. "Just let me in," she said.

"What is this all about?" the neighbor said. Her chest was dotted with flour.

"Let me in," Sarah repeated. "I'm not planning on murdering you," and she moved sideways through the door. The woman had a spatula in her hand, three children of different ages behind her. Sarah shuffled through the house to the back rooms. "I'm calling the hospital," the woman said, but she didn't. She followed Sarah through the rooms, kids trailing behind in a silent parade.

A bathroom with a claw-footed tub, plastic children's toys lining the edge—rubber ducks and colorful plastic cups. She had no plan. She had come here as an act of improvisation. It was a nice place, much nicer than the cabin she was renting, and she knew she would find something like this. "It's early," Sarah said. She ran the water. She pushed away the toys. Something strange had happened. Sarah had made the house her own.

"You're doing good," the neighbor said. "Keep doing what you're doing."

The water turned red with blood and then she was there, Celine, although Sarah had not thought of that name yet. The nameless baby spread its arms and entered the world head first, trailing the cord. "Like a little astronaut," Sarah said later, to anybody who would listen. She remembered the heat of the body against her, the pure need that ran both ways, but she didn't remember any of the suffering. It must have been there, but now it was gone, like the drowned boy's name, like so many things. The hospital might be one of those things soon, the sharpness of it at least. The acuteness of that particular pain was already leaving her.

But now they had found the hoodie girl's house, the starving dogs. More of them than she could have ever imagined and the sight reminded her of the poverty of tenements. She turned to look at Celine across the truck but the contentment on her face had drained away, the pinched expression returned. Her arms were folded and she was watching the makeshift city that spread before them: plywood boxes, almost fifty of them, surrounded by chain link and from each one a small face watching from the narrow rectangular window. Their bodies were hot and needful too, tucked nose to ass. The noise of the truck had broken that arrangement, roused them from half sleep and uncurled them to attention. Celine stood at attention too. She saw *something* in all those boxes—maybe it reminded her of a prison—but it was difficult to say exactly what except that it was bad. Someone had built all of them, but not the hoodie girl. She wouldn't be capable of such a thing. *Look at this*, Sarah wanted to tell her daughter, *Look at me, and understand what a person can do.* They had found the place and it hadn't even been very hard, although surely her sister was beginning to get worried about them. Let her worry, Sarah decided. A couple of the dogs stood on the flat roofs and these were the first to bark. Soon the others joined in and the senseless noise rose up around them into the sky and down the hill, something solid and heavy moving out of control. *Animals*, Sarah thought, and the idea seemed profound. It *was* profound.

The starting place was rage. Those two human shapes against the snow seemed the ultimate offense against them. But as it grew it warped into something else: anger so pure it became agony. Sarah was torturing them just by standing there. Three dogs moved forward against the fence. One tilted its head, biting at the wire. Its eyes, so bright blue it seemed impossible that it could see out of them, ears back, teeth grinding. Yes, it was pain. They whined—a high, keening wail—and then barked and each dog hurt the others with its private noise. Sarah had stood on a factory floor and heard music in the banging metal, but there was no music in this at all. Celine said, "Mom, let's get back in the truck."

"This might be the place," she said, but saying it made her less sure.

"Did she tell you she owned this many?"

"I don't know," Sarah said. "I don't remember."

This definitely *wasn't* the place formed in her imagination when the hoodie girl told her stories. A few more dogs had moved forward, forming a line along the fence, and she thought of herself stepping to them, reaching out to touch. The teeth of that one dog would find her hand, her wrist, instead of the wire, and how would that feel? The shock moved from her hand to her brain in slow motion—the shock of the imagined hurt, the shock at having such an idea in the first place. But she couldn't let the idea go, and the pairing—her flesh, the dog's snapping mouth—seemed as neatly arranged and balanced as any man-made thing.

"Mom," Celine said. "We really should go."

Leaving seemed stupid and staying seemed stupid too and so Sarah was relieved to see another human shape trudging through the snow toward the opposite side of the high fencing. It gave her an excuse to fall into action and when she noticed the rifle in his hand, well, enough was enough. "Get in," Sarah said, as if it were her idea, but Celine was already inside. Sarah arrived second, turned the key, twisted the truck around, and went back where they had come from in a single motion connecting her body to the vehicle.

"Dumb, dumb, dumb," Celine said, although there was a thrill to it too. Sarah could hear it in her voice below the anxiety.

"It's around here somewhere," Sarah said.

"Somewhere on this *mountain*," Celine said.

"It's something I have to do," she said.

"Explain it to me, Mom."

"I did," she said, but then she realized she hadn't, not really. She had just begun to talk about the neck burns and then they had spotted the side road with the homemade sign, the painted hippie sunflowers on the broken door set against the tree. Perfect, she thought, and she jerked the wheel. And now everything in reverse, past the broken-up outhouse she hadn't noticed the first time. They leaned into the bumps like horse riders and then stopped and listened for the barking. At least Sarah was listening. She cracked her window. Silence. Not even a single dog. For some reason it disappointed her. Like a joke had been played on her. Such incredible noise and then it was just gone.

"I should be in school," Celine said.

"And I should be in the ward?" Sarah asked.

"Oh, Mom," Celine said. "God, no."

"I'll try to explain it," she said as the truck moved forward. They were going higher.

She wanted to start with the boy's face, but that was ridiculous, so she said something about the girl on the phone, and the simple fact that she was somewhere else, and that it was both a comfort and an insult that she was so far away. She thought of the water turning to blood and the small person who would become Celine. She had spent hours in labor in that tub, her neighbor telling her over and over that they should go to the hospital. The baby was a month premature. Things needed to be done. But then there she was, moving through the water, the blood following her and then surrounding her. She was breathing through the cord. Sarah reached out for her.

"Mom," Celine said. "Watch where you're going."

She was trying to make all that stuff right in her head before spitting it out and she felt the tires spin and find traction again at another turn. She said, "Remember what I told you once? We take care of each other here. It's not like the Lower 48. It can't be or we're fucked."

She took the right fork down an embankment, tapping the brake all the way down. There might be cabins down there too, animals, men who didn't want to be found. "Once," Celine said, and she laughed.

"Love isn't just romance," Sarah added, but that was something she had said before too. Many times. They were going walking speed now. A light jog. The defrost was on full, but the outer edges of the windshield were still lined with ice: just two circles to see through, one for Celine and one for her. Up ahead she could see bright orange signs, piles of black barrels, a mound of two-by-fours and plank wood. Behind that must be some kind of shack. This time they left the truck running. Celine stayed inside. "I don't think this is it either," she said, and then, "This isn't it."

"I'm just going to look around," Sarah said.

"You're asking for trouble."

"I'm not," she said. She slammed the door and took it all in: the barrels half covered in dirty tarp, the wide sheet of snow unmarked by boot prints. She might be the first person to have come here all winter. She took a few steps forward and the snow went up almost to her knees. She could feel Celine's eyes on her back and she thought of turning around to see what she was up to back there—to have that last moment of connection before she moved even one more step away. She took a few more steps. They were close to the hoodie girl's place. She knew that. The girl had described the landscape, the direction, and there weren't many roads up here on the west side of the hill. The cold wasn't that bad and she had fur-lined boots and she decided that the good things in her life—the decision to come to Alaska, the decision to have Celine—had happened at the gut level. This was like that, and she took the hoodie girl and put her out here with three dogs and a meth addict for a boyfriend. Right out there in the shack, maybe one hundred yards. Smoke plumed from the chimney. There must be another access road to the place, an easier one.

Except that of course the girl wasn't in the shack. She was still in the hospital and there was no way of getting to her.

In a way she was safe.

Sarah hoped to see another human shape like the first one appearing from behind the building, this time with the gun raised. Had it been a gun? Thinking about it again, she decided that maybe it had been just a walking stick, a ski pole. Sometimes people used them to navigate through the terrain. She could use one now. The snow was getting deeper. She stopped and looked back at the truck. Twenty feet maybe. Celine was in there and she was probably thinking about Seattle. By next week she'd be enrolled in school there and in a month doing very well. They'd talk on the phone.

Each step back to the truck was a labor, made more so because she knew Celine was watching her. She lifted her legs high and refused to think of herself as awkward. "Fine," she said as she swung open the passenger's side door. "It's not the place. But we're close."

Out on the main road she was fed up with the silence so she added, "This is us being good people. Me and you. This is me teaching you something."

That didn't break the silence.

Celine curled to the opposite window, watching the birches slide by like posts on a fence. "An adventure," Sarah added, but she spoke the word with no force. And then Celine turned from the window and looked out ahead at the road and she started to talk. It was nothing new, but the delivery had changed. She sounded tired. She talked about the long driving trips to the south when she was younger, the beautiful mountain, but also eating out of cans or not eating at all, looking at all that beauty and starving because your mother forgot to pack lunch. Was she starving too and she just didn't care? Celine said, "I remember seeing those other people, the families, with their campers, and I'd think about what kind of things they had in there. All the conveniences, I guess. They just seemed so huge."

"And I'd floor it and blast by them."

"Slow as hell."

"That used to drive us crazy."

They were both smiling. Maybe this was the trick: to find some common memory and fix on it like a target, some little bit you could agree on. Sarah thought of those big RVs, the faces Celine made at the drivers as they blew by them. "They all looked so old and confused," she said.

"Confused by the bears," Celine laughed. "By nature."

"By the fresh air."

And this strange discovery—that there could still be humor between them, even on the edge of their separation—seemed to cause the second discovery: a road almost hidden by low-hanging branches. Fresh tire tracks and moose tracks too, when she slowed down and looked more closely. And further down the road the moose itself, head raised to listen. "Oh, there you go," she said. After years and years the appearance of one still called for you to stop and be amazed, be thankful. Celine knew that too. She felt it. Sarah could tell just by glancing at her rapt expression, and she remembered that it had been one of the children, the oldest, who had first used that expression. *Like an astronaut.* He had stood in the doorway, watching from behind his mother's big body, and exclaimed it with such joy that it had driven deep into Sarah's heart.

She had taken it from him the way she had taken the house, the tub, the warm running water.

Two miracles, one minor and one major—the sight of the moose and her premature baby in her arms. One was long gone so they followed the other down the road. It veered off into the trees, moving slowly, as if it had all the time in the world. Something about moose passing through the landscape had always reminded Sarah of string puppets, the lifting of the legs, the hanging bulk, and this one was no different, real and unreal at the same time. It hesitated at the roadside gully and then passed over into a place they couldn't go. But they had emerged into a ring of five cabins, a ghetto of one-room jobs, each with its oil tank on the side, each with its outhouse. A couple looked abandoned, with broken-out windows, and those were the most pretty, because they were half hidden by snow. A couple more were occupied. A truck was parked by one, a car by another. Dogs ran out to meet them, circled the truck, moved around behind, and chased it in. They crawled to a stop and the dogs ran back up ahead to intercept a man wearing a ski mask and holding an axe. They circled him too, ran back to the truck.

He drove his axe into a stump, pulled up his mask. It was a girl. Teenaged. A flat nose like it had been broken and a shaved head, dark with peach fuzz, black as a bruise. But a girl. She smiled and waved like she had expected them.

⁂

The bananas might already be brown, the yogurt hardening, four good apples gone hard from the cold. They had been talking too long in this small, warm place. "That sounds like Keely," the girl said, as she lit a cigarette. "Does anybody want any coffee? A beer?"

They sat around her kitchen table. Thirty-five below out according to the window thermometer and Sarah knew as a definite fact that the eggs were already no good. The oranges would follow. A lot of it could be saved, but Sarah didn't want to stand up and break the spell. The whole table had been used as an ashtray, its black surface marked by burns, scratch marks, drawings of screaming faces.

The fuzz-headed girl told them about what had happened, or at least her side of it. It was the latest in a series of fights, and Keely was the one to blame. She had tried to stab the other girl, the fuzz-headed girl, with a butter knife. Who uses a butter knife as a weapon? And then she ran outside. No, not ran. She walked. She stormed out, but she was thinking clearly enough that she stopped to zip up her coat.

The fuzz-headed girl frowned. How was she supposed to know she was suicidal? She had run out before, headed to town and picked up some guy and that was the end of it. The next day it was all normal again. "That's just how we do things," she said. "It's a habit."

"She said you were her boyfriend," Sarah said.

"Yeah," she said. "She hates herself. She hates who she *really* is."

But this was directed at Celine.

Sarah said, "She was worried about her dogs. I was worried."

The fuzz-headed girl ignored this. Everything was directed at Celine, who was silent and motionless except for the occasional nod of agreement. *Go ahead, go ahead, keep going.*

The fuzz-headed girl said she didn't drink coffee, but kept some around for Keely. For her, she said, the best thing in the morning was a light high and peace and quiet. She half closed her eyes and took a long drag and Sarah decided that, yes, her nose had definitely been broken, but she was still pretty. Her lips were full and exotic and she could see the girl from the hospital, Keely, becoming obsessed with that face. At least the feelings she had talked about had been truthful. It was disappointing though. Sarah had wanted to find a man. What would she had said to him, done to him? She thought of the silence of the dogs, that feeling of being tricked. She had missed some of what the fuzz-headed girl was saying, but she came back to the world now, the table and lowered voices. The cabin was hot. Two logs burned in the open stove. Their coats hung from the back of their chairs and the floor around their feet was dark and wet with melted snow. The girl was trying to explain something to Celine. What exactly was it though? That Keely, that the girl in the hoodie, was undependable. She didn't know who she was and that made her the kind of person who would let you down. "Don't fall for it," the fuzz-headed girl said. Did she think that Celine was a romantic rival?

Celine ran her fingers along the table edge.

The dogs scratched at the door and the fuzz–headed girl told them to shut the fuck up. Then she lit another cigarette. She offered one to Celine, who refused with a wave of her hand and a laugh. The table looked like a war had happened there, not all at once, but over days, years. A thumbnail scratching, scratching. The edge was serrated with knife marks. But maybe just from cutting fish.

"We talked a lot," Sarah said, but she felt like she was telling someone else's story—her daughter's—because the fuzz-headed girl had misunderstood. She thought Celine was the one who had met Keely, the one who had gone to the hospital, Sarah the protective mother. A natural mistake, and a compliment in its way.

Because if Celine were ill then Sarah would save her. She had saved her once already, that day she was born. It had been a half-mile walk up the road to the neighbor's house, but the hardest part was the stairs. They seemed to go on forever. Actually, the hardest part had been all of it: the walk, the conversation at the door, the birth.

Celine said, "I like your hair," and the girl laughed and rubbed her head with the flat of her palm.

"I did this when she went away," she said. "Monk style."

"Army man," Celine said.

"GI Joe," the girl said. She rubbed her second cigarette out on the wood. The dogs scratched and she said, *Shut up, shut up now*, but she was mocking her own contempt, playing around with it the way she did with her cigarette. Sarah had been wrong about the dogs. It went the other way. Pain to anger. She said, "I'm the one."

"The one what?" the fuzz-headed girl asked, and she looked at Sarah, the chaperone, for the first time. How to answer that? The fuzz-headed girl held her stare, like, *Hey, who are you talking to, Mom?* But Sarah imagined the poor hoodie girl's legs in full spasm, the flash of it as quick as a shutter clicking. How could you do anything less than comfort a person after something like that? How could you be cruel?

The dogs again, scratching and pawing. Sarah had been wrong twice. Not anger to pain and not the other way. It went back and forth, rising and rising until you were outside yourself, until your heart went crazy. "I'm the one," she had said. She was the person who had run away to Alaska and she was the one who was going to stay put, even though her daughter was running in the opposite direction. The wheel had turned, revolving slowly the way it always revolved, and completed one full revolution. It had taken two lives to do it.

"I was the one in the hospital, not her," Sarah said, and the fuzz-headed girl nodded. Maybe she had known this all along? Maybe she just didn't care. "The crazy one," Sarah added, just to be sure. The weak one. The stubborn one. The bad mother. She considered each label and then put them all aside.

"Don't listen to her," Celine said. "She's not crazy. She's just tough. You should hear some of her stories. Tell her one of your fishing stories, Mom."

"That's okay," Sarah said. "She doesn't want to hear one of those."

"Go ahead. Tell her."

But all this did was make her feel backwards all over again, Celine the mother figure prodding the daughter onto the stage to make a speech, to perform her well-rehearsed act. Sarah sniffled and leaned back and let the moment slide by her until it didn't matter anymore. "How did she survive?" Sarah asked. "Your girlfriend?"

The fuzz–headed girl grinned wide, arms spread. Oh, that was a story to tell. She had cut her own rope. Changed her mind at the last minute, somehow hauled herself up, gripped the crossbeam like she might do pull-up, and then found the jackknife in her pocket. Nobody was there to see her do it and the whole thing sounded impossible, but there was the evidence: the living, talking body, boasting about it to the paramedics. Sarah imagined her kicking and struggling for life. They sat in the silence the girl's story had hollowed out of the room. Finally, the girl said, "I should put more wood on the fire," but instead she lit her third cigarette and let it burn in her hand.

"When does Keely get out?" Sarah asked, but the girl didn't know. It could be a long time. She shook her head and laughed. And then they simply stood. It was Celine who did it first. She pushed back her chair and rose without speaking and then the rest followed. The dogs pushed their heads inside as they left and the girl kicked them back and screamed their names. Then Sarah sat behind the wheel again and they were going down the hill. They did not talk until they had entered the city and passed out the other side and then Celine spoke. "I used to think I was a horrible person on those trips," she said, "because the sight of the mountains didn't cure my hunger."

This part was new. A little extra twist.

Sarah thought of the dog's teeth again, her fragile wrist, and that twisting road from Anchorage to Homer, the apple cores thrown at their feet. Driving like now. Always going *somewhere*. Fifteen minutes to home, one day until her daughter's leaving. Soon the cabin would be a mess of newspapers and medication and unwashed dishes, but there they were, the two bodies, neatly placed against each other, arranged as simply as a knife and fork, a pair of shoes. "Remember last summer," Sarah said, "when all of this was green?"

"Of course I do," Celine said.

Outside of town the world recovered its mystery. The squat buildings of downtown gave way to dense layers of birch and pine, sloping hills, and narrow, winding roads. A fat raven stood out on a snow-covered tree, a singular dark embellishment against the white. Then it was above them, behind them, the tips of its bowed wings in full fan. The darkest thing in the world, Sarah decided, although she was also thinking of her cast-iron pan with eggs frying in it. She remembered cooking them when pregnant, three or four at a time, and eating them standing up with splashes of hot sauce, and then, when the baby came—when Celine was born after almost a full day of labor—the craving vanished and never returned.

ASMODEUS SPEAKS

PART I

STRENGTH

Imagine this: the place at the back of the shop where only the initiated are allowed. One kid's right leg has fallen asleep. Another one *is* sleeping, head on the table. His character died two hours before, immolated by dragon fire, and he has to work the third shift at Wal-Mart soon. His prone body is a form of protest, a way of saying, *I may be dead, but you can't forget me*, his bowl haircut greasy as a fish and hands curled into loose baby fists. What is he dreaming? What are we all dreaming?

A broken door across sawhorses makes a table, and the table is covered in books and paper and multicolored dice, some with six sides, some four, some diamond shaped, eight-sided and bright green, a few, almost as large as golf balls, with twenty. They spill across the table like gems or at least candy: things a person might want. People finger their favorites, the yellow four-sided with history of success, the large white twelve with a comforting heft. A kid checks the chip bowl out of reflex. It's the gravity around which everything else orbits, but it's empty even of crumbs.

Imagine it. The open eyes all red, bodies stiff in their folding chairs. With a slant of one's vision it's easy to believe that people aren't just tired—they've been crying. They are crying for the dead boy, and they are crying for themselves. The helplessness in the face of his death has called up everything they try to keep hidden. The sense of themselves as outcasts. Their timidity in the face of bullies and awkward dinners with family and the prospect of deep kissing. But they're not crying, of course. They're just tired.

Of course, the bravado papers it all over, but just barely. They mumble strings of swears when the rolls come up low. They slap the table edge and consider all the bad luck of their lives. So sick of their misfortune and hungry for more onion dip and just one more chest of gold pieces, one more magic sword or potion of underwater breathing. The place and the people are real and what goes on here is both medicine and illness to those of us sitting around the table, trying hard to get through another winter in Fairbanks, Alaska. What are we dreaming? We are dreaming about our other selves, the stronger and more courageous ones, the numbers on the sheets, the lists of treasure.

Imagine that this particular day is a good one, so I've got $400 in the cash register from sales of some vintage Shogun Warriors action figures. I'm in a good mood and I've only killed one person—the sleeping guy—and because the day is a good one everybody is there: the kid with the stutter, the coward with the ring of invisibility, the shy and the nervous, each one an outcast in a land of outcasts. And at the far end of the table, black coat open and loose around his shoulders: Peter Aquyittuq, his hair the usual mess. He's smirking because he has a plan. I'm trying to make a picture of it all and of him especially. Imagine the tattoos of ravens on his forearms, one on the left, one on the right, or maybe one on the chest, and then the way he tilts his head when I speak as if I'm mouthing nonsense, as if he's a raven himself, puzzled and amused by the stupid world and its words. I've never seen him in short sleeves, so it's my imagination that puts the black birds on his skin, the pulse of muscle up his arm. I can't help but follow my worst instincts. I *want* them to be there. I've made him into a character in a film, a picture in a magazine, a clothing catalogue, but he's real. It's that I can't quite penetrate into that reality, at least not yet, not until after he's dead too. A death that's real, but for a long time simply an absence, as if he's walked into the other room, or decided the rest of us are simply losers not worth his time.

Imagine that he's happy because I want that too. He has a plan and I'm sure it's a good one. More monsters charge forward, a battalion's worth, and the dice clatter down. The numbers reveal themselves. Fours and sixes. The monsters fall back. Peter produces his bow and fires one, two, three arrows into the dark. The others gather behind him and charge in swinging but the whole thing could turn on a new set of numbers. "Fuck, yes," one of novice players says. The word is fresh on his tongue, virginal. It's like he's saying *I love you* for the first time. I never swear, but I don't mind it when they do. It's as much an act of creation as the game I'm making, the story I'm boiling up in my head. The arrows hit their mark and the damage comes up nine. I describe the monster's scream and Peter Aquyittuq says, "Got him."

When most people remember him they probably think of that barely-there bicycle with the broken spokes, the rings of old electrical tape spiraling the handlebars, the ripped seat bleeding foam, and even more tape bandaged around that. Any person would recognize him as *that* guy on *that* bike, the one they spotted as they drove around town, the one they almost plowed into that one time. And they'd remember the way he rode: like he was walking, slow and lazy, one handed, sometimes with a paper coffee cup or cigarette or his boom box in the other. He'd slide along the sidewalk in front of the store that way, about an hour before game time, talking to the kids on skateboards. If he had gone any slower he would have fallen off, him and his little black boom box blaring Iron Maiden and Black Sabbath tapes. Peter Aquyittuq listening to "Number of the Beast," "Supernaut," "Run for the Hills." Peter Aquyittuq daring someone to say, "Hey, turn that down." Daring gravity to give the bike a push. The shape of his body, everything about him, feels like a challenge, including that grin, the difficulty us white people have pronouncing his name. *Good for him*, I think sometimes. We are certainly not the same kind of outcast, but that's part of boiling things up. You throw everything into the pot.

Once he did fall off, actually, and he jerked the bike up and shook it and then threw a leg over, as if it had been the bike's fault. Maybe he was a little stoned. A little busted up is what he liked to call it, and he was busted up relatively often. His eyes are red, and maybe that's why. Good for him. Good for him. He's saved everybody else, including the ones too proud to think they need saving. Every time I consider his body, his face, I feel as if I'm committing a great wrong, but I'm trying to save him too.

He rode the bike straight through winter, oversized gloves attached to the handlebars and a ski mask over his head. Not *that* unusual around here, except for the tapes. I could hear them from the warmth of the store as he approached the building. Peter Aquyittuq arriving early again because he had nowhere else to go. He'd come inside and pull up his mask to reveal his face, usually smiling, eyebrows white with ice, and he'd say, "I almost got hit by a car" or "I almost rode into a ditch." Always a brush with death. Imagine the peeling up of the mask, the revelation of the face. Anybody would sit behind the counter and later, remembering, think, *Okay, this tells me something about him*, even *before* the face is revealed, when he's stomping the snow off his boots and laughing at how cold it is out there. Until then he's closed to me. It's all real, all important, the snot warming on his upper lip, the laughter, the long black hair falling loose, the way his sentences end on a high note, as if he's always asking questions. The delight on his face is a kind of mask too when it's revealed. The high cheekbones might remind a person of royalty. The eyes squint as if into sunlight. A person could pick and pick at a moment like this, until it bleeds.

But when I think the name *Peter* there he is, reaching over his shoulder to unsheathe his weapon and then let loose the arrows at the obstacles I've put in his way. Or he's crouched in the woods, hair decorated with leaves and dirt. He's drawing a map on the ground with a pointed stick, explaining, "We can attack by going through this tunnel," because the journey is just beginning. He's not falling off his bicycle, or coming into the store triumphant, and he's not the picture on the front page of the paper or the story underneath it. He's not any of those things.

What are we dreaming? We are dreaming of a better place and better people. We are dreaming Peter Aquyittuq.

⁓∿⁓

Early March and everything's crazy white, including the sky, the branches, the parking lot hardpack in front of my store when I look out the window. Before heading into the shop, I always hit the trails out past Dog Mushers Hall. I pull on my boots and turn my feet sideways when going down a hill, the dogs scrambling up ahead because they're even happier now. Something in the cold air makes them a little wild, and they range further from me, cracking through the skeletons of blueberry bushes. Sometimes they stop in mid-run, just standing, listening, and I can see their breath and it makes me almost as happy as they are. It makes me want to laugh and laugh, because it's been dark since November and the sunlight is making me nuts too. It's like there's nowhere to hide anymore, nothing that's not revealed. That's the feeling, and it's terrifying, it's wonderful, and it's surprising even though it happens every year.

Even *their* bliss has sharp edge to it, something skidding toward madness or maybe just absurdity. One dog is a black lab and the other a white husky mix and in a winter like this one, when it snowed early and hard and steady, I can still track them both by finding the black spot and then sliding my gaze ahead just a little, to the thing she's trying to catch, that second dog who was born here. Sometimes it seems like he's just putting up with me and the lab: the two awkward barrel-shaped girls.

I'm not surprised when the man appears up ahead on the trail, a big bear of a thing. He holds one arm up to say, *Hello, I'm friendly, no worries*, and I hold up an arm too, but I *am* worried, because after ten more steps I recognize the face. I consider turning around as he quickens his pace. I consider walking right past him. "Hello," he says, and he's smiling behind his beard. "They're doing good, huh?" He glances around the woods for the fast-moving shapes, but they've scrambled on without us.

"Really good," I say.

"Me too," he says. "I'm doing really good."

"Then we all are," I say. "All of us are good."

The dogs push up to us, find his hands with their muzzles. He says, "Good to know they remember," and he shakes their necks, lowers his voice to a growl. It's like he's sharing a secret with them. Then they're off again. "Skinnier," he says. "Did you change their food?"

What can I say to that? I try to talk about the trees. His eyes narrow as I speak, as if he finds the words *birch* and *pretty* insulting.

"How's the shop?" he asks. "Have you changed that too?"

His mouth moves sideways and I realize he's chewing gum. I can practically smell the spearmint. That was the taste of his kiss when he'd grab me behind the register, spin my head around, let me go. Then he'd seem to shrink. "Customer," he'd say, under his breath, as if I had been the one grabbing him. But now he's transformed, booming with friendliness, ready to tag along on the rest of my walk. When I step ahead so does he.

I try to talk about the shop the way I had talked about the trees.

"Jesus," he says. "You might as well open a soup kitchen."

That's enough. We stop and watch the dogs running back to us. They head to him first, but this time he doesn't touch them, not a noise or a gesture. They spin around him waiting for something to happen. "I didn't change their food," I finally say.

"I don't expect you to make the same decisions I did, but I cut that anchor chain and you should too. I'm just looking out for you, Kim." His grimace shifts from annoyance to pain. "Really."

"I know how you feel," I say.

"Do you? I'm not so sure about that, Kim. For instance. I don't know how *you* feel. Before or even right now. I'm being honest when I say that."

"Well, that's a hard one," I say. "You're talking philosophy now. You're talking abstractions."

"I don't think I am."

I am trying to steer us back in the right direction. I'm trying to change his grimace back to simple annoyance. "The gaming is going well. That brings in a lot of people."

"Who don't buy stuff."

"Yeah," I say. "That's true."

"Losers."

"Idiots," I say. I'm not sure why.

He gives me another one of his looks and says, "Yes. Idiots."

"Scum," I say. "Worthless morons. Dickweeds and dummies."

He turns his back to me. I think of Peter Aquyittuq lifting his arm, the handsome profile of his druid, the arrows flying. My ex and I have separated now, a good ten feet apart, and he speaks out to the woods instead of to me. His voice is booming, echoing, and if Peter is here somewhere then certainly he can hear our argument. "I'm trying to help, Kim. Things happen for a reason. Meeting out here, for instance." And that's when I know he planned this. He came looking for me the way I've been looking for Peter.

"Moochers," I say.

"Stop it."

"Punks and nerds. Dim bulbs. Freeloaders."

"I'm not playing games," he says. "I'm trying to talk to you deeply and sincerely."

"You're scaring the birds," I tell him, and it's almost true. Everything has gone silent, and I can imagine a flurry of wings moving away from us, fleeing the sound of his voice.

"You're doing what you always do," he says, and he spreads his arms. "I'm not your enemy. I'm just trying to talk. This is just us talking."

"Sub-humans," I say.

"Stop it," he says, and I feel such a deep sense of satisfaction that I almost laugh. If I did, though, I'd be laughing at myself as much as him, because he's half right. I'd done this before, or at least something like this, in many variations, during those last days. I'm good at it.

"I don't know where the dogs got to," I say. Any mention of the dogs acts as a cure. I glance off into the woods. "Should we go?"

"I'll go this way," he says, and he points in the direction of my footprints. Then he points at his steps, large shapes in the snow. Even the pattern of his boot heel is familiar. "You go that way."

"Okay," I say. "Good." I do as he commands, and we separate, and when I've gone far enough I trudge off the path in my oversized boots, thinking *Peter, Peter*. My heart isn't in it anymore, though, and the dogs are a little extra crazy, so it's back to the car and off to town, first stop at the coffee hut, then at the store so I can open by eleven. Imagine a late Sunday morning, twenty below, a few of them already waiting for me with their cars running. I love these ones best of all, and not just because they spend a lot of money. It's their earnestness that thrills me, and when they didn't show up that first Sunday after Peter took that trip across the river, I have to admit I was worried about each one. And I'm still worried, because it's been weeks now and they're still not around. Imagine them speaking to me as I fumble with my keys, push open the door, unlock the second door—and then wipe that away because there's nobody outside, it's just me and the dogs and a couple of guys looking angrily into the engine of a snowbound truck. The dogs swirl around me as I work the door, and then they find their dog beds behind the register and corkscrew down into sleeping position. I roam around, restless, waiting for the first customer, drinking my coffee.

Peter always brought his own dice and jiggled them in his hand as I narrated. *You are going deeper into the earth,* I would say, or, *The skeletons rise from their coffins, broken swords drawn, their faces crumbling into grim death masks. Although their eyes are dark holes the heads spin in your direction. They know you're there and they move closer and closer along the stone floor, five of them, then ten, then twenty.*

"Twenty?" Peter would say. "You *want* to kill us."

"You wouldn't get in trouble if you thought before you entered a room," I'd answer. "Check for traps next time."

Being a dungeon master is close to godhood. I stand outside the action, but my presence is found in everything. I'm the voice of every monster and barmaid, the scheme of every villain, and the sage advice of every friendly wizard they meet along the journey. So in a way I was Peter's friend and his enemy too. "Motherfucking crazy lady," he'd yell at me when a creature got in a good shot. Then he'd laugh when he gave one back and the dice came up sixteen or seventeen. *You split its face in two,* I'd say. *It stumbles back clutching at its wound. The morning star clatters to the floor. It's screaming in its death throes. What do you do next?*

Always that question. What do you do next? Do you go left or right? Up or down or forward or back? I am thinking this question as I wander around the store with my coffee cup. I am concerned for them, all these missing ones, but also for myself, because they've abandoned me, and there's nothing I can do about it except wait. By noon a few customers have come in, but still no players. "Hear anything yet?" one of them asks, and I give a noncommittal shrug as I ring up his comics. "You know what?" he adds. "I wouldn't be surprised if he appears in here one Sunday and says hello. I wouldn't put it past him. Weirder things have happened. Don't you think weirder things have happened?"

Weirder things have definitely happened.

But I say, "You have to let go. Everybody just has to let go. There's a thin line between expecting something and thinking you deserve it." I'm not sure how much of this I've said aloud and how much I've just thought in my rushed inner monologue. My face is corkscrewed into an ugly shape, eyes tight and pinched. I can feel it and I can see it in the way the kid looks back at me. I'm holding his interest. I'm practically shouting. I'm telling him that of course weirder things have happened. I'm used to sudden twists in the plot. I come up with them all the time.

As the kid gives me the money he says, "You don't have to yell."

"I'm not yelling," I say, as I slide his comics into a bag. "I'm just telling you. The weird thing, it already happened. Back then. That's all we get. That's the thing."

⁓

Imagine the table surrounded by people, the people surrounded by walls of comics, stacks of them at the back of the store. And in the middle of it another woman, a girl, really, the newest player. Kids sneer when she asks about the rules, but she sticks it out and every Sunday her Ranger earns more experience points, more gold coins, more skills, and every Sunday she talks more. In the beginning it's a series of modest firsts: the first time she kills something, the first time she goes up a level, the first time she says *shit*. It's hard not to think of her as the *only girl* because I can tell that's how *they* see her. I'm something else.

I call her by her character name when we're playing and *Elizabeth* afterward, when I am closing out the cash register and she's talking to me about her life. Peter is on his bicycle, already heading home or to the bars, and our game is at rest, a Ferris wheel without passengers, a novel carefully bookmarked. Elizabeth says, "I saw what you did there. I saw the rolls. You let him live." I tell her, "No, that's not true, I don't know what you're talking about." I'm sliding an old issue of *Detective Comics* into a poly bag and I concentrate on that instead of the look she's giving me. Sometimes Peter needs a little help, that's all, a nudge or two to the right of my critical hit tracker. The arrows would have sprayed across his back. Instead they flew above his head. "Right," Elizabeth says. "He's just lucky. That's all. Is that it?"

What do you do next? Do you go up or down, left or right, forward or back? She said good-bye, but hovered at the counter, watching my face but also the more interesting things behind me: the most expensive comics in lines along the wall, the display rack of Japanese toys. Did she see herself as the only woman? I wanted to ask her and I wanted her to ask me something too. But her father was beeping the horn and my mouth wouldn't work right. All I said was, "I have something special planned for next Sunday. Things get a lot harder."

PART II

INTELLIGENCE AND WISDOM

So yes, I'm the voice of the old man at the bar and I'm every troll and skeleton and I'm the helpful wizard dispensing sage advice. But they aren't *who I am*, not really, because after noticing the way Elizabeth looked past me that day I decided to be somebody else, an adversary with a face and name, a true villain. I dreamed up the horned helmet, the lizard skin covering his back, the long sword shining but twisted like a burned stick. I borrowed a name, Asmodeus, to give him gravitas. I invented his stats and his motivations and then I put myself in his nefarious shoes. We had been playing the same adventure for months, from September into the winter, and people were worn down, a little bored. This would correct that.

Every villain needs a good entrance. The following Sunday he rose from a pit of fire, the tip of his sword first, then his hand and wrist, and then the tips of the horns. The helmet covered his head, but showed a second face, a crude painted mask in red, three sharp teeth hanging from a triangular smile. He stepped out of the pit the way someone might from the shower, lazily, hardly noticing the people watching him, and then he turned, as if thinking, *How rude.* In his left hand he held a great burned wing, the wing of an angel. He drew it up from the pit and let it drop to the ground and took a step closer. Just curious. That's all. Because they hardly merited his interest, these creatures from above. Fire trickled from the crooked sword. I had made a promise and then fulfilled it.

"He looks dangerous," one of the dumber players said.

"I think he just killed an angel," someone else said. "Fuck." This time short and sharp—fuck—like a period at the end of his sentence. He was thirteen years old with a Snickers bar in his fist, a New York Yankees cap on his head. His character's name was Nightshadow, an elven thief with a history of making rash decisions when in close proximity to treasure. In a few minutes he'd be dead.

Elizabeth told them, "I think that's *his* wing. One of them. He's a fallen angel." And again with the f-word, three times in quick succession, four, like a machine designed to say the word had just broken. The kid in the Yankees cap had just broken too. I had snapped his brain with my imagination and I couldn't help but feel awesome about it. Asmodeus made a clicking sound behind his mask. Was it laughter? Contemptuous laughter. Broken teeth clattering together. "Saving throws all around," I said.

The kid took the dice reluctantly, picked through them to find just the right one, then released it onto the table. An eight. Flames extended from the sword to the kid's elf, enveloped him, and in a snap he was dust. Another f-word, resigned, and then a bite from the Snickers bar. More clicking from behind the mask. The figure stepped forward, one footfall, then two, and the sword glowed brighter. I was having an extremely good time.

I had never played this way before. I wanted to kill a couple more.

Peter literally *stood* and held the dice between his thumb and finger, then flipped them to the table with a turn of his wrist. A nineteen. He was laughing, celebrating the sheer craziness of it, and he rolled again and the same number appeared. How was this possible? His spell knocked the creature backward, spines of energy bursting like fireworks. No clicking sound now, just the sound of fire erupting as the horned king fell back into the pit. I pretended bemusement. I reached for my own dice. Forty-two years old, divorced twice, and I was pouting like someone had stolen my milk money.

But I liked it too. It was good for the story. Because he would be back. The helmet sank below the fire. The sword vanished. The room grew calm and then even the fire grew pale. A placid pool of water now.

I would prefer not to consider the possibility that Peter was cheating. It would not surprise me very much, except he seemed genuinely amazed by what had just happened. Of course, acting surprised would have been part of the trick. But it's hard not to think of his reaction as genuine. I wanted it to be. I was luxuriating in my own defeat, because a moment before I had wanted to strike them down and laugh. People pushed back their chairs and stood up along with him. There was actual cheering going on. I mean, I wanted to cheer too. Forty-two and I wanted to cheer. "There you go," he said, when the numbers came up, and it felt like *anything* was possible, like this luck was something you could wrap around yourself and wear out into the weather. Yes, I had helped him before, just a little, but this was not that.

At the same time the moment was ending, a flame chasing after itself. The battle was over and people had to go to the bathroom and get rid of all that Pepsi. But he rolled the dice again, just for the panache of it, I guess, like someone taking a few extra showoff jump shots after a game of pickup basketball they've just won. He picked up each die one at a time, cupped them in two hands, and let them spill the length of the table. This time they came up low, a couple of two's, a three, and he let them sit there. A mistake for him to reach for too much, everybody saw that. Then he said a very interesting thing, something I've thought about often since his walk across the river. I remember it mostly because of the way he said it, I suppose. He screwed up his face, like he was feeling physical pain, and as he looked at the dice he said, "There you go. The real me."

I imagine his legs, lean as a cowboy's, and that black hair, worn so long in the way of a lot of the Yup'ik guys, tied back with a red rubber band. I want him to be the one appearing on the trail, raising his arm and saying hello. But it's my ex-husband I see again, the next Sunday I'm walking through those same woods. He knows the pattern of my day and how to insert himself into it. "I'm sorry about last week," he says right off the bat, and then "Really I am." The dogs go to his fingers. I notice his thumb is bleeding at the cuticle when he scratches his face. I guess they're interested in his little wound.

"Did you sell those early issues of *Spider-Man*?" he asks while we walk.

"Which ones?"

"The single-digit ones." I don't answer. I'm listening to our feet on the hardpack. "They're priced too high," he adds.

I call the dogs, but only the black one appears. Then she jolts back into the woods to join her brother. I say, "I like the one when he has to fight through the flu. It really shows his heroism."

"I should have taken a few of them," he says. "Split right down the middle."

"You said you wanted to cut all that loose," I say. "You said you wanted to walk away clean."

He bows his head and grins. He sniffs. "I did say that, didn't I?"

"And there was what's-her-name."

"Let's not talk about her. What a piece of work. She's in California now with her sister. And her name is Judy, by the way."

"I remember," I say.

I consider them making love on our couch. It's a quick route from that memory to our bedroom in the old house, his body pushing against me from above. It would end in frustration more often than not, and the last time we tried he used that word *rock* to describe me, although his face had been covered in hurt. My sweatpants had been pulled to my ankles and I did feel like a stone in the middle of a stream, water rushing by me on both sides.

"You made me feel like I was raping you," he says. "That's how you made me feel." We've been thinking the same thing: the creak of the headboard, my closed eyes, the sweet syrup pouring from the radio. We still co-own that particular experience. For some reason I almost reach out and take his hand.

         —⁂—

What do you do next? That is always the question. You keep going forward, because that's always the answer. What else are you supposed to do? You go forward into the next series of rooms, the next Sunday, the Sunday after that, downward and ahead.

Imagine Elizabeth becoming the toughest one: strong, fast, a master tracker, good with a knife and a bow. One with the forest. Younger than some of them, fifteen maybe, although she could have been older. She had to be good. When she showed up that first time she was quiet, in her dark lipstick and heavy eye shadow and expensive down parka. Army brat, I decided, and I was right. I liked how her presence made the rest of them nervous. "Powergirl is way hotter than Wonder Woman," one of them would argue, and the other one would answer that Batgirl was the hottest because boobs weren't *everything*. Yes, they are, the first would say, and they'd laugh, and I'd tell them, "That'll be $72.56. Do you want a bag?" But now here was *one* of *them*, right there, sitting at the table, and she wasn't forty-two years old, with a deep voice from a lifetime of smoking, a mind sharpened from two bad marriages. Would she make me more visible? No, she made me more invisible, if it's possible to be *more* invisible, but that was okay, it is okay. The second time Asmodeus appeared she was the one who grabbed the dice and said, "Let me do it." But this time I had something different planned. She saw him from a distance, across a ravine, and behind him stood a dozen hunched figures, each with a spear and sword. He raised his sword, slowly, in a kind of greeting, as if to say, *Hello, I remember you.* And then the arrow flew from Elizabeth's bow. Fifteen.

He raised his free hand and caught the arrow inches from his red painted face. The obligatory swears of awe, the reaching for chips.

And then he raised his sword higher, slowly, and the cave walls sprouted eyes. Then arms. The chamber became the enemy, and the players began kicking and screaming. I was invisible, sure, but they were living in my world. Elizabeth broke the grip of a demonic hand, but Asmodeus was already gone. She said, "That should have hurt him."

Dungeon Master's prerogative. That's what I wanted to tell her.

Peter had moved from his chair and was crouched next to Elizabeth. Contempt and affection seemed to mingle in his expression. He probably guessed at her background too. She lived in a place with neatly arranged furniture, a bathroom that smelled of Lysol and potpourri. Her father loved her enough to wait in the car even as her brothers' slapping turned to punching, to Indian rope burns and pinches; just a simple *Hush it on down a notch, boys* was enough to still them, but then they'd start up again, around and around. Peter said, "She's right. That should have hurt him," but he was pushing his chair back, standing up. He had places to be.

One of her brothers appeared at the door and said, "We're here to pick up my sister. Is she done yet?"

But she lingered at the door, her hand at the back of her brother's head, fingering his shaved hair. Her dad, she said, was in the army, a captain, and her mom was a housewife. Dead, she corrected herself, for two years, but before that she had been a housewife. In Tennessee. This made the group even more nervous. They looked down at the tabletop, at all of their plans. People did not talk about their personal lives here at the store, especially not on Sundays, when the smallest thing could cause the fantasy to come crumbling down around you.

Her brother coughed and said, "It smells in here."

"Hush," she said. I could see her tighten her hand at the back of his little shaved skull.

"Dad's mad," he said.

"At you maybe," she said. "Never at me."

We could hear the bleating of a car horn, once, twice, and Elizabeth and her brother turned their heads to look outside. I lowered mine deeper into my imagination. "Patience is a virtue," Peter said, and the smirk widened. "I have a lot of brothers," he said from his folding chair. He was looking at me but speaking to her. "I have a father too, although I haven't spoken to him for a long time. He wasn't patient either." And I thought of my Asmodeus rising from the fire. This was Peter's dramatic entrance. "I remember this one time," he said, and then we were all in the car with him when he was fifteen, driving with his family, his father at the wheel. Or at least I was there. I wanted that. "We used to go on these trips," he said.

Elizabeth's hand held her brother steady when the horn sounded again. "I can't say I enjoyed them. You think this store smells? That car. Oh, man. It smelled like all of us. My mom and dad and all my brothers and cigarettes and the thermos of strong coffee my dad cradled between his thighs." He told us about the hood ornament, an angel with outstretched hands, and the crucifix hanging from the rearview mirror, how these important objects wavered as the car wavered. The whole family leaned into turns, held their breath as one. Several times the car crossed the yellow line and back again and his mother, his brothers, they didn't say a thing. "Now that was a smell," he said.

The horn blared and Peter's face scrunched up like he could smell it all again, half listening to his father's long-ago voice, and although he was really speaking to Elizabeth I could, with a little turn of my mind, place myself between the two of them. "I was a little nuts back then," he said, as he geared up for the meat of the thing, the point when things would happen. I was imagining the heat of all those bodies, the rush of wind from the open windows. Was this supposed to be a funny story, something with a punch line? "The cross is swaying back and forth and I can hear my mother's heart beating from the back seat."

She was nervous. She was sick to her stomach.

So he told his dad to stop the car. In fact, he yelled so loud that his father *did* stop the car, and Peter opened the door, scrambled outside onto the edge of the dirty highway, his T-shirt soaked with sweat almost instantly.

Did Elizabeth's hand tighten even more at the back of her brother's head? I stared at a spot on the floor, a two-year-old stain that still made me feel guilty. The horn sounded again. Knocking at the door: the second brother. He said, "Are you guys okay?"

"Everything's fine," Elizabeth said. "Come in."

He moved to the other side of her, bookending her, the eldest, his head also shaved, that same open face that would be handsome someday soon. She touched the back of his head too. Peter turned to me, as if he had only just then realized I was there. "You haven't heard this one before?" he asked, and he seemed surprised when I said no. Then he was back into the stream of it. "Everybody is terrified," he explained, "but they're not saying a word. The radio is playing 'Rocket Man.' I remember that because my father turns it up. His lips are moving to the chorus, but he's not really singing along. Was there something extra in that thermos? I bet you're all thinking there was, that's what you guys always assume, but it was just who he was. He only had one foot in this world. That's what my mother used to say about him."

I *had* assumed that, and I flinched inwardly, hopefully not in a way anybody could notice. I was mostly invisible, after all.

"Is this your game?" the second boy asked, but nobody answered and I don't think he expected us to anyway. He fell into the background. We all fell into the background. It was just Peter and the car and then the horn again from outside, longer now, so that it sounded angrier, but sorrowful too. One long blast with two short honks at the end. I could see why one man, a man like Elizabeth's father, might want to interrupt a story like this one, a story about another father, a very different kind of father, long ago. That's what the honking seemed aimed at: to bring back his daughter, yes, but also to stop this kind of thing from being passed on. Possibly they had to stick together, these men behind the wheels of large cars. Possibly they were instinctive enemies. Both seemed equally true, though opposite. The craziness of the logic made it more compelling and I imagined the tightness of his jaw line as I anticipated the next keening honk. We were all waiting. Peter had stopped talking.

There it was: a single blast, a pause, then another.

"He *is* mad," Peter said, and he laughed.

"We should go," Elizabeth said, but it was Peter who stood and said, yes, we should, we should go, as he opened the door for them. The boys left first, then Elizabeth, and Peter said, "Thanks. Good game today."

What happens next? It's always the same question and it's always the same answer. That's what I wanted to ask Peter. What happens next? He threw his leg over his bicycle while I watched from the doorway, stood up on the pedals, lurched into a wavering motion across the ice. I would have asked him to tell me more, but he would have said no, I was sure of it. He had lost his audience.

I had heard stories *like* this one before from my ex-husbands. They stood for the conflict to which some men dedicated their lives: a battle with his parents first, then high school bullies and difficult teachers, then the police and government, like the system was just another bully, another version of your father. I imagined the way his dad held the wheel from below, one handed, all lazy, like he couldn't be bothered, the thermos warming his thighs. He is the villain, but I don't understand him, not really.

My ex is there again on my next walk and I'm not surprised. It's like we've arranged it, like this is something we *do* now. We walk in silence, looping around to the place where we started. Just before we're about to say good-bye he says, "Did they ever find that Yup'ik guy?"

"They will," I tell him.

·ᴎᴵⱬ·

Imagine sitting in front of the character sheet, staring at your strength and intelligence and dexterity scores, and you're holding a fistful of dice and it's like anything is possible. The world is as small and manageable as a number. A two and you're in serious trouble. A twenty and you've changed everything.

Peter did it all the time. It would be like, bam, and all eyes would turn to him, the hero, the *reluctant* hero, because he'd be smirking like it didn't matter, his character scaling a wall or slaying a dragon or whatever the hell. Or you could get a five, a three, even a one. You fall to one knee and your only choice is whether or not to make a pretentious death speech. The monsters have won. Which is not saying that *I've won.* I'm the good guys too, after all, so part of me celebrates and part of me mourns.

On the best days the store felt like the center of town, the only place in Fairbanks these particular people could call home. Sometimes not even their actual homes fit this requirement, so it's an obligation I take seriously. "We should start playing again," someone says as he flips through the comics, and I can tell he doesn't believe it. It's colder, thirty-five below, and he's skipped school to come here. "We should play," he says, with more emphasis.

"Maybe," I say.

"Let's do it anyway."

"Remember," I say. "You died. You don't even have a character."

"I'll make someone new," he says. "I can use Peter's druid."

I don't even acknowledge that stupid idea. It's Peter's character, after all. It's *Peter.* Except I say, "You embarrassed yourself. Remember?"

He titters and puts his fist to his mouth, begins biting his thumbnail. He remembers. "Who was that guy anyway?" he asks.

"Asmodeus?" It's the first time I've spoken the name aloud and I laugh at its pretentiousness. It's a sort of confession. That's all he's going to get. It's fun to see the reaction, the genuine nervousness. "I want to play," he says, and this time it's almost a whine. "I think it would help all of us. What's stopping you?"

I remember him standing at the end of a corridor, a long shadow cast by fire, and again he raised his sword and this time the fire spread, ran along the walls and ceilings, flooded the space. The skinny kid's dwarf stood first in line and as his character burned he stood from his chair and, for the first time ever, raised his voice. "This is some cosmic-level bullshit," he said. "This is not how it should have played out."

Nobody replied. He deserved his moment in the spotlight. After all, it was his final moment. "You're *picking* on me," he said, and his voice cracked. His eyes moved past us, over us, and I prayed for him to sit down and play out his final moments with dignity. There was still character work to be done: he was allowed his last words, a description of the corpse, a final flourish. But instead he aired his grievances. "You guys get in much worse situations and you don't get killed," he said. "Kim is always cutting you breaks. Jesus Christ. Last month Peter was poisoned and he survived. What was that all about? He rolled a nine."

I was afraid he might smack the table and send the whole thing to the floor. It was a delicate arrangement. He looked to Elizabeth when he said that last word, *nine*, as if it were incontrovertible proof that we were all against him. And she looked away from him, to me, and then to the others. The next thing I knew he was storming out of the store, or at least he was leaving, striding away from the rest of us. "You don't have a ride," I called after him.

"I live three blocks from here," he said. "That's how much you know."

He was gone. We could all feel the rush of cold air he had let in. We switched back to the game, the jumble of papers, the image of his burned body we held in our imaginations.

"This is awkward," Elizabeth said, "but can I have his battle axe?"

Peter smirked.

"I don't see why not," I said. "That's how it is."

So she picked it up and threw it. "Try to catch this," she said, and she rolled three six-sided. A seven. "It falls harmlessly in front of him," I said, "and then he's gone. The flames die down, the walls burned black. The corridor leads further, deeper and emerges into some kind of cave."

"A grotto," I added, because I had always loved that word.

"Motherfucker," someone said.

"What do you do?" I asked, although I knew they would keep going. That was the most interesting thing, after all.

Afterward she stayed behind. She flipped through the Player's Handbook, scanning the charts and graphs. "It's all math," she said. Maybe she had expected something more magical, because the complexity of the charts seemed to frustrate her. "Does that always happen?" she asked, but we *still* hadn't reached what was really on her mind. This was all preamble.

"What?" I said.

"The drama. That kid leaving like that."

"Not often," I said. "Sometimes. He'll be back."

"I doubt it," she said.

"I'll talk to him," I said.

"So," she said. "Tell me."

"What?"

"The end of the story," she said. "Peter's story."

"Isn't your dad waiting for you again?"

"I have a little time. What else did he say?"

"You have to be careful with Peter's stories," I said.

"Sure," she said, "but what did he tell you?"

"He started walking," I told her. "Do you know what his father did?"

"I don't know."

I didn't have to stop to consider. I did what I always do. I started making it up, and it was clear as anything.

It was as if I had been one of the family members squeezed into the back of the car, shoulder to shoulder with his brothers. I could practically smell the sweat, the beer in front. "He drove alongside him. Half in the breakdown lane. He was screaming at him to get back inside." I stood at the other end of the table with my hands on the back of the folding chair. "This is what he said. He told me after you were gone. He said he walked along the side of the road and the car followed him. The passenger's side door, it was open, but he drove along anyway, leaning over and yelling at him to get in."

"That doesn't sound right," she said.

So I tried to *make* it sound right. Sure, maybe the door wasn't open and maybe the rain wasn't pouring down as hard as he had said, but the rest of it was true, could have been true: the mountains strung along the horizon, his father screaming his name. Why not believe it?

Elizabeth said, "What got him back into the car?"

"His mother," I said, and she nodded. Of course, of course. She could identify with that, right?

I believed it now too. Peter stoic in the face of all that.

What did I know? I knew his father was a big man. A white man with a white man's anger, Peter told me once, a sliver of information dropped in the middle of the game. He kept the engine running, the turn signal on, but he was the only one looking at his son, and I saw his face softening from anger to sadness as he regretted his miscalculation of his son's willpower. The other cars sloshed by and the kid just *stood* there. What lesson was he trying to prove anyway?

I imagined his mother looking down at her hands. One word from her and maybe things would change. I knew nothing about her except that she was born in a village on the Seward Peninsula, another small sliver of information Peter had mentioned in passing, but I could see her there, hands gripping a crumpled fast food bag, the sound of water and her husband's booming voice in her head. How fast? A walking pace. Cars leaned on their horns as they passed. Peter was thinking clearly, with *wild focus*. A term he had used once in the game to describe himself when attacking a bugbear.

That's what I told Elizabeth and her body relaxed into the story. I said, "He was ready to walk all the way back with his thumb out."

His anger felt like something to keep him comfortable all the way home, like a bag of snacks, a cozy coat.

Elizabeth said, "You're making this up, man."

I said, "I'm not," although what I wanted to say was "Please believe me."

"You're exaggerating. Peter was exaggerating. You both are."

"No," I said. "Let me tell you more."

But she opened the Player's Handbook and flipped through the pages, looking at the drawings of men with swords, orcs, and half-elves. "I could have been a paladin?" she asked. "Why didn't anybody tell me? They look cool."

"There are no female paladins," I said. "It's a very male profession."

"Joan of Arc," she said, and her expression shifted—not Peter's smirk but something subtle. I'd never seen anything like it before and even as I watched it take shape it was already vanishing and I was mourning its loss. In a few years she would be living somewhere else, and would we be part of what she told her new friends? She closed the book and added, "He's going to lean on the horn any minute. Can I take this with me? I don't have any money."

"Sure," I said, although I had always answered other requests like that with "This isn't a library."

She moved to the door.

At some point I had picked up a Godzilla action figure and I turned its head around and around as if winding a watch. I only realized this because I followed the line of her vision to the center of my body where my hands were performing their nervous experiment. I glanced down at the thing I was torturing and willed my fingers to stop. I said, "Do you want to hear the rest of Peter's story?"

But she stepped through the door and out into the cold. I don't think she expected me to follow her but I did, and she stopped and scanned the lot. Outside it was already dark and a row of headlights at the Chinese restaurant across the strip mall signaled that the buffet was open and the Sunday night crowd had arrived. Sometimes I joined them, eating alone with my head deep in a comic book, but not tonight. A few of the lights blinked off and heavy-set shadows moved across the lot. They had their comforts and we had ours and it seemed best then to keep them separated. Elizabeth pulled her hat on her head, her eyebrows pulled in with deep concentration. "He should be here," she said. Then she stepped away across the lot and became a shadow too, a floating shape losing its human outline as it stepped deeper into the dark. The feet lifted high over a ridge of snow at the road's edge and I still waited. More lights went out, more men headed inside, more families. I could see the faintest hint of the northern lights above the shallow valley, a thin green ribbon undulating like a part of the river had been elevated from the earth to the sky and made beautiful. I put my hands in my pockets and then I heard the gunning of the engine and I saw the Lincoln Town Car, brand new but splotched with road dirt and ice. It slid up to me with the window down and he spoke from behind the wheel. "Is she inside?" he asked. One of the boys leaned forward and we exchanged a look before my eyes slid back to the other face leaning to me, almost out the window. I felt like he was driving through a fast food lane and it was my job to serve him, but he was smiling, he was friendly. He added, "I'm a little late."

"She walked that way," I said, and set my eyes on the far road. He narrowed his eyes into hard lines with crow's feet splintering at the ends, as if maybe he had decided he was talking to an idiot, and he said something about not being *that* late, and did she say where she was going? I fumbled around for some kind of answer that didn't sound even more dumb but I could tell he was only half listening. He was looking me over, deciding what to make of me, my wide face and nest of messy hair and stilted way of talking, like I was failing at my first job interview. He reached into his pocket and fumbled around and the two boys in the back of the car started asking questions. Where is she? What happened? What are they going to do now? Did she decide to walk home on her own? I wanted to tell them, hey, it's fine, it's going to be okay. This is not a big deal.

He held something out to me from the warmth of his car. "Would you mind taking this and listening to it?" he asked, and I stepped forward—still his servant—and held it without looking at it. He smiled harder. From the way his face tightened it seemed to take real effort. "Really consider what that man has to say," he told me. "It's important. You have a good evening, okay?" And the car separated itself from me, off into the darkness, the empty road slick with ice and snow.

The tape bore a name, Pastor James Cameron Funke, and a primitive drawing of Jesus fighting the devil, although they looked like old friends embracing, arms around each other, the devil smiling at a joke, and not just any regular joke; a really good one, something to split your sides.

Inside I sat at the long table and assessed the empty chairs, the arrangement of dice—pockets of chance and hope at various positions. What next? What next? I set down the tape and thought of her father looking for her and then slowing down next to her as she trudged along the side of the road. She'd recognize the irony and maybe that—along with her annoyance—would make her silent as he called out to her. Is this how Peter felt? She wanted to know how he felt and so she didn't answer even when he said, "I'm sorry, okay? I'm sorry." The whole thing was serious business and silly too, but only to her, only to me, the two of us.

So imagine her finally sitting in the warmth of the car, in the passenger's seat, and he's saying something boring about school or about the sky. His words make even the aurora, the green ribbon of light above them, as tedious as study hall. He would talk about church, but that would come out as boring too. He had become the boring father, the kind of man who was late, and his anger grew as her silence stretched deeper into the ride. It wasn't her fault, of course, but it was: hers and her mother's, whose fragility had left him alone in this frozen world. Imagine him saying, "I know you didn't want me to do it but I gave her the tape. She needs to hear those words and you do too."

"I've already heard them," she said, but so low that it seemed as if she had remained silent, and anyway she was thinking of Peter at the side of the road, his anger drawing him forward step by step. The boys in the back told her she would have gotten frostbite taking off like that. Who did she think she was anyway? What a dumb thing to do.

But admiration and envy when they said it.

I played the tape and heard the pastor's fever-pitched words about how devil worship comes in infinite forms: in the Ouija board, yes, but also in the Catholic Mass, and in this strange game stealing the innocence from the very souls of our youth, a game featuring devils and monsters and the most ungodly of creations. He held up the pictures and described them and the crowd gasped. He read from the books I had in front of me and the crowd gasped again. I felt good, almost imperious, as the tape spooled and his pleading quickened. He was angry, mad at me specifically, but the more he talked the less hold he had on me. I was the one walking on the side of the road.

The only bad thing? I was alone, but I knew the moment would have been impossible *without* my aloneness, and it gave me time to plan out the next Sunday: Asmodeus appearing again at the crest of a wave of trolls, raising his sword, the army charging, following the arc of his blade. The voice wanted to save me, or save people *from* me, but it was only a voice.

PART III
DEXTERITY

One of the dogs, the lab, emerges from the woods on a Sunday morning in early January with gashes crisscrossing her face, tongue lolling, still happy. The cuts are deep and I take her head in my hands and try to hold her steady for inspection, but all she wants to do is follow her brother. I turn around and head back up the trail to the car and in my mind's eye I can see my ex waiting for me, wondering where I am further on up the path. The sight of his hand rising in the air, even in my memory, twists my concern for the dog into annoyance. She needs twenty-two stitches because someone's decided to erect a barbed wire fence in the middle of nowhere.

That night she whines and kicks in her sleep and the worry about the vet bill mingles with my worry for her. I'm expecting a phone call from at least someone from the store, but the phone doesn't ring and I'm in bed early and awake early the next day. I still have his number—there's no reason he would have changed it—and I consider sitting up, reaching for the phone. After all, I have news to tell him. It's easy to imagine his voice rising, berating me for not being careful enough, then the gradual softening, welcoming me in until he finally says, "It's going to be okay." I just need to reach across the nightstand. But what I really want to do is call Elizabeth. Would her father pick up the phone and if he did would I have the courage to say something?

Second best involves simply thinking about her as I toss and turn. The dog curls at the foot of the bed.

To imagine Elizabeth's life outside the shop I have to put part of myself in it. So I take my two dogs, the black lab, the husky, and I give them to her in my mind, let them roam around her house. "You shouldn't let them sleep in the bed with you," her father tells her, but since her mother passed away he's not been much of a disciplinarian, and anyway, he loves the dogs too. Sometimes he lifts one up into his arms like a baby and walks around the house with it, repeating its name in a singsong voice. Maybe they have cats too. It's a house full of motion, pairs of boys, dogs, cats. Maybe Elizabeth and her father make a pair too.

Because Peter is gone and so is the game, my imagination finds its way into other places, water finding its way to low ground. The father, the army captain, does the dishes while his daughter dries them and he says things like, "If the boys keep eating those cookies like that they're going to be climbing off the walls," and Elizabeth thinks, *I'm not Mom.*

It's easy to take that stationary image and turn it into more. Once one of his men died—he calls his men boys too, like he does her brothers—and for a week he walked around the house just *staring* at stuff. He'd sort of walk over to something—the unopened phone bill, the TV set—and just *look* at it. In my imagination I can see him trying to think of the word that matches the object. Toaster. Coffee table. A bright yellow tower made of Legos. Daughter. Sons. One of his boys is gone, for Christ's sake. I can imagine what he might feel like. He wants them all to be safe.

In the game I sometimes give villains complicated motivations, bad childhoods, deep traumas, but I keep them to myself. They inform my decisions, make things interesting, move us way past the math underpinning it all. What do I share? The horned helmets, the menacing speeches. Every villain has a chance to express himself, even when all the words do is indict the person speaking them. I can picture him coming home one day and finally telling Elizabeth about the dead boy, the way he might have told his wife if she wasn't dead too. The weight of it is heavy on him like a physical thing. He arranges the forks and knives in four settings around the kitchen table. His mind is going 100 miles an hour, but his uniform is crisp, and arranging the table set-tings soothes him. A forklift accident, and someone not following the rules, and a kid from Tucson, Arizona who was probably the same age as the boys who hang out at the comic shop.

Imagine Elizabeth telling him, "There was nothing you could have done. You weren't even there when it happened." Would she have the courage to speak to him like that? Because as he talks the back of his neck turns deep red. There's an imperfection in the world, some-thing that causes things like this to happen, and arranging silverware neatly on a table is not sufficient medicine for it. He wants to put a fist through the plaster. He wants to scream at his two idiot sons playing video games in the other room. The noise is maddening.

His daughter puts down the water glasses, each one full with a cube or two of ice, and then a beer for him, smoking with condensation. He'll drink half of it, pour the rest down the sink. I can imagine her telling her two younger brothers, "It'll be fun."

Because she's taking them out with her to look for Peter. I know this is true. I'm up early and I like to think that she's up early too, her father even earlier, up and gone, already an hour into his day. I see him stooped at his paperwork, running his hand through his peach fuzz haircut. In a way the day hasn't even begun. Still gray out, just me and the radio coughing up chatter, news from the Lower 48 about poison Tylenol and artificial hearts but it's all news from a foreign land. The dogs watch my every move for the sign that we're heading out into the woods. Even the injured one wants to go.

I suppose I have rough stuff on my mind, and the news doesn't help. Now they're talking about local tragedies again and he's included, right there among the short list of names, all but one a young man, all but one drinking when last seen. I hear something about them all popping up when the snow melts, and I imagine a shoulder and hand poking out of a snowbank. The rest passes like noise. Then they talk about the weather and someone makes a joke about finally moving to Hawaii. I can imagine Peter out there in the winter, not so much a ghost as, well, just a part of it all, like the trees. "Ten below at the airport," one of the radio people says, and they agree that's good news.

The day opens so slowly that it feels like it might never arrive. I can look out the glass double doors onto the deck while I drink from my favorite coffee cup, at the glowing porch light and the woodpile, which is covered with plastic and pockets of dead leaves and snow. I need this time before the gears of the day begin grinding against each other, when everything's suspended and you're outside it all, like looking out the window of a plane or inside a fish tank. This morning it's different. I'm thinking about Peter, of course—that's what I do—and without anyone around to soften my thoughts it's like he's right there in front of me. Looming, I guess, like the woodpile, like the voices on the radio. In my mind's eye he's telling stories, moving his hands in crazy patterns, but his face is twisted up. I don't know how to look at him to make him beautiful again.

So I return to Elizabeth and her brothers. Imagine one of them holding his favorite toy, a plastic light saber. Obviously, he's been pretending his brother is Darth Vader. "Cut it out," she says. "It's way too early for this." But she stoops down and gathers them in for a group hug. "I have a plan," she tells them. "Want to hear it?"

"Definitely," one of them says.

So she lays it all out, and they're both as excited as she's ever seen them. She's had her learner's permit for a few weeks and just the sight of her behind the wheel is amusing and transcendent. She drives slowly because the roads are slick with ice and she shouldn't be doing this anyway.

"Wait in the car," she tells them when they arrive at the dirt parking lot. Most of them are already here, standing around in groups talking about guns and old friends. They're allowed to smile and laugh, just like they would at a funeral, but to Elizabeth it feels rude: rude for them to do that, rude for her to condemn it.

She trudges over to Peter's younger brother and he says, "Hey, you. Good to see you. Thanks for coming out." His hair is even longer than Peter's and he's just as good-looking too. He seems a lot like him but without the manic energy, that distant smirk. She likes him and she wants him to like her, but she doesn't know how to make that happen. "I have my little brothers with me today," she says.

"The more the merrier," he says.

It's a double pleasure: bringing them here without her father knowing, and then having them accepted so casually into this cluster of strangers. This trudging through the snow calling his name, it's a family affair, a tribal affair, and now she feels like part of the family. Not part of the tribe, but yes, the family, as if she's found her way into it in a manner more devious than marriage. When she turns to head back to the car they've climbed out and are standing by the bumper, watching her. "Every time we do this I grow even more sure it was murder," one of the older relatives says. Another one calls it an assassination, and a third, the oldest of them, starts a prayer, but everybody has heard it all before and it's hard to get interested. There's no sign of a person I would recognize as a father.

Elizabeth doesn't feel like part of the family anymore, especially when one of her brothers begins playing in the snow. She heads off down one of the trails, the boys just behind, but after about twenty paces they've passed her. It's like a game of hide-and-seek to them.

That's how I see it, how I make it in my own mind. It's not a difficult thing to do. The voices call out through the trees. *Peter, Peter, Peter, are you there? Can you hear us?*

I had created something and we all wanted to see it through. People stopped making conversation with me while buying their stuff. They hated me a little bit, for killing their friends, but liked me more too, because I had made their lives more interesting. Also, the cold had dipped again, and once it reached twenty below or lower everything became slightly unreal. It was easy to let the game slide into the foreground. The next Sunday, Elizabeth stood when Peter entered, gave her chair up to him. He looked in bad shape: unshowered and unshaved, hair splayed around his face, but grinning. But then again, we were all in bad shape. Again, it was cold, and I had brought out the space heaters. I was drinking strong coffee from a thermos.

I didn't speak as they arranged themselves around the table. I looked deeply into my Dungeon Master's Guide.

I could see Peter as a teenager walking along the road with his brothers. Maybe he was happy then too, laughing, breaking into a run. Maybe his father had been too. It could all have been a joke, the cold rain sliding across the sound, turning his T-shirt translucent as the sky. But I could only slant the story in that direction for a second or two before it pulled back in the opposite direction.

"Where were we?" Elizabeth asked, and then it came back in a long trail of events: the traps I had laid and had yet to lay, the last difficult battle. And then they moved down into the dungeon in single file, holding swords and torches and, in one sad case, a long bo staff. From up ahead they could hear the sounds of snarling beasts, something guttural and angry, and when I described the black shapes swirling out of the darkness I found myself smiling. They struck them with such force that the group had to retreat. The monsters chased after them, growing in size along the walls like long shadows, and then, emerging from the crowd, came Asmodeus, sword trailing fire. One of the cowardly boys had turned invisible, hugging the wall, and then the half-elf fighter died, pulled down into the crowd of trolls. *Enveloped*, that was the word I used, and the pimply kid at the far end of the table winced as the number came up five. His head vanished, his outstretched arm holding its plus-three battle-axe, and that was that.

"I hate this," Peter said.

But Elizabeth was having fun. She killed one of the enemies, then a second, and rallied the other players behind her. Soon she was leading the charge, chasing the trolls back down into their holes. She stabbed another in the back, then ran after the one who had pulled the battle-axe from the dead man's hand. He shambled down the hall, his long arm trailing the axe as it skittered on the stone floor. This was it. The first true confrontation.

The troll ran to Asmodeus like a child running to its father: the horned helmet, the painted face, and the outstretched hand touching the top of its head. Elizabeth stopped, expecting him to speak, to finally reveal his intentions, but I let the moment gather importance. She was alone with Asmodeus. He did not move except to scratch the troll's chapped skull. She had made a mistake. Peter said, "I run to her."

"You don't know where she went," I said.

"Bullshit," he said. "Fucking Christ," he said.

This was genuine anger. For a moment I thought he might reach across the table and shake me.

She spoke to the painted face. "Who are you?"

The dead kid said, "Why do I die and she gets to talk to the thing?"

"Life isn't fair," someone else said.

"What do you want?" Elizabeth asked.

He reached up and removed his helmet and long, blond hair fell loose around his shoulders. A handsome face with a touch of the feminine, eighteen, nineteen years old, high cheekbones but a tint of red in the eyes. I had invented this the week before after watching her walk away from me as I sat listening to the tape. No monster. A boy. I was also making the story up as I went along. The troll handed him the axe, a small present for its master, but he dropped it to the ground. She did not shrink from him and she didn't fight. "I'm trying to find her," Peter said. "We all are."

A damsel in distress trope, but not really. The rest of them seemed much more distressed than her.

Asmodeus returned the helmet to his head, masking first his eyes, then his nose, his mouth, his entire beautiful face. Up close she could tell now that the painted hand was a bloodstain, the imprint of a real hand, a victim who had reached up to tug at the helmet in his death throes. She said, "I don't know what to do. Should I try to kill him?"

"You can't answer her," I told the other players. "She's alone."

Why was this so thrilling for me? He didn't speak. I made a point of this. He didn't attack, although the troll growled and snarled as it hung to his leg. She said, "What do you want from us?"

His right foot stepped forward, but his sword hung by his side, dull and black and crooked as a burned branch. I was making this up too, inventing it as I watched her eyes, and I didn't know if they should fight or not. For a moment I thought of the satisfaction of killing her, crossing that line and testing the reactions of the others. What would Peter do then? She had thought herself immune to harm when she set out on her own.

"I think I need to fight him," she said.

"So fight him," one of the kids said.

Except my imagination failed me. My will. Because what if she were to win? What if she were to lose? Both scenarios ended in my defeat. So Asmodeus retreated, the troll scuttling after him as he moved deeper into the dungeon. Elizabeth picked up the axe from the floor. "Weird," another kid said.

The rest of them found her. I made it easy for them, and it was a kind of victory for me, because I had drained away the dramatic action, made things boring. It was a kind of attack, but more invasive. I glanced at Peter and he glanced back because he seemed to know.

But that wasn't the most important part.

They scanned the room for treasure, digging their fingers into cracks in the dungeon walls and shining lantern light in every corner. I gave them gold pieces and emeralds, rubies and platinum necklaces, so much that it felt gluttonous. How unsatisfying to receive so much for so little. It was a kind of trick, and part of my ridiculous victory. They gathered it all up.

Except for Peter. He crossed to Elizabeth, calling her by her character name, and said, "I'm going to kiss her."

"What?"

"Elizabeth," he said. "My character. My character is going to kiss her character. The druid is going to kiss the ranger."

He spoke their character names again. He described the gesture. "Just a little kiss." That smirk again.

"Really?" I asked.

"Yes, really," he said, and I looked to Elizabeth, and she nodded the way she had at my story, at Peter's story, with a sort of casual interest. "Just a small one," she said.

Now I was the one in distress. He had found a way to subvert my victory. I tried to describe it, but it was so much harder than blood and guts and armor clattering against armor. The rest of the players lowered their heads, moved papers and dice around. One of them stood to go to the bathroom as I was saying, "You part her hair and wipe mud from her cheek and then you kiss her. She returns it, hesitantly at first. You are locked in an embrace. Then you have to return to the others, to the difficult work of burying your dead and moving deeper into the dungeon."

"By dead you mean me," the dead kid said.

Elizabeth looked across the table at Peter. She wore his smirk. The kiss had passed it to her.

What did she know about him? That he was good-looking, in his late teens, and that he seemed lucky, but much of that luck was my invention. She knew something about his family, but a lot of that was mine too. She knew his class, his race, his fighting level, and maybe she knew something else, something that I didn't know.

"She should have to roll a saving throw to avoid herpes," one of the kids said, because the shock of the gesture was wearing off.

"You don't catch herpes from kissing, dickweed," someone else said.

"Of course you can, asshole. How do you know so much about herpes?"

More monsters roared into the room, six trolls brandishing clubs and spears, another five orcs in scale mail. The numbers came up bad and blood sprayed the dungeon walls. Asmodeus had revealed his face, but it had been reduced to a catalyst, the thing that caused the important thing, the *remembered* thing. They were still arguing about herpes as another player died, and I was just going through the motions.

I'm thinking about the kiss while riding Peter's bicycle: the kiss made of words, some of them mine. When I arrive at the Skyline Ridge trailhead I'm out of breath and ridiculous and nothing like him. As I disentangle myself from the bicycle all I can hear is the ragged pumping of my own heart and lungs.

I'm also thinking of my second husband and his thousand refusals. He refused to get up early in the morning, and he refused to apologize, and he refused to watch sad movies or read sad books. "There's enough pain in real life," he'd say, and I think that's what finally did us in, although I don't pretend to understand what breaks the back of a marriage. What I'm really thinking about is his mouth against mine, his hands on my thighs, but the reality always pushes away the fantasy. I'm always falling away from him, apologizing, rearranging my hair and clothes.

I don't know how Peter ever did this. I'm taking deep, raspy breaths by the time I dismount the bike. *Pete*, they are calling out. *Can you hear us, Peter?* There's always the small chance that this might be the day they find him, but my ambitions are more modest. I want to find Elizabeth.

One guy is already finished, sitting there on his tailgate drinking from a thermos, and he tells me he thinks that she went that way. How does he know? I wonder, and then realize that yes, we're probably the only two white women out here. He gives me a sly look, high school all over again, the cool kids with their private jokes and me always on the outside trying to edge a way in. "Thanks," I say. "Did you find anything?" He seems to think this is funny. He smiles and considers his plastic thermos top. And of course, *because* he's smiling—because he doesn't give a shit about me—I start making small talk with him. I tell him that this is my first time coming out on one of these things, and that I should have done it earlier but I've been really busy, and then I ask if they have any clues, like they're detectives or something. As I talk I can see his smile eroding on his face, smearing into a tight scowl, and that makes me talk more, and pretty soon I'm dropping details about Peter and about Elizabeth and about me.

"I just want to find her," I tell him.

"You're her mother," he finally says.

I let him believe what he wants to believe.

I look around, hoping to find her emerging from one of the trailheads. Nothing, so I just pick one, and as I step away from the guy he says, "This is serious work we're doing, you know."

Ten minutes and my fingertips hurt from the cold. I'm about to give up, but then I see one of her brothers there, hiding behind a tree, his arm raised: that familiar gesture. I recognize him from his brief visits to the store. He's still as a deer, watching for something, and spotting him like that slows me down. There's drama unfolding, his brother further down the path, hiding behind a different tree. I can see his bright blue cap.

I'm not sure if they can see what I see. In fact, as it happens I'm sure they don't. I'm in a privileged position, an audience member.

The brother closest to me cocks back his arm, digs a foot into the snow. He's the younger one and I'm rooting for him.

I fight back the urge to tell him where his enemy is crouched fifty feet away, squatting behind a rocky hill.

But the scene changes when I see Elizabeth moving down the path to me. They're not enemies, they're collaborators, waiting for *her*, the victim, and I don't know why but I'm disgusted with myself for jumping to the wrong conclusion. I call her name and the brothers stop, lower their snowballs, turn in my direction. They size me up. The closest one looks like he might let loose at me instead.

"What are you doing here?" she asks, and I want to point out that I've just rescued her.

"Nothing," I say.

The boys are already absorbed in something else, moving away from us, the younger chasing the older. Elizabeth watches until they disappear past the line of birches, and even then she's eyeing the distance as we walk. "Why do you come out here?" I ask her, but she gives me this look because, of course, I'm here too. *Why don't you like me anymore?* I want to ask her, because everybody but my ex-husbands likes me, and even they never looked at me the way she's looking at me. I want to tell her that it's a free country the last time I checked and that I can be out here too, right? Instead I say, "You should come to the store again."

"What would that do?" she asks.

Do I need to explain it? The storyline is incomplete. They're only two-thirds of the way down the dungeon hole and the most difficult things—the most interesting things—are still in front of them. But how to put this in a way that doesn't make her want to slap me? The boys come up alongside her, one on her right hip and one on the left, and they eye me with suspicion, and I think about that last scene: the ring Peter had pulled from the bony finger of the illusionist they had just defeated, Elizabeth injured, the chip bowl empty and the ice in the cups melted to brownish Pepsi water. They were paused there, in a way, waiting to be released back into the flow of events. "It's not the same," I tell her.

She says, "You shouldn't be here."

"You shouldn't be here either," I say.

The boys move in tighter against her. They don't know me at all and I must be frightening in oversized hat and heavy coat. I'm a stranger encountered in the woods, after all, and I'm making their sister upset. "I'm sorry," I tell her, because I am, and then, "Are you okay?" Because her face is twisted up into something I don't recognize. The voices are still calling out his name, or maybe they aren't. I'm not paying attention to that. I'm just looking at her mouth, her eyes, and she's looking past me at something else. The forest behind me, but no, something beyond that too. I step in to touch her, but the kids hug in closer, parentheses around her body.

Maybe her father is just now getting home. He scans the living room and is surprised to find it empty, but he knows where she is, and he feels like a fool for trusting her. He's made so many mistakes and this is just the latest one, but getting angry about it would only compound the problem, so he sits on the edge of the couch and tries to gather his complicated thoughts in a tight line. He misses his wife, her physical presence next to him, her calm advice, and it's easy to think of him as a victim, but he's also the villain. Middle-aged, but his body is sleek and muscular and he sometimes wants to slam a hand down on the table and say, *Enough*.

⁓

The day of the first kiss. I went so far as to describe Peter touching Elizabeth's cheek. I went that far and a little more, because then I described their coming apart, the awkwardness of the gesture, their silence, as if I had expected this all along.

Of course, the fighting had to return. I was obligated to keep the story moving forward, but the violence didn't seem quite so interesting anymore. Green claws stretched from the dark. Teeth gnashed. The standard descriptions, always reaching toward fierce poetry, never quite getting there. I did my best to restore the order of things. The next battle turned into an enjoyable massacre. What a relief to submerge ourselves in battle after all that romance. People laughed and swore. Someone else died, dismembered, pulled apart at the waist, fingers eaten, but this player didn't care. He had never liked that character anyway, he said, and anyway he had to be home soon. A couple of characters hovered around single-digit hit points and the group fell back out of the darkness into a torch-lit room. Elizabeth managed to kill one final troll as she scrambled backward and it screamed in outrage as it died. The others reversed direction, gave chase, climbing over the corpse, and one player's knee began to bounce, the table quivering with the pulse of his anxiety. Asmodeus was nowhere to be found.

This fake fear sat just on the edge of the genuine.

The kiss had made everything else just a little more real. At least that's how it seemed in the moment.

The players extinguished the torches and stood stock-still. Rocks clattered out in the corridor, upset by misshapen feet. Seven o'clock and parents would be arriving soon. I said, "You hear a voice from somewhere. From nowhere and from everywhere. From deep within the earth. It's saying that you must leave. This place is not for you. Go now and no harm will come to you." They knew who spoke to them. They must have liked that little touch.

Elizabeth said, "I'm going to kill him. I want to kill him so bad."

"Good. Right. Yes," I said. "Next week. We've gone more than an hour over."

She shrugged and stretched her neck and we all fell back into the world of the shop, the smells of our own bodies and the unsatisfactory sound of our own voices saying, "See you next week." Peter left the shop without even saying good-bye to her and when he was gone I noticed his bike out front. A chain wrapped around the seat post, but he hadn't bothered to lock it. Who would steal such a thing anyway? I didn't have his number so I'd have to look it up in the phone book and that's when I realized I didn't know his last name. I walked down two stores in the strip mall to the pizza shop. The man behind the counter smiled. He knew me because I ate there four days a week. "Do you know that kid who comes in here sometimes? The one with long hair."

"A lot of people come in here," he said.

"You know," I said. "The good-looking kid. Really long black hair." He gave me a look so I added, "The Native guy?" I had resisted saying that for as long as I could, and finally speaking those words seemed to reveal something bad about me, about the person across from me. He thought about that, flour-white hands resting on the counter. Sure, okay, he knew the kid, but he didn't know a thing about him. He just knew what he liked on his pizza. He said, "Did he steal from you?"

I didn't bother to answer his question. I said, "His name is Peter. That's his bike out front."

I was becoming too involved, by which I mean I was a little involved. I decided to stop trying right then.

But the next day I found out his last name by asking customers who came into the store. Everybody seemed to know except for me and the pizza guy. I looked up his number and gave him a call from home. "Your bike," I said.

"Keep it," he said.

"I have your *bicycle*," I said, because I thought he hadn't heard me right.

"Yeah," he said. "Keep it."

"I'm not going to do that."

"I don't need it."

"Of course you do," I said. "Tell me where I should bring it."

"Walking is good," he said. "I've always loved the woods. Walking through the woods is one of my favorite things to do. Although I haven't done it in a long, long time."

"I have time free," I said. "I could be over now."

He told me that trees were alive, like this was important, possibly subversive information, and that once, when he was ten, he had slept in a tree for an entire evening. In a tree house, he added, but a tree nonetheless, a large one, the tallest tree in all of Napakiak, which must not have been very tall at all. A minor miracle it didn't fall over when he climbed it.

I said, "I brought it into the store so it wouldn't get snowed on."

His tree story didn't seem particularly believable, but he wasn't the only one with that sort of inclination.

I could see forever. I remember him telling me that and the way he said it, like he was there again. I couldn't escape the feeling that he had just told this story to someone else and I was getting the afterimage of it, the bones of the thing, the story of the story.

I told him that it was a good bicycle and it would be waiting for him next Sunday, but maybe what I should do is just bring it by right now. We could talk more then.

"The tree house had a trap door," he said. "It had a pile of stones to throw at my enemies. Although I didn't have any enemies. Well, everybody was sort of my enemy."

No, not very believable at all, I thought, but I liked him for it.

When his parents told him to climb down, that dinner was on the table, he placed his ear against the trunk and listened and felt like there was some kind of pulse there, something that held him to that spot and comforted him. His parents were down at the bottom of the tree by that time, calling up to him, and he asked them—he was trying hard to be calm and reasonable, but he knew how he must sound—if he could just stay a little longer.

His older brother called up the tree, "You're an idiot."

It was growing dark out and he wanted to see what would happen next, what he would *discover* next, and he knew that he could outlast his parents, who looked small and frail and very perplexed down below there on the ground. His father was already heading inside, in fact. To bring his dinner out to him, he would find out in a few minutes, because once in a while he was capable of surprising acts of kindness. Just to set you up for the next bad thing, Peter joked.

They put the food in the plastic beach pail he lowered down with a rope: a peanut butter sandwich his father had made and even cut carefully into four equal pieces, a bottle of orange juice, a hooded sweatshirt. No, his father did not usually act like this. Every kid in the family knew that crossing between him and the TV on the way to the screen door was a good way to get yourself kicked with a steel-toed boot. But there it was, the peanut butter sandwich in equal parts, the juice, the sweatshirt, one of his brother's sweatshirts. Peter put it on and drank the juice and ate half the sandwich and then he thought of a song his mother used to sing but didn't sing anymore, one about a tree squirrel.

"But later on my dad came out and started shaking the tree like a crazy man," he said. "I thought he was going to rip it out of the ground. Maybe he wanted his sandwich back."

These were his words, and as he said them I patted the husky's side, making a satisfying hollow thump, thump, thump. He raised his head from his dream.

"My hands are shaking," Peter said.

I considered telling him that his hands were probably *not* shaking, and that he was not talking quickly at all, but steadily and forcefully, as if he were making a speech. "Your father reminds me of someone," I said. And he did. But I couldn't decide which one: the other father, Elizabeth's father, or my ex, the man who never wanted to have kids but seemed like a father anyway, a father and a boy at the same time, one parenting the other. I wanted to tell him that my hands were shaking too. I wanted us to have that between us, even if both were lies.

"Ah," Peter said.

"So should I come over?" I asked.

The line hissed with the absence of his voice and my hands really were shaking now. I had to grip the phone with both and the dog raised his head as my hand rose away from his fur.

"You don't listen," Peter said. "You act like you listen but you don't. You haven't heard a single word I've said to you."

"I did," I said. "I was listening."

He began swearing at me, not just a word or two, but a whole stream. The words emerged from a dark hole I was just now imagining inside his head and they kept going, different than the ones shared around the table, all single words, each one as simple as a hammer. And not yelled. He didn't even raise his voice. He was practically whispering, like he was telling me a secret.

"I think you have me confused with someone else," I said, but he didn't stop. He seemed to be searching for the perfect insult and as he continued he grew madder and madder in his attempt to find it. Finally he gave up and just said *busybody* over and over and over, clenched teeth biting at each iteration. Then the snapping became something else: laughing. He was laughing and saying *busybody, busybody, busybody*, and even though I didn't laugh along I did smile, because something *did* seem funny. It was funny and I never wanted to see him again.

But then I thought about him up there in that tree, the sandwich, his father wrapping his arms around the trunk and shaking. He had built a tree house and had wished he could stay there forever. Maybe that was all. I thought that story had been finished, but right then I knew it was as incomplete as the other one, the one he had told before and the one we were playing and the one between my ex and me. All of them. He said, "I've got to go. I'm in a bad place right now. I'm sorry. I'm sorry about calling you that awful stuff and I'm sorry that I have to go. You probably won't see me again. I should tell you that. Things are difficult right now. Sometimes I do things I shouldn't do. You wouldn't understand. Not the way you live." He groaned as if in pain. "Your life," he said. "How can you stand it?"

His voice broke with sympathy and that bothered me a lot more than all the little swear words. "Please," I said. "Don't say that."

"Just look at it," he said.

"I want to come over," I said. "I want to bring you your bicycle. Let me do that for you."

He said, "Haven't you been listening?" I thought of him saying *busybody* and *bitch* and *dyke*. I had listened to all of it. "I'm not anything," I said. I had meant to say, "I'm not any of that." But the line went dead and the dog's head sank back to my lap, back into dreaming. And I worked hard to think of Peter climbing the tree, and it grew taller and taller the more I thought about it. Imagine him deciding to live there, imagine his hands on the white bark and then imagine he climbs even higher, the small crowd of his family below. I put myself with them, and felt their amusement move to frustration and then dread.

~~~

He did not vanish the following week. The next Sunday he appeared early wearing a nice button-down shirt, untucked and wrinkled but clean. A slight bruise around his eye had darkened and yellowed, a split lip scabbed over, but he smiled as he took his usual seat. "I feel like we're going to get him today," he said. "I know we are. Did you have a good week?"

"Yes," I said, as I shook the chips into the bowl. "Really good."

Elizabeth appeared next, face bright red from the cold, and I wondered if she had walked this time. Her eyelashes were covered with frost and she flexed her hands to warm them. Then she took her seat too, at the opposite end of table. More came in, the fighters and wizards, the paladin, the cowardly thief, and made the usual arrangement, coats on the back of the chair, rubbing their eyeglasses clean on their sweatshirts. They moved forward through the dungeon, through chambers of broken statues and sunken tombs, descending into the deepest of the catacombs. *The only sound you hear is your own footfalls on the damp stone,* I said. *The least courageous of those among you begin to tremble. You come upon an earlier expedition, travelers and warriors like you who met a sorry end. Their corpses have been run through and beheaded. But it all happened a long time ago. Now it's all dust and bones.*

"I turn invisible," the annoying kid with the gap tooth said.

"I check for gold pieces," another one said.

"I keep going," Peter said.

I described the growing heat, the oppressive mood, while they reached for soda refills and Wheat Thins. They ate as if watching a movie: without really tasting much of what they swallowed. *Men appear,* I said. *Soldiers in horned helmets. Each wears an amulet with a crimson insignia.*

"Just like that other guy," the gap-toothed kid said.

"No shit, Sherlock," someone else said.

Rolls were made, the enemies defeated, bodies splayed on the dungeon floor. One of the soldiers whispered something. Peter moved his ear close to the man's mouth to listen. Of course, this was dramatic embellishment—they had made their rolls and the guy should have been dead—but breaking the rules was okay if it added color and texture. The soldier said something Peter didn't catch, so he lowered his ear even closer. I've read the stories and seen the movies. Important things are always spoken in moments like this.

"You fools," the soldier said. "You shouldn't have come here."

"Do you think we're afraid?" Peter asked.

"No," the man said. "That's why you're fools."

Of course, the man died before Peter could quip back.

His dying words had elevated him from a bit character to an important piece of the storyline. The words had real dimension and weight, and showed a personality operating behind them. My personality, of course, but maybe not. Did this soldier have ambitions, a family, brothers who would want revenge? It was fun to think about these things and I hoped the players thought them too. Peter wasn't satisfied though. He shook the man's corpse and said, "Fools, huh? I'm not the one who's dead, am I?" Those were the words exactly, and he said them with such defiance that even though he spoke them to a corpse they were effective and cool. Maybe the important thing was that Elizabeth was listening.

Elizabeth, who had been quiet through most of the battle, chose this moment to push herself into the story. "I kiss him," she said, and Peter lost his power to smirk. As I narrated he ran his thumb along his upper lip. It began to go red with fresh blood, and I imagined her father striking him.

The battle has been hard and you embrace as much from sorrow as from passion. How long have you been traveling? It feels like weeks. And for what? A few gold pieces. A jewel or two.

"But I'm not sad," Elizabeth said. "I'm not tired and I'm not unhappy. That's why I'm doing what I'm doing. Not sorrow."

And what could I say to that? They were her own thoughts, after all, and she had a right to them. Best to move on to the next room, the next challenge, but no, they held the kiss. "Get a room," the gap-toothed kid said, and the whole table tittered. I had run out of words to describe it, so I let it just hang there while they made jokes about it.

Imagine Elizabeth entering her home, her father at the kitchen table. He's made dinner and it's had time to go cold. The boys don't care. They run to their seats and begin gobbling it up, but *he* cares—he's angry with himself for caring so much, in fact, and angry with Elizabeth for making everything so complicated. He rises from his chair when she says hello but refuses to ask where she's been. She refuses to tell him. The stalemate continues on through the evening, past the washing of the dishes and the watching of TV and the boys going to bed. Maybe that's when he finally speaks. He says, "Come over here. I want to talk to you. This is important."

But who's to say?

I spoke to him for the second time the Tuesday after the second kiss. DC Comics had just killed off the Flash and Supergirl and the place pulsed with outrage, and not just because these characters were fan favorites. Everybody could see through the pathos to the crass commercialism. Sales would spike and then, eventually, the characters would return. One guy was talking to me about just that when a middle-aged man in uniform came into the store. I didn't notice him at first, but he joined the line without actually picking up any comics, waiting as I rang up each person's stuff. Military people in the store were nothing new, but they were all young, usually in groups of three or four, joking as they flipped through the stacks. This guy looked like he had entered a church after years away from religion. He held his knit cap in both hands, just under the slight curve of his belly, and when he moved up to the counter and spoke to me he looked at the back wall of rare comics instead of my face. "I'm looking for my daughter," he said. He took a step back to let the next kid move in with his comics, but he continued to talk. "She's been here a few times. Do you own this place?"

I recognized him, of course, but he didn't recognize me. He had spoken to me and then somehow forgotten. "That's right," I said. "I do," and then, "We met before. You gave me something."

"Oh. Yes," he said, but his expression didn't change. "Now I'm just looking for my daughter."

"She might be here," I lied. He turned and let his eyes arc across the store and then back to me, at the wall behind me, the framed comics selling for 30, 40, $50 a pop. Maybe he was just worried about her or maybe he was looking at the titles and prices. "You seem upset," I said. I couldn't tell if he was a colonel or a captain but he was *something*, I knew that, and I thought of a thing my first husband had told me once in one of his more lucid moments: that the enlisted man knew his true enemy, and it was the officer directly above him. But I put that tablet of wisdom aside and tried to wear my friendliest face. "Could you describe her?" I said.

"It doesn't matter," he said. "It's fine. I'll find her."

"Are you sure?"

And then he did the saddest thing. He turned to a toy display and found two creatures, bright yellow, identical, lifted them up, checked the prices, and returned to the line. One for each boy. His politeness was heartbreaking, and I wanted to admit to him that I knew some of his story and that I thought it was lousy that life gave some more troubles than others. *Speaking as someone who has had my fair share*, I would add. "I'm sure she's somewhere," I said, sounding like the queen of all idiots, and then I bagged the toys.

He put his hat on his head and took his bag and then he thought of something—he paused with his hand on the door—and produced a pen from his chest pocket. He tore off a bit of the bag and wrote down a number. "Call me if she comes in this Sunday," he said. "Would you mind doing that?" But at the end of the day when I found the paper in my pocket I placed it on the kitchen table, and then the next day it went from the kitchen table to a bowl by the sink, and by Sunday, just before I headed to the store, it was in the garbage along with eggshells and used tissues.

~☆~

The dog's face bled through the stitches, although she lay still across my body, the blood milky with pus. An infection. Why hadn't I noticed before? It must have been going on for a long time. Her legs kicked. In her dream she must have been running, and that seemed like the measure of a good life: to dream the thing you did in your waking moments and find happiness in it even when sleeping.

Imagine Peter and Elizabeth meeting at someplace public, the library maybe, in the rear stacks, or at the McDonald's near the grocery store. The floor is wet and dirty from tracked-in snow and nobody will clean it anytime soon. Some machine in the kitchen hums beneath the sound of their talk. He's drinking black coffee and she's eating french fries two at a time. Sometimes he takes one and streaks it through the catsup on the napkin, taps it, plays with it, does everything but eat it. The fluorescent lighting makes them look ugly. This is a thought she has—that he is ugly and she is uglier—and she wallows in it as she eats. Maybe she's annoyed at his behavior, but the last time she criticized him his body jerked to stiffness and his face froze. It was as if she had struck him. How do you argue with someone like that? He's looking at the little french fry as if he's considering popping it into his mouth. It's burned black like a match.

"This is nuts," she says. "I feel like I'm going nuts."

Or she says, "Talk to me."

Or she says, "I would never come to a place like this if you hadn't told me to meet you here. I didn't care where. I just wanted to see you. But you look disappointed. Aren't you happy to see me?"

Or they move up and down the library stacks, scanning the spines of books. The titles flow into each other, forming one gigantic sentence, and she thinks, this is paradise. Maybe they are holding hands, her in the lead. It's one of her favorite places in town and she wants to show him everything: the spot at the back wall where she sometimes sits cross-legged on the floor and reads, the children's room with its tiny tables and chairs, the study room where vagrants sometimes sneak a smoke. He is thinking about his family, his many brothers and their wives and children and here he is holding hands with this teenager, this stupid white girl from Tennessee or Texas or wherever-the-fuck. "It's hard to believe that people wrote these," he says, or "I'm hungry. Let's get some food."

Or he says, "You're like a moving target. Slow down. I want to spend time with you. I don't want to chase you around this place." Maybe he's smiling and so is she and they go just slowly enough for him to read the titles too. The order of the place is as clear and exotic as a picture of blue Hawaiian water, except that he's actually *here*. He's in it like he's swimming. They move to the rear windows of the building, where she left her book bag and he left his jacket. He doesn't understand the route he has taken to arrive at this bizarre happiness. A good day but they need to get home soon, him to his small room and her to her big house, to her father, who will be wondering where she is and what she's been doing. She doesn't have a lie yet but she'll think of one and he'll hope she's finally making friends.

"I like being your tour guide," she says. "It's kind of fun showing you around places in your hometown. Places you've never been."

Of course, this might anger him—the gentle arrogance of it. "I wasn't born in Fairbanks," he says, but yes, he likes it too. Maybe he shouldn't. His joy makes him feel stupid. Uncomfortable. Easier when his smile doesn't match what's on the inside. He says, "I was born in a town of 400 people. This is the city. I'm still getting used to it."

"Me too," she says, and she feels stupid too. She wants to be his friend. She wants more than that. She thinks of touching him but it's as if the long table at the comic store still rests between them. "I want you to show me things too," she says. "Tell me about your town."

"It's not very interesting," he says. "Mostly snow machines and drunk uncles." He pauses, reaches for his coat. "We should get going."

They part without touching. Or he reaches out, shakes her shoulder and grins. Better to have done nothing at all than that.

Or something else. I move through the possibilities as if they are photographs of the same face, sometimes showing small variations, but sometimes not even looking like images of the same person. The differences can be startling. I don't have the determination to consider some for more than a moment. I am running ointment over the black dog's facial scars and I'm holding her big head steady. The scars grow uglier, darker with scabs, as they heal, and I have to remind myself that she's doing well even though she's whining. My ex calls and says, "You've been avoiding me," and I tell him that the dog is fine, I'm fine, the store is fine, everything is fine.

PART IV
CONSTITUTION

I think of the next Sunday as the day of the third kiss, although no kiss happened. Still, it's written in my head like a memory.

I had planned for one. That was a mistake.

That day Elizabeth came in first, a good hour before the game was due to start, and she began sharpening pencils, putting out the dice. A couple of the other kids came in shortly after, but they ignored her and went straight to the graphic novels. They were still talking about Supergirl. One of them said, "She didn't even die heroically. They tried to make it heroic, but it's not like she defeated anybody. Superman and Batman are going to have to do that."

"Will you shut up," the other one said. "Who cares. She's just a made-up person."

"She was my *favorite* made-up person," the first kid said.

"Good week?" I asked Elizabeth as she came to the counter.

"Boring," she said. "School here is boring." She had been to five schools, she said, and this was the second worst. Texas was worst, but that one didn't count because it was so off-the-chart bad. She sat down at the table and gathered some dice around her. "Where's Peter?" she asked.

"He'll be here," I said, although I didn't believe it.

And yet he did arrive. He had taken a cab, he said. Who knew they were so expensive? His face was healing, and his hair was wet and pulled back. He sat across from her at the table without removing his coat.

You have come very far, I told them as we started the game. *Some of you are wounded and one of you has given everything a warrior can give.*

We all looked at the kid who had died. He had stuck around waiting to see what might happen and we admired him for that. *The heat is intolerable*, I continued, *and as you move deeper you all suffer up to six points of damage. Each of you make a roll on a D6.*

They all did so except for Peter, who grimaced and said, "Just from the heat? Really?"

"Yes, really," I said.

"Okay, okay," and he gave it a roll. They made the appropriate adjustments on scrap paper. The next opponents appeared, lizards walking like men, four of them emerging from the shadows holding spears, and then more behind them. Their eyes glowed in the dim light.

The lizard men parted for their leader. Asmodeus, of course, with his sword of fire, the bloody hand print across his face.

"I'm already invisible," the annoying kid said. "You heard me, right?"

"You didn't say that," someone else said. "Suffer with the rest of us."

They fought and fought. It was already beginning to feel tedious, like a task assigned to you at your cubicle. A dozen lizard men. Another dozen. The bodies filled the cave. "You know who I'm going to attack next," Peter said, as he climbed through the scaled bodies.

"Too late," I said. "He's standing by the ranger."

He raises his staff and your mind is made strange. Your eyes glaze over and you drop your sword.

All this spoken to Elizabeth. Then to the group about Elizabeth.

She leaves with him. The other lizard men block your way.

A test. I looked to Peter to see what he would do.

So yes, it was a mistake, but it was a mistake I couldn't simply erase. She was still standing, but her eyes were glazed, secreted away from the others. I had already established all this. The wizard waved his hand in front of her face and she said, "I want to make a saving throw," and I said there wasn't a saving throw to make. Her sword and shield were on the ground, among the bodies of the lizard men she had killed. Her compatriots were in a different room still fighting for their lives.

I revealed the truth again. He lifted the helmet to show the teenager's face. I shouldn't say that this is the person I wanted to be, but it was a version of me. How could it be otherwise? Closer now, and he was not eighteen. Sixteen maybe, with the tiniest scar on his chin, a counterpoint to his beauty. He spoke in a low voice about his history, men he had murdered in their sleep, children and innocents. Nothing was beneath him. But he barely touched her shoulder, as if he might break her.

"Fuck," one of the kids said.

He spoke to her as if he knew her, as if he had watched her from afar for a long time. His fingers on her shoulder tightened and he tugged her in closer. *The spell is fading but you do not want to do violence to this one.*

Two lizard men unshelled her armor, took her knife from its scabbard. Reclined in some smoke-filled room smelling of alchemy and death. He crouched by her side and continued with the story of his life. His father had been a wizard, had made a deal for power and paid a price. These spells, they were his father's spells, these slaves, his father's slaves. He had never seen a human woman except for his mother and that was ages ago.

Half the tales were lies. His hand rose from her shoulder to her cheek. I had prepared this, fortified myself. The hand moved to her forehead, her mouth.

Imagine him touching her cheek. A stock villain's gesture, but a certain kind of villain they had not encountered before. It would call for a stock response. Imagine her turning her head away, or insulting him, or biting the meaty side of his palm. Imagine Peter wondering what might happen next, his nervous surprise. But she didn't do anything. All she did was look disappointed, bored, as bored, as she must have looked at school. I was sorry, but I didn't know how to undo it all. I wasn't used to someone simply opting to not play.

This was the point when he was supposed to lean in for a kiss. Imagine them coming together roughly, and then Peter charging into the room. Imagine him striking his enemy to the ground. I felt like I deserved it.

Except he was counting his gold, picking up her sword and shield, making his way to her but taking his time. "Now you can roll," I said.

She spilled the dice. A twelve, but I let her free herself. She rolled again. An eighteen. Her enemy fell to one knee, his long hair falling around his face. I did not speak my thoughts—that it looked like he was praying, that he was proposing to her, his head hanging in shame. She said, "I'm going to kill this motherfucker," and the dice rattled in her fist. In five seconds Asmodeus would be pierced by a sword, fumbling for his spells, and in another five he would be dead. A fifteen. A seventeen. I allowed it to happen.

That's when I first considered the idea of resurrection. I wanted to see the surprise and pleasure in their faces when the villain returned, but more than that: I wanted to give him a second chance. He had been better than what he had shown in that moment. By the time Peter came into the room Elizabeth was fine. She pulled the spear from the body, hefted it up above her shoulder in a gesture of victory. The eyes had gone gray. "What do you do?" I asked.

But the third kiss didn't happen then either. They glanced at each other across the length of the table and then searched for treasure.

It's this last kiss, the one that never happened, that I'm thinking of when I grab the phone. When he answers—when my ex answers—I tell him that I'm sorry I missed him the other day. I had something going on. He says, "I wasn't there either," and I nod, ridiculously, because even though I can see him in my mind's eye he can't see me. I tell him, "Okay, I don't want to bother you," and before I know it the line goes dead. Then it rings again, in my hand, and I say, "Hello?"

"I didn't mean to be a jerk," he says. "It's just that I have a friend over."

"Then go," I say. "I had nothing important to talk about anyway. The shop is good. The dogs are good. I'm good." He makes a sound at the back of his throat and I say, "Hello?"

"They found that kid," he says. "Didn't they?"

"No, not yet," I say, and he makes a second sound, softer than the first. I wonder if he's listening to me deeply or if he's mouthing something to his friend. I say, "Really, truly. Everything is good."

"Okay," he says. "I believe you."

"You were a prick to me," I add.

"Here we go," he says. "Oh, boy. Finally. Do you know how long I've waited for this? Tell me what you really think." But that's all I have, the start and the end all in one sentence. If we were out in the woods we could separate, one south, the other north, and I could listen to his feet crunch on the snow as he walked away, but now all I can do is hang up.

Imagine the McDonald's full of teenagers. A high school hockey team has just won a state championship and big, meat-headed kids are running around laughing and shoving each other. Elizabeth and Peter sit there trying to talk while one of the kids, a real bruiser with ripples of skin on the back of his neck, holds another in a headlock. He counts down from ten as the victim's face grows redder and redder, but this kid, the kid trapped in the headlock, seems to be enjoying himself. So does the crowd around them. They join in on the counting. Everybody is shouting out the numbers, and even the people working there are laughing. "Neanderthals," Elizabeth says.

Peter is trying to ignore the whole thing. He knows there's no future in any of this so he wants to make the seconds count, and one way to do that is to look into her eyes and ignore everything else. But it's too loud and he finally says, "Jesus, he's going to suffocate him."

"What's your problem?" the kid says, without looking in Peter's direction. He's looking at his captive's red face as he gives his head an extra little twist. The count reaches zero and the crowd cheers.

Possibly this is how Peter's face ends up bruised, his lip bloodied. He cheers along, louder than the rest of them, mocking them but also shaming them with the complete joy of his scream. They could never lose themselves like that. Peter knows Elizabeth's eyes are on him. He raises his arms above his head like he's just scored the goal himself. They should be screaming along with him. He could be their leader.

In this scenario it's not the father's fault. The punches come from several boys and he doesn't fight back. I imagine him bowing his head, falling, his hand on the greasy floor, almost welcoming the contact, and of course all of it feels wrong. It's the father—it has to be—but every time I picture him throwing the punch it doesn't come together right, and not imagining it—allowing myself to just let it exist as a mystery—is even worse. A story needs its villain.

It's been more than a week since I saw Elizabeth in the woods, still four days until another Sunday, and he is alive in my imagination when I hear the news. They've found him. "Okay," I say. "This is good," because it is, right? We all knew there was no chance.

The story arrives by phone, spoken in the voice of his oldest brother, and I'm not sure how he found my number or why he even feels the need to call me. Surely I'm not that important that they feel I need to know? But he asks me how I am doing and thanks me for my help. "I didn't do anything," I say. I'm trying to be honest. If there's anybody who deserves it then it's this person. He even *sounds* like his brother, and he's treating me like the news may run a crack right up through me, from bottom to top.

"You did," he says. "You were his good friend."

"Thank you," I say.

"No need," he says, and I can picture him surrounded by children from five or six different brothers. They're running around his legs, in and out of the house, and there is food—caribou, salmon—arranged on a long table. A stranger, walking into such a place, might assume that two people have just been joined in matrimony.

I am thinking of stock gestures, familiar tropes, Asmodeus and his villainy. He never really became unique. Terrible to consider, but possibly they thought of him as a joke, despite my best efforts. I am trying to push past the surface of things into the genuine.

"Talk to me in Yup'ik," an elder says to one of the younger boys, "and I'll give you a dollar." Another child, not his own, bumps into his leg and he feels the contact as pleasure—the kid's body is so alive that it *has* to run. It's as easy to imagine as the parking lot outside, the images in the comic book making their faces screw up. It's as easy to imagine as anything I've ever imagined and I don't know why. He asks me to repeat what I've just said because the line is bad. I am trying hard to focus on his voice.

"Are you calling Elizabeth?" I ask.

"Who?"

"Never mind," I say, and someone comes up to the counter. I hold up a single finger to tell him to wait and he nods, hands in his pockets. He has a question and it's important enough that he's going to stick around. I turn away, my shoulder dividing one business from another.

"You sound like you're really far away," the brother says, and he apologizes about the noise. Then he calls out to the crowd, *Keep it down, keep it down*. His voice is relaxed but hard-edged. He's someone who expects people to listen and to agree. He begins talking about the wake, the funeral, but I ask him about the exact place they discovered the body. It's hard to think of it as just a body.

"So it was you?" I ask. "You found him?"

"No, no," he says. "The police. The police found him." He pauses. There are more details here and he's thinking about sharing them. But he's thinking twice. "We think he was trying to cross the river to the bars on the north side," he says. "My guess is that he had already gotten kicked out of the ones to the north. Or he never got into them."

Except that's not the kind of thing he would do.

He could have simply been going home from seeing Elizabeth by the shortest route possible, mad enough that he didn't care. I remember what he had told me about that time in the car, the impervious feeling his anger gave him. Possibly there had been a fight and he left her crying. Or he was the one who was crying as he reached the river's edge. "He must have known how dangerous that was," I say.

"I loved my brother," he says, "but he didn't have very good radar for stuff like that."

I want him to tell me the story I've already heard, the one I'm thinking about. I'm forced to imagine a whole family in the station wagon, not just Peter, and it's two of them, Peter and his brother, who are walking along the side of the road. Except he's telling me something else about Peter's bicycle. He trails off, apologizes for talking so much. Maybe it's exhausting for him to finish. I'm sure he's been talking all day.

"You've heard it before," he says.

"Yes," I lie.

"You *were* close," he says.

"Not that close."

The customer stands with his hands in his pockets and I smile at him with my best can-I-help-you grin. He glances down and then back to me. I take the phone away from my ear and say, "What do you need?" He begins to ask me a question but it quickly transforms into something else. He knows speculation is wrong but if he could buy, say, fifteen issues of the death of Supergirl it would be a good investment for college and he disagrees with the rest of them. It was actually pretty well done. The art was good.

"I don't have any more of issue 7," I tell him. "I have 10. It's on the shelf."

"Behind the counter?" he asks. "I'm willing to pay extra. Maybe out back. You must have saved some up, right? It's the death of Supergirl. Of course you would. You're smart that way." He goes up on his tiptoes and leans over the counter, as if I'm hiding them right back there, poly bagged and backed by acid-free cardboard.

"Hold on," I say.

"It was done with dignity," he says. "They could have made it lurid but they didn't. I thought it was very well done. Maybe out back?"

I walk him to the stacks while Peter's brother is saying, "My mother is the real mess. She drank all the way through the pregnancy. And I'm sure Peter told you about our dad." He laughs and adds, "It's weird. The rest of us turned out okay. I'm not sure why Peter was so unlucky."

"We all could have done more," I say.

"True," he says, and there's a sense he's losing interest.

The customer is still talking. "I'm not saying that they couldn't have done it better. I think what they really should have done was kill off Superman and leave her alive. That would have been more daring. And it seems like the series is getting worse as it goes on. The latest issue doesn't even make any sense. There are too many characters and I can't keep them straight."

"I have two copies of issue 8," I say.

"But none of 7?" he asks.

Peter's brother says, "Hello? Are you there?"

"Yes," I say. "I'm sorry. I'm at work."

"Oh, well, listen, I have more calls to make and you have things to do. Take care of yourself."

The customer is talking about some other issue of Superman from years ago, when Lois Lane found out his secret identity. She was always finding out his secret identity and he was always tricking her into thinking she got it wrong. The issues were classic. "Wait one second," I say. The phone goes dead but it's still pushed to my ear. This is when I realize the kid is older than I thought, in his early twenties, and that he's irritated with me. I can see it in his face, the way his cheeks are flushed, and the way he's moving his hands around when he talks. I tell him, "Well, dig in. See what you can find. Maybe there's something in there." He narrows his eyes like I've just told him to go to hell, so I add, "I have things to do, okay? I'm going to be at the front of the store."

"Okay," he says. Now I've hurt his feelings. He doesn't say anything, but I imagine him calling me a hippie, an old lady, a string of insults: all the words Peter called me. They could all come out of this man's mouth if he would let them. But I don't go to the front of the store. I have more to say. "Don't think you're special," I tell him, "because you're not. Nobody is."

"I just want issue 7," he says. "The one I've been trying to tell you about."

"Which is fine," I say, "but you don't know anything about me."

I return to my position at the cash register and think about Peter moving across the ice. At what point did he realize he'd made a mistake? Maybe early on, but he kept going anyway, or maybe it wasn't a mistake at all. It would not be that bad a death, falling into a crouching position, then onto your side, the cold and snow cradling you. It would be quiet out there on the ice. I can picture him walking down the embankment, sliding, rising back up and duck-walking his feet forward. He is smiling, but it's the smirk, and he wipes his arm across his hot face. He's forgotten his gloves, but he doesn't care. The other side seems close enough that he could reach out and grab it: a cluster of lights strung from pole to pole, a few headlights in the parking lot. He has friends there and when he gets inside he will charm one of them into buying him a drink.

Or he'll just settle down and sleep because life is hard. It's a decision he makes without any real difficulty. He drops to one knee and then to sitting. His face touches the snow. But then he rises. He thinks about rising anyway. It could be as easy a decision as the one that got him here, face down on the ice. This isn't how it happened, of course, but I can see it in my head, and the aftermath too. The body out there on the ice in plain sight—that would mean it was everybody's fault, every single person who ever even glanced at that white expanse of the Chena. That seems right somehow, but I pull myself back closer to the logical, to the shallow water and scrub brush along the shore. Why doesn't he make it? All he has to do is push himself forward, screw his face back into the smirk, keep going. It's not that far.

"Don't get upset," the customer says. He's followed me to the counter. "I'm not."

"You're crying," he says.

"Excuse me," I say. I have not cried in a very long time, since the first divorce, and this does not really feel like me crying now. Something is happening, but it doesn't feel like anything I've ever experienced before. The customer, he just stands there watching, wide-eyed, and I guess he's never *seen* anything like it before either, just the two of us, the performer and the audience, and the more the audience looks the more the performer is obliged to put on a show. My body shudders and I try to apologize—usually I'm very friendly to people who frequent my store. My business depends on it. I'm sorry he couldn't find what he wanted. Really.

"It's okay," he says. "It's not that important."

"It is," I say. "Everything is important."

That night I stay up late drawing dungeon chambers: a series of boxes on graph paper with numbers corresponding to descriptions in my notebook. They form a straightforward scheme, from largest to smallest, least to most dangerous, as they move deeper and deeper into the earth. I extend my unfinished ideas, place monsters and treasures in each room, and by the time early morning rolls around I've written out the climax of the story—the rest of the imaginary crucible. Fourteen pages of maps in a sturdy ring binder, each one leading to one below it, where the most lost souls reside, the most disgusting creatures. Asmodeus and his servants.

A good night. I stand and stretch and crack my knuckles above my head. Each small thing rests in its proper place, and I am in mine, and as long as I don't turn on the television or drive my car or look out the window that's how things will remain. I sit on the edge of the bed and give my work one last proofread: the crypts where men lost everything—their lives, their names, their souls—and the things that reside in them. I call my ex and tell him, "Everything is good," and he tells me, *good, good,* but why am I calling so late if everything is perfect? The lab's head is on my lap, eyes closed, and I'm stroking her heavy skull. "Well," I say. "Sandy is sick. I think it's an infection. I thought it was good but it's not. How can you tell these things? She's always so happy."

"You need to pay attention," he says.

"I do," I say. "Jesus Christ. I'm petting her right now."

"I love that dog."

"I love her too."

"I'm going to come over tomorrow and pick her up. So help me."

"I'll take care of it," I say. "It's fine. It's just a little swollen. It looks so weird. But I have medicine."

"I know you so well," he says, and his voice turns from a snarl to a low whine. It seems like he is changing as we speak, shifting from an animal into a small child. And then he is back again, snarling, telling me I had better stay on top of it. I can't see him in my head though, or at least I don't want to see him.

No more kisses. I only saw Peter once after that. That Sunday after the game he sucked his split lip and talked about a fishing trip he had taken with some of his brothers. Salmon practically begging to be caught, he said, and he was as lucky as ever. He had caught eight of them. They had practically given themselves to him and if I didn't believe him I should call his brothers. The river ran silver and pink with them.

"What a day," he said, and the electricity came off him with such force that I wanted to touch him just to feel the shock of his personality.

"I have something big planned for the game," I told him, although my mind was a blank and he seemed disinterested. I had been wanting to know him, but somehow, maybe, he was the one who knew me. If I could just think of the next thing, the right thing.

And now I am telling my ex, "I can take care of the dog. I took care of you, didn't I? I take care of everybody. You should see everybody I take care of. They all depend on me."

PART V
CHARISMA

Imagine discovering something about yourself. You enter a room half expecting to find a dead man on the floor and there's nobody but you to do the things that have to be done. So you try to do them in the right order. You click the light switch and the room reveals itself: Aerosmith and Guns n' Roses posters on the walls, a stack of tapes on a VCR, a couch with a blanket and pillow, and there he is on the yellow linoleum. You kneel and touch his wrist, the back of his neck, gentle at first and then more forcefully when you pull him up to a sitting position. He coughs and tells you to leave him alone, but no, you're in too deep, and you ask him, "Peter, are you okay?"

"Fuck, yes," he tells you. "I'm fantastic."

A kind of joke. But maybe not.

I asked around and found his address. It wasn't hard. So I headed over with his bicycle in the back of my truck. It was only when I had just arrived—when I was standing in front of the scratched rectangle of his apartment door—that I wondered what I was doing. I knocked and knocked and there was no response and then, just when I had convinced myself I should leave, I tried the doorknob. I opened the door.

I had come in at the end of things. His face was splotched with pinholes of blood, but his lips were locked in that same smirk. I helped him to stand. He separated from me, gave my hand a squeeze, and found a chair, slid in closer to me. His right eye watched me from the nest of a bruise, left eye as clear and untouched as a stone in a stream. "Sorry," he said. "Rough day." He stood up again and walked—unsteadily, dreamily—to what seemed like the only other room in the place—the bathroom—leaving me with a dirty plate set on a stool next to me, a line of beer bottles on the back of the sink. His voice shouted out above the sound of running water, "You didn't need to come."

"We were worried," I said. "You didn't show up for the game. Neither did Elizabeth. I thought she might be here."

The water stopped, but he didn't reply. "I really am okay," he finally said. The water started up again. I picked up the plate from the stool and waved it under the kitchen faucet. I imagined him throwing water from his cupped hands to his face, at his injuries, then throwing more water, opening and closing his damaged eye. I washed the forks and knives and other plates. I stacked them in the plastic dish drainer and scrubbed the sink and turned off the tap. I could hear his boots as he moved around. "Hello?" I asked, but he didn't answer. He coughed and the toilet flushed. But still the door didn't open. "I think you should open the door," I said.

"I'm not going to open the door. Why do you people always think that talking is going to solve all your problems?"

"I know it doesn't," I said, because my experience had taught me a thing or two, "but I want to know what happened to you."

"Because you're *curious*," he said.

"I've had my share of difficulties," I said, although I'm not sure why I said it. It had nothing to do with what he had just told me.

He said, "I'd like to be alone now."

"Okay," I said, but I moved closer to the door, set my fingers against the wall and stared into it like I might see past it if I only looked hard enough. "Something bad is happening and I want to help," I said.

"You just want to hear another story," he said.

"If that's what helps."

"They don't," he said, "but let me tell you this. What if I told you that there was a black dog after me? He's been following me for weeks. For months. What if I told you that? What would you do about it?"

"I don't know," I said.

"But you make up stuff like that all the time, don't you?" he said. "You make up a lot worse and send them after us. So what would you do to help me? If I told you about a black dog."

I said it again. "I don't know."

"Of course you don't know. Because you don't know about the black dog. You've never heard of Keelut. You don't know about Tizheruk or Qualupalkik in the sea either. Kidnappers and tempters from way down deep. Bugbears, yes, and definitely orcs and goblins. But no black dogs. Keelut is a tricky one. Maybe he's following you too and you've never turned around quick enough to see him."

"I know about dogs," I said. "I have two."

But I felt like an idiot, standing there at the door, waiting for it to open a crack. I could hear him pissing into the bowl, a hard stream, a silence, and then more and more. More running water. It seemed possible that he might spend the rest of his life in there.

"If you don't know about these monsters then you don't know what I'm going through," he said, and all I could think of was my own dog with her damaged face and then the two of them, the injured and the uninjured, running through the snow, almost touching nose to tail. I gripped the doorknob but just cradled it for a moment before letting go. "But I don't really know about your monsters either so don't feel so bad." And it was like he could tell what I was thinking—like he could see me through the door even though I couldn't see him—because he added, "I'm not talking about those. Goblins and orcs. All of that is just stuff you use to escape from the real monsters, you know? It's the cure. We all have our cures and some work better than others. You know what I'm talking about."

"Can you open the door now?" I asked.

"Asmodeus," he said. "A devil. But most importantly a man, so macho with all the fire and brimstone and killing. How does it feel?"

The sarcasm had drained from his lowered voice. "How does it feel to be a man like that?"

"Please," I said. "Open the door."

"Because you asked politely," he said, and the door opened and so did his arms and he hugged me, very quickly, before releasing me, so quickly that I wasn't sure if it had really happened or not, or if I had accomplished anything at all. His hair was wet but tied back in a rubber band and I felt good because he had touched me and bad because I had already forgotten the names, even worse because I guessed that he knew this and the hug was forgiveness.

None of this is true, of course. I never went to his place. I never spoke to him through the door. But there has to be *something*, because this is the night. He leaves me out front and heads across town to the river and then across the ice. As we say good-bye he's smiling. He smacks my shoulder and I can still feel it, hard, through my heavy coat. We're like friends who go all the way back to grade school. We've been through wars. I could be one of his brothers. Music blasts from a bar across the street and it would be natural, at least for that second, if I just went with him. We'd walk together with him doing most of the talking.

Why has everything changed? You were the obsessed one and now it's me and I don't know how to go back to the way it was during those first couple of weeks. I don't even know if I want to because I like this feeling. I just want you to feel it too. Peter says this to Elizabeth before he disappears. They're the words I put in his mouth so that his disappearance means what it *should* mean, but he's still smirking, walking up and down the stacks of library books. Or he says, *I know you feel this way too. You're just being dishonest.* He's holding her tight around the shoulders, the way he wanted to grab the wizard in that last fight, and maybe he wants to shake her too. I'm not sure. It's a balancing act, and it's difficult not to fall too far one way or the other. I'm stuck between the mundane and the sensational and all I can have him say is *Don't lie to me* or *I didn't plan any of this.* My second ex-husband told me similar things once, and they seemed fake even then, spoken aloud in a real moment.

But there has to be a final meeting between the two of them. There has to be something. Life might be too disappointing otherwise.

Maybe Peter speaks these words at her house, standing in the driveway, and he's making a speech he planned out on the way over. He's mad enough, desperate enough, that he's forgotten his gloves, so his hands are pushed into the pockets of his coat, his hair loose around his shoulders, and he's crazy and beautiful. He'll be walking down to the bars on the north side of the river soon and a few hours after that crossing the water. It's twenty below out but his face feels hot as a stove.

He's thinking of her father, the racist prick, the GI Joe, the born again, the sad man.

Or he's not. I don't know if I'm moving closer or further away, but those are the words. She's on the porch, in the doorway, or right there in front of him, and she's not wearing a coat. Occasionally she looks at the house and wonders about simply taking a first step back there, a second and then a third. Would Peter try to stop her? And where is her father? I imagine him sitting in the kitchen with the two boys, but what holds him there? Shame at what he did before, though I still cannot imagine it. The boys are talking television shows and it's easy to ignore them: the buzz of their voices and the scraping of forks. Outside she tells Peter that now is not a good time. She has a family *right there*. She points to the kitchen window with two fingers and he watches her hand, her resigned frown, and decides that she's gesturing toward her future—not just the house and the people in it but something beyond all that. He'd give anything to go with her. And that's why, when he's finished yelling, he'll set off in the *opposite* direction.

⚶

The nurse at the vet's office tells me, "I don't believe this. You should have come in weeks ago. What were you thinking?" She holds the dog's head in both hands and looks her in the face, then raises her eyes to me, and if she stood up and slapped my face it would not seem unusual. She's a big woman, with a heavily made-up face and complicated hair, but her voice is simple and direct. She's used to working with horses, sled dogs, burly men with bad attitudes, but from the look she gives me I feel like the most difficult of them all. The lab pushes forward and I pull back on the leash.

"I don't have much money," I say. "I thought she was okay."

"At least you didn't wait any longer," she says, and she stands and I know it's time for me to leave. Outside at the front desk another nurse gives me a stare. Apparently, they've been talking about me. But look, the dog is eager and happy, pulling at her chain, hungry and healthy, and when I lower my hand she nuzzles it so desperately that I want to say, *See, there's proof.* Proof of what I'm not exactly sure.

Eight in the morning and I call Elizabeth, speak to her voicemail in a rambling, high voice. "Did you hear?" I ask, and then I remember to identify myself. "Please," I say. "This afternoon? I'll see you there."

The dog's scars have become a bright pink cross, a target on her eager face, and I pull her to my chest and then release her down the path. She's lost vision in her left eye but doesn't seem to even notice. It's early on a Sunday morning and the trails are empty except for one other person, a skier who appears and then vanishes further down the line of trees.

Everything has to be like before, better than before, right down to the potato chips and soft drinks. I scatter the dice around the table, set up all my reference books at the far end. So much of it is in my own head, but I need the maps, the monster manuals.

The youngest kids show up first, driven by parents and older brothers, then the teenagers, the dead paladin, the snide elf with the southern drawl, the suspicious ones. They move around the table and sure, they all notice that the sheet is there in its normal position: a level 9 druid with high marks in almost everything: strength, wisdom, dexterity, and charisma. Two eighteens and a seventeen and nothing below a twelve. A character to be coveted, like a fancy house, a nice car, but it's more than that too, of course. It has a name and history. The paladin says, "I could play him. You know, if you need the help."

"I don't need the help."

"Who's going to play him then?"

I ignore that because Elizabeth enters, and at the sight of her I can't help but grin. I pretend I'm grinning at my plans because my pencil is moving across the page behind the screen. We're ready to begin. "Disgusting," the dead paladin says when I describe the black hole of the mouth, the bile around his lips, his hollow eyes. Asmodeus has returned in all his glorious stupidity.

But I'm just trying to put them there. I know that's what they want. I complete the arc of the action. It's as easy as following the trajectory of a ball thrown underhand across a field. "Like a voice emanating from a tomb," I say when I describe the wizard's words.

Elizabeth rolls an eight. Someone else rolls an eleven.

I have to speak in *both* their voices, repeat Peter's words from a month ago and add new ones. The wizard speaks back. It calls the druid a fool. It calls him worse. Everybody seems to be enjoying this, but all it takes is one small mistake and the illusion is ruined. What might happen next? A simple touch could kill the druid, blackness running from the animated corpse up the hands, the arms, into the body, the heart. It might be as easy as that. The symmetry is attractive.

But the stories don't have to align so simply. What if the battle spins out of control, druid fighting alongside ranger, both injured but still struggling? It's the others who might die, the youngest ones, driven by their burdened parents, the cowardly one with the ring of invisibility. That would leave just these two. And they could defeat him—it would be hard but not impossible—and then go deeper still. There are treasures there in the catacombs. I've put them there.

Or they could all die. We could just start from scratch next week. I imagine them falling one by one, enveloped by skeletons.

Elizabeth says, "Do I have room to swing? I'm going to aim for the neck. Get out of the way. I'm going to take its head right off." I tell her okay, she can try that. She's fierce as anything.

The youngest ones, they're the ones who can see it all most clearly. I can tell from their faces, their tense positions in their folding chairs, their hands balled into fists. It's only ten below out and by next week, if we're lucky, the thermometer will hit zero and keep going up. The dead paladin, he'll make a new character, and I'll make a new story, and soon instead of hiding from the cold we'll be hiding from the constant sunlight.

Elizabeth says, "Are you clear?" and I tell her yes, but there's still a chance something will go wrong. Everything is happening so fast. The sword swings. She rolls and it comes up fifteen.

She came back to do this. That part is real. The head spins free. The body falls. People are laughing, slapping the table, swearing, because they don't believe what just happened. But it's still not finished because the ideas keep coming.

The head speaks from the floor. I'm improvising, checking how far the whole thing can be pushed. What words can it say? A warning? A curse? Then it occurs to me. The eyes grow dull and it says, *It is cold here.* Just that and then its face turns dull as a stone. That's almost the end, except for the embrace, the moment when I feel what Peter must have felt. I say, "The druid has strength enough to run to you."

Except Elizabeth says, "I need to make sure." She says, "Give me the dice," and she reaches across the table. The sword comes down again and again and I'm at a loss. I don't know how to describe what's happening.

"Hey," I say, "It's okay. He's dead."

I'm not sure what voice I'm speaking in.

The sword comes down again and again. I know that desperation.

Imagine this: he wants his bicycle, but the lady at the store has it and he'd rather have his pride, and he wants his family, but they wouldn't understand. And for a second, in my mind, he's pursued by the black dog through the city and he's the black dog itself, following his brothers, not just down the roads but through the years. Because being followed like that turns you into a shadow too. And in my mind it's not me on the other side of the door listening to him talking about the black dog. It's her. She has her hand on the doorknob, but she's twisting it hard. It's locked and he's speaking the names to her.

Except she says, "Tell me more."

And he says, "Okay. If you really want to know I can do that."

And she says, "I really want to know."

Except she keeps turning the knob, *click, click, click*, and the door doesn't open. Except she does it now for the simple pleasure of the motion and sound. And also she wants him to know that she's trying.

But why does it have to be this way?

Maybe there's another kiss, a real one, a small one, in front of the house, or in his apartment, when he *does* open the door, and they promise to see each other the next day and the day after that, and then on Sunday he'll save her, or she'll save him. They'll save each other, because why would I be so cruel as to not let that happen, at least in my own imagination? Her father is waiting so they have to rush. She apologizes for having to go back inside and he's sorry about vanishing before, but he's sick of the game. Life has supplanted it—this other thing between them. And that's how they separate, and it's his *happiness* that sends him down to the river and then across it.

He thinks it's the beginning of his journey.

About the Author

DAVID NIKKI CROUSE is author of the short story collections *The Man Back There*, winner of the Mary McCarthy Award in Short Fiction, and *Copy Cats*, winner of the Flannery O'Connor Award, as well as many uncollected stories, including work published in *Prairie Schooner*, *Agni*, the *Colorado Review*, *Witness*, the *Kenyon Review*, and many other fine magazines. David also writes and enjoys comic books.

David is the Grace Pollock Professor of Creative Writing at the University of Washington–Seattle, where they direct the MFA program. David lives in Seattle.